Dream Lover

ROBIN LANDRY

NewLink Publishing

Henderson, NV 89002

info@newlinkpublishing.com

Dream Lover

ROBIN LANDRY

Contact the publisher at info@ newlinkpublishing.com.

Line/Content Editor: Janelle Evans
Interior Design: Donna Raymond
Cover: Richard Draude

p. cm. — Robin Landry (Young Adult-Paranormal)
Copyright © 2020 / Robin Landry
All Rights Reserved
ISBN: 978-1-948266-05-5/Paperback
ISBN: 978-1-948266-38-3/E-Pub

1.   Fiction/ Science Fiction/Time Travel
2.   Fiction/ Science Fiction/Action Adventure
3.   Fiction/ Science Fiction/Romance

NewLink Publishing

Henderson, NV 89002
info@newlinkpublishing.com
Printed in the United States of America

Dedication

I'd like to thank first and foremost, my husband for always supporting my dreams and helping me to make them a reality. I'd like to thank my family, those who are with me now, and those who have passed on, and help me from the other side.

I'd like to thank Jo A. Wilkins for taking a chance on me, Janelle Evans for polishing my writing, Donna Raymond for interior design and Richard Draude for the perfect cover for my story.

Lastly, I'd like to thank anyone who takes the time to read my story, it was a joy to write

One

"**I don't know** how you managed to talk me into coming here, Diana," Kristen whispered to her friend sitting next to her. She looked around the room filled with excited — mostly women — in the local television studio. A stunning redhead sat on an on-stage couch with her long legs crossed. She looked into the camera off to her right and smiled as if she had just been told she won the lottery.

Diana grinned and pointed at the stage. "Did you forget how to have fun?"

Kristen closed her eyes and took in a deep breath. "Of course I know how to have fun." She glared at her best friend.

Diana grinned back, smoothing her long, straight, blonde hair. "Smile, I think the cameraman is looking over here."

How had she ended up here? Waiting with her best friend — the girl voted most likely to end up married to a millionaire — to be part of a television audience to see the internationally renowned psychic, Cynthia Brown

"All you know how to do is study and work, work and study." Diana lifted her friend's long, dark ponytail. "See? You haven't even been to a hairdresser, in what? Five years?"

Kristen sighed. "You're right, but I've been busy. It is my last year of medical school, you know."

Diana's eyebrows made a dramatic rise. "No woman should ever be too busy to see her hairdresser."

Kristen gazed at her friend. She wanted to protest, but she spoke the truth. Yes, she worked and studied, but what else did she have time for? Becoming a doctor and working her way through school required sacrifices. Sometimes she fell asleep with her clothes on, too tired to even undress for bed. How could she manufacture the time to have her hair done?

"Seeing your hairdresser at least every other month is a woman's God-given right," Diana said patting her own beautiful blonde hair. As usual, she looked perfectly turned out with everything in place, leaving Kristen looking dowdy in comparison.

Her jeans had three days of wear, her button-up blouse had wrinkles, and her boots had scuffs. Things she's been in too big of a hurry to notice before. At least no one here in the audience knew her.

"Well, it's not like *I'm* the one on stage." Kristen ran her hands over her shirtsleeve in an effort to smooth it out.

A mysterious grin came over Diana's face.

She frowned at Diana. "I'm just here to watch, right?" The rumor going around the studio about Diana, the on-air talent of the local Seattle news—at least for the moment—suggested she would soon be moved into a national slot.

"Sure," Diana said patting Kristen's hand, "but I do wish you'd have let me dress you. We're about the same size…" Diana's eyes ran up and down Kristen's figure. "At least we were until you decided to starve yourself to death."

"I've been too busy to eat," Kristen mumbled under her breath. Why had she decided to go along with this? Probably because they had been friends since grade school, and it might also be the last time they would be together before her best friend left for New York.

Diana shook her head. "No one's too busy to eat. Too busy to die, maybe, but never too busy to eat."

Kristen shrugged. She did not want to talk about her life. Actually, she did not have a life to talk about. She spent her time at the hospital from morning until night, and then she cleaned offices until nearly midnight. She kept telling herself it would be worth it someday when she finally became a doctor, but she had no time to even think that far into the future.

A grinning young man in jeans and a flannel shirt over a white t-shirt with a ball cap declaring his allegiance to Washington State University Cougars came on, eliciting scattered applause from the audience. He put his hands together encouraging more applause.

"I know you can do better, people!"

The applause grew louder.

"That's better! Now, whenever you see this sign..." He pointed to a sign hanging overhead, out of range of the cameras. "...just do what it says."

Kristen leaned over to Diana. "I had no idea you trained the audience."

Diana laughed. "You have to, otherwise they just sit there as if they were in their own homes watching TV."

"Isn't that guy a little underdressed for TV?"

Diana smiled and waved at the young man. "Are you kidding? Seattle invented grunge, and besides, the camera's never on him."

The young man raised his hands high, causing his t-shirt to show his chiseled abs. "You guys are doing great! Now, how about a warm welcome for the star of our show, Cynthia Brown!"

Kristen looked from the young man to her friend. "Don't tell me you and —" She pointed at the young man. " — that youngster are —"

"He's not that much younger, and I'm single." Diana smiled.

"And leaving town."

"Exactly," Diana said. "Who knows how long it'll take to find a date in New York?"

"Not long, I'm sure."

The applause sign lit up. The audience clapped. The lights dimmed on the audience and brightened on the tiny stage. The hostess walked out into the light with a bright smile. She appeared much shorter than Kristen would have imagined, and painfully perky. The audience cheered with rising enthusiasm.

After greeting the audience both in the studio, and on camera, the hostess introduced the day's guest. "Today we have someone really special. She's written a book on her adventures as a psychic — and it's number one on the New York Times bestseller list. Please give a warm welcome to Seattle's own Cynthia Brown."

The applause sign was not needed. The studio audience cheered to a fifty-something woman walking out on the stage. She smiled and nodded at the boisterous crowd. Brown looked nothing like a psychic, with her shoulder-length, tinted-blonde hair, and her conservative dress. The giant purple crystal she wore on a silver chain around her neck the only indication that she might be something other than someone's grandmother.

After a few questions from the audience, which left several women crying, the hostess turned to smile into the camera. "There you have it folks, Cynthia is the real deal."

"How accurate do you really think she is?" Kristen whispered out of the side of her mouth.

"Who cares?" Diana said grinning. "She really brings in the ratings, and it's not as if we have these people on again to ask them if they found what they were looking for."

"I think it's just a way to sell books," Kristen whispered back fiercely. "Look how she's getting these women all worked up about their lost kids and dead relatives." Kristen folded her arms over her chest. "Cynthia Brown is taking advantage of vulnerable minds. I think it's terrible."

Saying nothing, Diana just raised her eyebrows and smiled, which brought on a sudden bout of nervousness for Kristen. When she heard a call go out to the audience for a volunteer, Diana's grin grew wider.

I'm just being paranoid. No one would do that to a friend. Just to be safe, Kristen sunk lower in her seat. When she heard her name called out, she thought she imagined it.

Diana tapped her on the shoulder. "I'm pretty sure you've been chosen."

"I can't!" Kristen whispered as loud as she dared. "I'll die of embarrassment." Some of the women around her gave her envious looks.

"You're almost a doctor, so you know that's not true." Diana laughed. "Now just put on your big-girl panties and get up there."

Kristen put her hand over her heart. It beat faster than the hearts of the mice she used for experiments. "Yes you can, I'm almost a doctor. I know these things!"

"Stand up." Diana stood, pulling Kristen with her.

Kristen looked around for someone to intervene but she only saw smiling faces of the audience looking at her as if she alone had been blessed. Once the producer started up the stairs toward her, she no longer had a choice.

The producer smiled and offered his hand. Kristen took it as if in a dream—no, more like a nightmare.

Kristen hoped that no one she knew would be watching. The only friends she had were at the hospital where she should be right now, not wasting her time being embarrassed on local television.

"So," the hostess said offering Kristen a seat on the couch. "You're the lucky one to be regressed by Cynthia Brown."

"Regressed?" Kristen repeated. Her face heated up, sweat beading on her brow. She folded her arms across her chest after taking her seat.

"Regressed means you're going to be hypnotized so that we can hear about your past lives," the hostess said as if she'd just announced that Kristen had won the lottery.

"Oh, that sounds nice." Kristen looked over at the psychic who smiled at her from across the couch. *She looks just like my dead grandmother.*

It surprised her how oblivious the psychic, Cynthia Brown, seemed to be to her obvious distress. *I knew she was a fake. All I have to do is get through a few minutes of this nonsense then I can be free to go back to work. After I strangled my best friend for getting me into this mess.*

Cynthia Brown got up from the couch and stood over Kristen. "If you lay down, I'm sure you'll be more comfortable."

"I'm not sure anything will help," Kristen muttered under her breath. She laid on the couch hoping to spend a few minutes listening to nonsense before she could creep back to her seat— or better yet, the back door.

Once settled on the sofa, the psychic pulled her chair close to Kristen's head and said, "Now close your eyes."

Kristen closed her eyes, able to hear the audience in the background whispering.

"You should start to feel sleepy."

That's right. I'm about to fall asleep on a couch in a room full of people staring at me, with a camera pointed at an angle that probably makes my chest look flat and my behind look five sizes larger than normal.

Cynthia Brown continued in a soft, sing-song voice. "I'm going to take you back to an important past life."

Kristen could not help but smile. *Not if I don't believe in past lives. I don't even have a life in the present. Good luck trying to find one for me in the past.*

"You start to hear voices," the psychic said. "Maybe something in a different language?"

Kristen groaned inside. *When is this going to be over? I'm not sleepy. The only voice I hear is the psychic's soothing voice. Ha! As if I can be hypnotized!*

Without warning, she heard people speaking in a foreign language. At least it sounded foreign because of a heavy Southern accent—a male voice that had to be the producer's voice.

"Kristen, wake up! It's time for me to get going."

I couldn't agree more! She opened her eyes hoping to get off the couch as quick as possible.

She sat up expecting the see the psychic still standing over her. Instead, a handsome man scowled down at her. His dark, straight hair fell in strands across his high forehead, contrasting nicely with a pair of emotion-filled blue-gray eyes that peered down at her.

Kristen said a quick prayer then smiled at the man who stared down at her with such fierceness. When he did not smile back, her own smile faded. *What is going on?* Had she done something to offend this heavenly man? Until five seconds ago, she had never laid eyes on him. Turning him off in such a short amount of time had to be a new record, even for her.

His delightful eyes narrowed. "I'm not going to fall for another one of your fainting spells."

"Fainting spells?" Actually, she did feel a little light in the head.

With his fists clenched, he paced around the room running his hands through his hair.

Kristen watched fascinated. He had to be just over six feet tall, broad shoulders and lean muscular thighs under a tight-fitting gray uniform with stripes down the side. She forced her gaze to his face again. She found herself attracted to him a physical level even though his features appeared

handsome in an unconventional way. It must be the raw mas-
culinity that had her so entranced. Kristen could not remember
the last time she had seen a man so confident in his bearing. He
exuded strength and power, like a lion. Like the king of beasts,
he bore confidence of his place in the world, ready to take on any
challengers.

Happy to continue gazing up at the man as he paced like a
caged panther, it took a few seconds for his clothing to finally
register in her befuddled brain. Gray?

*Is that the uniform of a Confederate soldier? Why is this perfect
specimen of a man dressed up in a Confederate uniform?* She smiled
and nodded. *Of course, I'm in a television studio. He's probably an
actor. The show must be over, I've fallen asleep. The next show is
getting ready to start.*

"Kristen!" He moved closer to her. "You're not listening to a
single word I'm saying!"

She shrank back on the couch. "I'm not?"

"No, you're not." He laughed without humor. "But then you
never did listen, did you?"

"What are you talking about?" She tried to stand up. For some
reason, she could not untangle herself from the couch. What's going
on? She looked down at her feet.

"My dress is caught?" Kristen could not believe what she saw.
She took a handful of the most beautiful dress she had ever seen.
Of a fine quality, the heavyweight silk had been dyed a lovely
shade of violet. *But why am I wearing it?*

"Let me help you up."

Still trying to understand, Kristen barely looked at the man
holding out his hand. Tearing herself away from his searing blue-
gray eyes, she gaped at the room. It looked like a visit into the past.
Heavy burgundy-velvet drapes hung across windows, reaching up
to a twenty-foot ceiling and back down to a polished wooden floor.
A brightly colored rug reached almost to the corners of the huge space.
Everywhere Kristen looked, she saw perfection. From the gold silk
embroidered Louis IV chairs to the gleaming ornately-carved grand
piano. It looked like a museum, only everything appeared new.

Kristen fought to orientate herself. "Where am I?"

Jerking his hand away, the man turned and stormed out of the room. She smiled at the way his tight buttocks strained against his form-fitting trousers. Knee-high black riding boots ground into the thick rug and then echoed on the hardwood floor.

Kristen looked down at her chest. "Oh my!" The dress she wore did not reach all the way up to cover her bosom. Half her chest was exposed. "I'm naked!"

"Ma'am?"

A slender, young, black girl came into the room, but she looked as though she wanted to disappear. "Master told me you needed help," she said in a voice that barely reached a whisper.

"Help?" Kristen tried again to stand up. Giving her skirt a yank, she managed to get to her feet but she still felt faint. "I can barely breathe." She put her hands around her waist. *No wonder, I'm two sizes smaller because of this dress.* She turned to the girl. "I need help all right, and a lot more than you're going to be able to give me."

The girl flinched as if Kristen had struck her. *What's going on?* She stood slowly. *Where's the television studio?* She looked down at the couch. The camel-backed velvet sofa had dark wood across the back carved in a swirl pattern.

She looked at the frightened young girl, who stood trembling in front of her just out of reach, as if afraid that Kristen would strike her. She reminded her of a dog she had found once as a child. She remembered counting every bone in the flea-bitten animal and asking her mother why the dog always flattened itself on the ground when anyone came near. "Because someone has beaten him," her mother said. Kristen had cried in grief for the poor dog.

"I'm not going to hurt you," she said, softening her tone just like she had when trying to befriend that dog long ago.

The girl's eyes almost rolled back in her head when she took a step closer.

"I need you to tell me where I am."

Frowning, the girl took a step back. "You're home, Mrs. O'Conner."

"I am?" Kristen said surprised, yet not. Somehow, this room did seem familiar though she knew she had never seen it before. "Okay, who was that man who was just in here?"

The girl smiled as if she had told a delightful joke. "That's your husband, ma'am."

"My husband?" Kristen's vision narrowed until she could only see the girl standing in front of her. Then, even that disappeared until the whole room went black.

Two

O nce again, Kristen's mind pulled back from a dream, except in this one she did not want to leave any time soon. Visions of a man teased at the back of her mind. Black hair and gray-blue eyes were all she could remember. She buried herself in a stack of soft pillows.

Wait a minute. Since when are my pillows soft? And why hasn't my alarm gone off? She opened one eye. *So far so good.* The white sheets seemed softer somehow and much finer than anything she had ever slept on before. Much as she would like to keep sleeping, she knew she had to get up. *I have to make rounds with Fowler.*

When she began working with Dr. Fowler she had been informed by other students that her name should be spelled F-o-u-l-e-r because of her perpetual bad mood, and her willingness to take it out on anyone under her. This week Kristen had that honor.

Kristen groaned. "I don't want to go to the hospital today."

"Why would you go to a hospital?" A deep voice demanded from somewhere beside her.

"Eeee! Who said that?" She jerked upright. "Who is in my bed?" Thoughts of picking up a stranger while drunk entered her mind, but she brushed them aside. She never could hold her liquor, even if she had the time to waste to get drunk.

As for picking up men — well, she would need a pair of hand-cuffs and a badge to get a man. She was no great beauty. Her mother, when sober enough for speech, made sure to tell her that on a regular basis. Best to use your brain if you do not want to starve to death, her mother always said. Her mother had been a great beauty in her day, before cigarettes and gin had robbed her of what nature had so freely given.

Shaking morbid thoughts from her mind, Kristen raised the heavy silk comforter to see what formed the lump next to her. The lean, tan body of a man lay there. She should have dropped the covers back over whoever lay beside her but that would have been like taking food from a starving man. She stared at the chiseled perfection of the still form, drinking in the sight—even lifting the blankets higher. The tan line ended at a muscled pale rear that sent chills down her spine.

Surely, dreaming. Kristen smiled. This was quite the dream. At least she had good taste. Too bad she would wake up in a moment, back in her own bed with the cheap poly-cotton sheets and pale pink comforter she'd had since high school.

"Kristen, what are you doing?"

To her shock, the man lying beside her turned over.

"Oh, my God!" She dropped the covers and nearly jumped out of the huge bed. She stopped, realizing she wore only a night-gown, if you could call it that. The lacy cloth colored her naked body a pale scarlet. She gathered up the covers and tried to cover herself.

The man glared at her. "What is wrong with you?"

"Y-Y-You're my husband?" Kristen stuttered, alarmed to hear her childhood affliction making a reappearance.

"Kristen, what is wrong with you?"

She could think of nothing to say so she said nothing, afraid she would stutter again in front of this man. She bit down on her bottom lip and tried to move as far away from him as she could get.

"Yes, I'm your husband," he said. "Jeffery, your husband of three years, in case you've forgotten." He arose from the bed, walked over to a chest of drawers, and pulled out a pair of pants. "Look," he said still bare-chested as he turned to her. "I know you haven't been feeling well lately, and I'm still not sure if this is another one of your stunts, but if you continue with this strange behavior, I'm going to have to send you to the place Dr. Shelby recommended. He says there are some good doctors there who can deal with people with the mental problems you seem to be having."

Gazing around the room, Kristen once again felt as if she stood in a museum. Every piece of vintage, federal-style and early American furniture appeared very new. The bed, chest of drawers, armoire, dressing table, paintings, everything, yet nothing looked old. In fact, everything shone from the care it received and its inherent newness. It even smelled like fresh wood.

"What problems?" Since she had first woke up things around her made no sense. Now thinking about the series of events, it started to make sense. It just did not seem possible. The more she thought about the situation and looked around, the less it seemed like a dream. Something had happened since she laid down on the couch at the television studio. Well, only one way to find out.

"What year is it?"

Jeffery frowned as if he thought she was trying to trick him. "I know you don't have a head for figures, but I would have thought—"

"What year is it!" Kristen said, fighting with the panic welling up in her throat.

"Eighteen and sixty-one."

"Oh, no." Kristen groaned and fell back into the mountain of pillows. "This has to be a dream."

Growling something under his breath, Jeffery grabbed a shirt, a pair of boots, and left the room.

Kristen closed her eyes but opened them with a start at the slamming door. While trying to sort everything out, she heard a timid knock on the door.

"Come in?" Pulling the covers over herself, Kristen peered out from under them. She expected to see her "husband" coming back to berate her more, but instead she saw the same slender, black girl of the day before.

"Who are you?" She vowed to herself, not to scare the girl who seemed terrified of her.

The young girl frowned. "I be Missy, your house slave, ma'am."

"Slave?" Kristen groaned. This had to be a dream, but it didn't appear to be since everything stayed the same. She must have

13

really been regressed, the only other plausible explanation for the scenario. The psychic really had somehow managed to send her into a past life. How had it happened? As far as she knew regressing someone meant hypnotizing a person and then they talked about some past life. How had she actually ended up in the past? Unless...

She considered the possibility for a moment. Yes, it made sense in a warped way. She had been regressed to experience her past life. Or someone's past life. What did it all mean, exactly? That any minute now Cynthia Brown would say the magic words, count backwards or whatever psychics do and Kristen would wake up?

That made sense. She would stay right here in bed until she woke up. Then everything would be fine and her life would go back to normal. Kristen scooted down into the warm cocoon of blankets ready to wait out her fate.

"Ma'am. You are gonna be late if we don't get you dressed."

"But I'm not going to need to get dressed, because I'm going to be leaving here any minute." Even as she said the words she wondered if she really wanted to leave. The thought of being married to Jeffery O'Connor *did* have merit. Waking up next to his warm body gave her chills just thinking about it. She chided herself for her lustful thinking.

Missy's eyes went wide enough to show the white all the way around her rich chocolate-colored pupils. "You gots to get dressed, ma'am. You can't leave the house without your clothes!"

"Oh, you don't understand," Kristen said, assuring the shocked young girl. "I'm not from here and I'm not staying."

"You're starting to scare me, ma'am. You're starting to sound like Mrs. Fullerton just before they took her to that place where all the people are crazy." Missy shuddered.

Kristen frowned. Things were not looking good. If she did end up staying here, she could end up locked in a mental institute. Considering what she knew of the care this era gave the mentally ill, being locked up in an institute for even a day would drive her mad enough to be a permanent resident.

"How about I get dressed and we forget what I just said?" She leapt out of bed, grabbed the comforter and wrapped it around herself. She did not want to ask who undressed her after she had fainted yesterday afternoon.

"I have your blue-velvet riding gown all ready for you," Missy said with a shy smile.

"Sounds wonderful." Kristen wondered about the riding gown, thinking that maybe it would be worn while riding in a carriage, or whatever passed for transportation here. History had not been one of her favorite subjects, but she wished she had paid more attention in school. Judging from the Southern accents and the slaves, this was sometime before the Civil War. *What year did the Civil War start?* Or as the Southerners would say "The War of Northern Aggression." Judging by Jeffrey's uniform, the slave standing before her, and the sticky heat, Kristen guessed she had landed in the Deep South. She hoped they did not live in one of the cities like Atlanta that took the brunt of the war. Kristen had watched *Gone with the Wind* so she knew that the war started sometime in the spring of 1861.

A startling thought occurred to Kristen. "What year is this?"

Missy shook her head. "I ain't been schooled. I don't know about important stuff like that."

"Figures." Kristen didn't want to think about how oppressive this century was for slaves. Having been raised in the twentieth century and the north, Kristen had lived her life assuming equality between the races. In her time, women had more prejudices to overcome than blacks to survive. Medical school had demonstrated that fact to her.

Brushing aside her thoughts, Kristen turned to Missy. "So where is this gown you're talking about?"

Missy smiled. "It's my favorite," she said going over to a chest identical to the one Jeffery had taken his clothes out of, except twice as large.

Kristen would have thought a dress would be hanging up but apparently not.

Missy drew out a long, exquisite gown in rich hunter-green velvet. Holding it out in front of her, Missy smiled shyly. "It brings out the color of your eyes, ma'am."

"It's lovely," Kristen agreed. "I'd like to take a shower first, though."

"Shower?"

"I mean a bath," Kristen said hoping they had one in the house. She had no idea what one did in the nineteenth century to bathe.

Without a word, Missy dropped the dress and ran for the door. Kristen's curiosity about her hasty departure would have to wait. She decided against asking, in case her probing might trigger an unwanted consequence. Maybe, the girl always ran off like that. Better to just keep her mouth shut and pretend she understood the habits and rituals, at least until she managed to wake up in her own century. "And body," Kristen said aloud, ruefully dropping the comforter. She belonged to this body and yet she didn't quite belong in it. This body seemed softer and fuller, although she seemed to be about the same height.

"A mirror!" Kristen said searching the room. Did she look different? If everything had changed and she had really become someone else now, what did she look like? Praying she did not look too hideous—Kristen found a silver hand-mirror on a table against a tall window. Fearfully, she brought it up to her eyes.

"Oh my!" She let her breath out with a whistle. She peered at the face reflected in the glass. She had known this face all her life, but she had not seen the sensuousness before. Her eyes, still leaf-green and large, but now they smoldered with something more. Her hair, still a rich russet, but it appeared sleep-rumpled and fuller. To her own eyes, she felt beautiful for the first time in her life, and she had more than a passing resemblance to her own mother. How had it happened? Had the previous owner of this body known things Kristen had not? Obviously so.

The urge to urinate hit Kristen full force. She nearly collided with a pair of boots in her hurry for the bathroom. Stepping over the tall, black, shiny boots and through the door, Kristen stood for a moment wondering what was wrong with what she saw in the room.

"The toilet," she groaned. Of course, toilets hadn't been invented. Not yet, anyway. So what did a person do? Surely, they did not go outside.

A small round pot with a handle on it jogged Kristen's memory. "A chamber pot?" She found it difficult to use, but it *did* relieve her.

Now ready for a bath, she noticed a large, claw-foot, copper tub resting beside the wall. Kristen nodded. Well at least she could take a bath. She reached for the handle to turn the water on and met only air. "Where are the handles?"

Before she stared too long at the space where the faucet and handles should be on the bathtub, Missy reappeared and interrupted her. A sheen of sweat coated her face, as if she had just finished running a marathon. Kristen looked down and saw the young slave had carried two large buckets of steaming water. She set them down spilling a large amount on the floor at Kristen's feet.

"I's sorry, ma'am." Missy dropped to the floor cleaning up the water with the hem of her dress, muttering apologies the entire time. After she cleaned up the floor, she tried to wipe the hem of Kristen's robe.

"It's okay." Kristen pulled on her robe trying to remove it from Missy's clutching hands. "Let's just get the water into the tub so I can take a bath."

Missy nodded. She picked up one of the heavy buckets. Kristen took the other side and helped pour it into the tub. Missy looked at her in wonder. When Kristen smiled, Missy quickly put the bucket down and started to lift the second bucket. Again, Kristen helped. As if ready to burst, Missy poured the water in the tub, picked up the empty one, and ran out of the room.

"Well, it's not much, but it's better than nothing." The water was barely an inch deep. Kristen did not know if Missy had gone for more water or just ran away, so she slipped out of her robe and sat down in the warm water. She washed herself the best she could with such a small amount of water. A bar of lavender-smelling soap sat on a table within arm's reach so she used it, washing quickly.

Missy came back with two more buckets of water. Kristen could only imagine how many buckets filling such a huge tub must take. She let the young girl pour it over her head. It felt wonderful to have someone wash her hair. Kristen even forgot to be embarrassed at being naked in front of someone. She nearly moaned aloud at the luxury of being dried and then helped into her elaborate clothing.

If anyone had told Kristen that having a maid would be nice, she would have laughed. Doing things for yourself, although much easier and more efficient in the twenty-first century, she would not have known where to begin in the nineteenth century. Clothes were so different. She could hardly believe her eyes when Missy brought out layers of petticoats and then a corset. The barbaric waist-tightening device cut off her breathing, leaving her barely enough room to take even the shallowest of breaths.

When the velvet gown went over her head, Missy pulled a full-length mirror out from a corner of the room. Kristen gazed at herself in the mirror and finally understood the value of spending time and effort to create a pleasing appearance. She looked and felt more feminine than she had her entire life. No high school prom dress could compare with the richness and fullness of this gown. Her now tiny waist and the fullness of the petticoats underneath accented the gown's beauty. Her creamy white breasts pushed up to heights Victoria's Secret could only dream about made a vivid contrast against the hunter-green of the gown.

"Thank you so much for all your help." Kristen looked over her shoulder at Missy, who stood smiling shyly behind her in the mirror.

Missy blanched. She backed away as if afraid of what her mistress would do next.

Kristen closed her eyes and sighed. *No doubt, I'm the first white woman to thank a slave for doing her job.* Or maybe the former occupant of this particular body who never would have acted with kindness.

What now? Kristen waited.

Missy seemed to know her job. "I can do your hair now, and then you'll be ready for your ride."

"My ride?"

"You always go for a ride after breakfast." Missy frowned.

"Oh, of course. Just have the carriage brought around while I eat." At least she'd remembered that cars don't exist yet. She noticed the look of horror on Missy's dark face. Her good mood interrupted, she wondered what she had done now.

"You don't want to ride your horse?"

"My horse? Oh yes, my horse." Kristen hoped the girl could not see in her face the despair overtaking her insides. She had not ridden a horse since the fair where a nasty tempered pony had tried to bite her. That pony gave her a lifelong fear of horses. She had stayed away from large animals, including dogs bigger than a cocker spaniel.

"Diablo would surely miss his morning ride." Missy nodded her head as she brushed Kristen's hair. "That horse gets all upset if he don't see you every day."

"And I'd miss him too." *Diablo? I'm supposed to ride a horse named Diablo? Maybe it's a misnomer, one of those plays on words.* The possibility that the horse would be a tiny, gentle lady's horse with a name like "Diablo" seemed remote. She needed a horse that walked slow in deference to the delicate Southern belle perched on his back.

Yes, Kristen assured herself. *That's probably it. Someone named the horse Diablo as a joke. Besides, how hard could it be to ride a horse? Just sit in the saddle and hang on, right?*

Three

*J*effery sat alone in his office drinking coffee and trying to read over the plantation reports. Tobacco prices were doing well, but for how long? The war would surely come. Tempers had risen too high for either side to back down now. Cooler heads could have prevailed at one time, but it was too late now. In his opinion, which did not count for much, slavery would have come to its natural conclusion—eventually. As the new nation progressed, the majority would realize the unfairness of the institution.

He had no interest in politics or the people attracted to the profession. Many planters like him quietly freed their slaves and gave them small plots of land after several years of indentured service—the only realistic way to solve the problem. A war freeing all the slaves at once, with no land to call their own, would cause chaos and prevent the freed slaves from creating a productive life on their own.

The war alone should have been enough to keep him occupied, but Jeffrey had another more pressing problem—his wife. Just the thought of Kristen sent his blood boiling. He could still remember not so long ago, when it boiled with passion. Somewhere along the line, his passion had turned to hate. Certainly, he could still appreciate her beauty. Everyone admired her charm and good looks. He could find no fault with her appearance. Jeffrey's love turned to disgust after getting to know his wife's temperament and her lack of integrity. He now saw how she used her beauty like a sharpened instrument of war, cutting off her enemies and friends alike with her sharp tongue and lack of compassion.

When he married her, she had been hurt deeply by someone or something. He had tried to help her, but instead of accepting her husband's unquestioning love, Kristen had used his feelings for her against him.

She laughed at his weakness for her body, ridiculed him for his need for closeness, but the fatal blow came when she rid herself of his child. A child he had not even known existed until Missy ran to him with the news that Kristen needed him. Jeffrey learned that his wife had been thrown from her horse, and the fall had caused her to lose the baby.

Nursing Kristen back to health, Jeffrey finally questioned his wife. Even in her weak state she laughed at him, telling her husband she would never ruin her figure to bear even a single child for him.

The image still stung when Jeffrey brought it to mind. Never again had he bothered his wife with his needs, preferring to visit the ladies in town who were happy to see him and men like him.

This morning when he had awakened to find Kristen staring at his body, Jeffrey thought she must be thinking of some new way to humiliate him. He would never let his guard down with her again, because she would eat him alive.

It had come as a relief of sorts when he first started hearing rumors of Kristen and other men. No one ever said anything to him, but the looks that passed between his wife and a certain governor at the recent Tobacco Growers Ball had not gone unnoticed. Out of sympathy, Jeffrey had danced with the governor's sweet, round, little wife, while forcing himself to ignore his laughing wife in the governor's arms.

Running a hand through his thick, dark hair, he forced his mind back to the plantation's affairs and away from his wife's. It might have worked if Kristen had not come into the room at that moment.

As usual, her looks stunned. Like an object he could never possess, only admire from afar. He had built a wall between himself and his lovely wife. Luckily, her selfishness outshone her considerable beauty so he could see through to the ugliness inside.

"Jeffrey?"

What did she want now? She seemed flustered, which he doubted she had felt since she turned thirteen, when she first gauged her effect on men. "Yes?"

"I just wanted to tell you good morning and that I'm sorry if I made you uncomfortable earlier." A shy smile played on her face.

Jeffrey could not have been more shocked if she had pulled a gun out and shot him. No, actually, that would have been more in line with his wife's personality. She never found fault in anything she did, therefore she never apologized.

"You're apologizing?"

Kristen looked confused. "I-I-I'm t-t-trying t-to."

Jeffrey's eyes widened in disbelief. What kind of game was she playing? Stuttering like a shy schoolgirl? This must be some new wicked way to draw him in and slice his heart out for the final time? He would never recover from the blow she had dealt by killing his child and then laughing about it. "What's wrong with you?"

Taking a deep breath, she seemed to need to compose herself. "Nothing is wrong with me. I just wanted to say I-I'm sorry."

"Fine, you've said it, now leave me alone." Jeffrey turned his head to face his books.

He heard footsteps running down the hall, his concentration shattered. He pushed his chair back and stood. He needed a good, long, hard ride. Anything to take his mind off the impending war coming between the states and the ongoing war he fought at home with his wife.

Four

*T*oo **upset after** her run-in with Jeffrey to eat anything, Kristen decided to get her "ride" over with. She would just climb on the horse, take a short jaunt and be done with it. A young slave named Noah led her to the stable. He, too, seemed afraid of her, keeping his distance. He walked ahead of her and constantly looked over his shoulder to make sure she followed.

"Could you slow down a little, Noah?" Kristen said to the skinny figure ahead. If this dress was meant for riding on a horse's back, she did not want to see what she would be expected to wear for a formal occasion. She could barely breathe because of the tight corset and her long skirt with its petticoats tangling around her legs. The half boots had pointed toes that pinched her feet, and a small raised heel that made her wobble on the gravel walkway. She longed for a pair of jeans and a pair of broke-in cowboy boots. She might look good but she doubted whether she could control a car in this outfit, much less ride a horse.

Double doors opened up to a stable almost as large as the high school Kristen had gone to. It smelled of fresh hay and clean horses, with only a faint hint of what horses did in stables.

Walking in with as much confidence as she could under the circumstances, Kristen looked around. In stall after stall she saw the gleaming backsides of horses. *Which one is mine? Do I just call out his name?*

A groom came out from deep within the stables leading a tall black horse saddled and ready to ride. The closer they came, the faster Kristen's heart beat. *This is just a dream, surely my heart won't shatter in my chest.*

Kristen hoped Diablo hadn't earned his name. His shiny coal-black hide brought to mind the darkness of hell. The large, rolling eyes of the big horse made Kristen step back as the groom brought him to stand in front of her.

"Here's you are, Mz. O'Conner," the groom said grinning from ear-to-ear. Did the man enjoy scaring her to death? *No, I'm not supposed to be scared. This is my horse.* Hopefully, the horse knew and liked her because she wondered how she could keep this huge animal from doing exactly what he pleased.

"Let me help you up, ma'am." The groom grinned, his white teeth contrasting with his black hair and skin.

"Um, sure." *What am I supposed to do next?*

As if sensing something wrong, Diablo laid back his ears and started prancing. The groom yanked on the reins, bringing the horse around. Standing against the animal's left side, he flung the reins over the Diablo's neck and then he leaned down, forming a cradle with his hands and waited.

She looked up to the saddle and then back to the horse looking down his long nose at her. The moment she started toward him, Diablo bared his teeth.

"I think I'll skip my ride this morning." Kristen stuffed her hands in the ruffles of the dress to hide their shaking.

"Oh no, ma'am. You can't. The governor's groom done told me that you was supposed to meet the governor up on the big hill this morning," the man said.

"Right, I must have forgotten." Kristen put her foot into the groom's hands and felt herself being lifted onto the horse. She tried to swing her leg over the saddle but her skirts hampered such a move. Hanging onto the saddle horn, she noticed for the first time that the horn protruded halfway down the saddle on the left side, instead of on top. *There's something very wrong with this saddle. How am I supposed to sit on this thing? What's going on?*

"I think there's something wrong with the saddle," she said to the groom who held her in place as she lay across the saddle.

"It's your usual saddle, ma'am."

"A side-saddle?" Kristen now understood how she should sit on the saddle, but it still looked unnatural. Sitting on the back of the saddle, she lifted her right leg over the horn with her skirts trailing over the top. She put her left leg in the stirrup.

Although, not as uncomfortable as she would have thought, she felt unsteady. Diablo, done with standing still, started prancing as the groom handed Kristen the reins. She assumed pulling back meant stop. The rest she would have to figure out because the horse had decided to move.

The countryside went by in a blur. The springtime flowers and trees burst with color and fragrance, none of which Kristen could appreciate as she struggled to hang onto the saddle horn – the only anchor between herself and the rushing ground under the horse's thundering hooves.

The reins, which she had held for a brief second, danced just out of reach on the long-arched neck of the black demon. She clung to the saddle for dear life.

It seemed she'd been hanging on forever, but in reality, it probably had been about fifteen minutes. Fifteen minutes of a never-ending nightmare.

Out of nowhere, a ghostly-white shape came up beside her. An angel must have come to take her to heaven because she had died while riding this runaway horse. When the other horse slammed up against her legs, she realized the horse had a rider. A man who seemed determined to pull Kristen off her wild mount.

Why would this crazy man want to drag her off the horse while she hung on for dear life? *What's wrong with him?*

"Kristen! Let go!"

The voice held such command that Kristen did not even think. She just let go, falling into the space between the two horses. Certain she would hit the ground – she tensed for the fall and her death. If the rushing ground did not kill her, the eight hooves pounding through the high grass surely would.

Arms like steel held her. She sailed through the air landing on the front of the saddle. Her layers of petticoats and gown saved her from hitting the saddle horn too hard as she slid back into the arms of her savior. Both horses slowed.

"What on earth were you thinking?" Jeffrey shouted in Kristen's ear.

"I was taking my h-h-horse out for h-h-is morning ride," she sobbed.

"You could've been killed!"

Kristen nodded, not trusting herself to speak. The thought had occurred to her also. Then what would have happened? Would she wake up on the couch in the television studio? Or would she die altogether? She had no idea.

Jeffrey shifted as if uncomfortable. His movements made a blush creep up Kristen's cheeks. The sway of the walking horse replaced her fear with a new emotion. Unaccustomed to the feelings that accompanied the tingling sensation running up and down her spine, warmth spread throughout her body and lodged itself in her core.

Against her back, Kristen could feel his response. It became increasingly more difficult to breathe as the big horse picked his path though the long grass. The horse slowed to a stop, oblivious to her raging emotions. He reached down and nibbled on the wildflowers within reach.

Kristen leaned back into the warmth Jeffrey provided. Why not enjoy the time she had? Her husband in this life would expect his wife to act like a "wife." She had to at least try to behave as the previous owner of this body, being married meant intimacy. Judging by Jeffrey's reaction to her sitting so close in front of him, this marriage had some passion. In order to keep up appearances, she would have to continue to be his wife in every sense of the word. A new bolt of electricity shot through her body.

With a sigh, she leaned into the strong arms that held the reins around her body. She tilted her head allowing his lips access to her neck, his warm breath delicious against her skin. She leaned in closer feeling the roughness of his chin on her skin.

Well, here goes. Kristen turned her face until her lips grazed his. Touching for the first time sent a shock, like touching a hot stove, through her body. The warmth came not from his lips but from her own. Shocked, she pressed against Jeffrey's lips and discovered that he was not the fire, only the match. Her body smoldered with urgency, which sparked a desire to fall to the ground and drag him on top of her.

The kiss deepened. She opened like a flower to the sunlight that fed its very existence. Helpless to the force that gave her life, she drank it in like a greedy child tasting sweet for the first time. To Kristen, it filled her with something that she had never had before. *Had Jeffrey felt this way before? Was it like this with the other Kristen?*

When his mouth forced hers open and his tongue slipped inside, Kristen met it with her own hunger, tasting of a fruit that should have been forbidden for its mind-numbing sweetness.

A voice out of a fog broke through to Kristen. She almost wept when Jeffrey broke off the kiss, leaving her gasping for breath. She held onto his arms, helpless against the spinning world.

"Mr. and Mrs. O'Connor." A dashing man rode up beside them, tipping his hat and smiling. "Glorious morning for a ride."

Jeffrey sat up straight and let go of her arms, almost toppling Kristen from the horse. She grabbed for the saddle horn, with no other support except what the saddle offered.

"Governor Gustave, what brings you all this way to our land?" Jeffrey said politely. At least the words seemed polite, but Kristen could hear a note of challenge running just under the surface.

"Why, I was invited for a ride by your lovely wife." The governor gave a self-satisfied grin and rubbed his goatee. "I was interested in sketching some of the birds in the area, and your wife was kind enough to offer to show me where they were nesting."

Something passed between the two men that had nothing to do with their conversation. The air shimmered with tension.

Jeffrey slid off his horse, leaving Kristen sitting alone on top of the big beast. "I'm sure my wife would be more than happy to show you the birds you wish to sketch, Governor." He patted the horse on its rear setting it off at a fast walk. The governor reined his own long-legged thoroughbred in the same direction.

Kristen turned in dismay to see Jeffrey standing still as a stone watching her. He wore a look that told her exactly what he thought of her. She wanted to turn the horse around and ask him what happened. *Why is he sending me off with a man I don't even know? Is this proper? Was the governor a relative of some kind? Would she be safe with him?*

The governor urged his horse into a trot. Kristen's own horse followed suit. She hung onto the horse's reins and turned away from the man who had just touched her soul with only a kiss. If she could have controlled the horse under her, she would have turned him around and sent him running back to Jeffrey. Instead, she hung on for dear life praying the animal would not run off like the black demon from hell had done only minutes before.

Five

A sharp whistle brought the big black horse trotting over to Jeffrey. Grabbing the reins, he stroked the long nose before unfastening the saddle and laying it across the back of the horse. He climbed on and rode back to the plantation house, barely able to keep his temper under control.

Jeffery brought Diablo, well lathered, to the groom. The tall black man raised an eyebrow at the sight of his master coming home on a different horse than he had gone out on and with a woman's saddle slung over the withers of the horse.

Jeffrey swung his right leg over the saddle while his horse still moved and landed stiffly on the ground in front of the groom. "Diablo deserves extra grain in his feed tonight. At least *he* doesn't forget who he belongs to."

Taking the reins of the horse, the groom bowed his head and then turned to walk the animal into the barn.

A large, white-haired, black woman met Jeffrey at the back door.

"You don't look so good, Mr. Jeffrey."

"I'm fine, Lila." He swept past the large woman who nearly blocked him with her enormous hips.

"You certainly don't look fine, Mr. Jeffrey."

Shooting her a look that would have struck fear in any man, Jeffrey shook his head. "Tell my wife I'll be leaving tonight to meet my troops."

Clucking, Lila shook her head. "I just knew t'were something doing with Mz. Kristen."

"Just tell her, okay?" Jeffrey said in a softer voice. "And send someone up to pack my things."

"Sure, enough, Mr. Jeffrey. Sure, enough."

Once alone in his office, Jeffrey poured half a glass of scotch whiskey and drank most of it in one swallow. The burning, amber liquid numbed the pain from Kristen's kiss. How could he have ever forgotten what it felt like to kiss her? The taste of her still drove his senses wild with desire, and she knew it.

Today had been different. The passion had something more to it than just lust. Something he had never felt with his wife before burned him down to his soul. Today, Kristen finally reached the one part of him he had kept secret and hidden from her. Finally, she had the power to break him completely. He knew he had no defenses left. He had to get away from his wife, as far as possible, before she could work her wiles on him. With any luck, the Yankees would see to it that he did not live long enough to come back to his self-created hell.

He finished off the scotch and poured himself two more. Then he walked unsteady up to their shared room, certain his wife would not be home for hours. He would be gone by then.

Six

When Kristen's horse finally came to a stop, she wanted to be on steady ground again. The swampy ground suggested to her that she must be pretty far south, however, she needed confirmation to be sure of her location. *How can I find out without the governor catching on to anything?*

Sliding off his own horse with ease, the governor moved to her side with unexpected speed — given his gray hair. He looked at least fifty. His hands traveled up her waist stopping at her breasts. Kristen yanked away, stumbling on the uneven wet ground.

"Don't tell me you're suddenly shy?" The governor's eyes traveled up and down her body.

"I believe I'm married." Kristen backed away.

The governor stepped closer. "So am I, as a matter a fact." He laughed as if he had just told a joke that Kristen should understand. "But you *did* invite me out here."

"I did?" Kristen almost swallowed her tongue.

"You most certainly did, my dear. I do believe you had something special in mind for the two of us." He stepped forward pinning Kristen against the horse. The horse whinnied and moved sideways causing Kristen to lose her balance and fall backwards. She landed in the wet grass and mud, her body sinking into the muck.

The governor seemed to take this as an invitation. He threw off his hat, dropped down on top of her, sinking her farther into the mud. "This might be fun." He brought his face down on Kristen's chest, covering her bare bosoms with wet kisses.

"Get off me!" Kristen pushed against him with all her strength.

This seemed to make the governor more excited. "Playing hard to get, are you? I've heard you like it rough." He grabbed her chin, forced her mouth to his, and pressed hard enough to bruise Kristen's lips.

When his tongue came out in a mocking replay of Jeffrey's searing kiss, Kristen could stand it no longer. She bit down hard.

"What that hell!" The governor sat up and glared at Kristen. Blood dripped from his tongue and down his lip. With a cold smile, he drew his hand back and slapped her across the face. "Bitch!"

Sure that would be the end of it, Kristen tried to sit up. Her cheek stung with the slap and she could taste blood on the inside of her mouth. Nobody had ever struck her before.

"If you ever do that again, it'll be the last time!" The sound of her own voice shocked her.

The governor laughed but moved off, as if seeing something he had not noticed before in Kristen. "I guess this means you don't want my help when the war comes."

"I don't want your help for anything." Kristen could hardly believe the gall of the man. "I happen to love my husband."

The governor's jaw dropped. Then he laughed, picked up his hat, grabbed his horse, and mounted. His laughter didn't even stop when he tipped his hat to her. "Just to hear you say that was worth everything." He turned and rode away.

Pulling herself out of the mud, Kristen looked around. *Now what am I supposed to do?* The white horse she had ridden grazed a few feet away. *How am I supposed to get back on the beast?*

Brushing off the mud as best she could, Kristen made a tentative grab for the reins. He walked along when she pulled on the reins, following like a contented dog. *This isn't so hard.* At least it did not seem to be until she realized that she had no idea which way to go home. Having heard stories of how a horse would go directly back to its stall when given its head, she considered letting the animal go and just following. She pictured the horse making a run for it the moment she let go of him. At least with the horse, she could always try to mount it and then let it find its way home. If she let it go, she might be doomed to wander the countryside, probably forever. Everywhere she looked, Kristen saw nothing but grass and fields with some sort of plants growing in neat rows.

"Now what do I do?"

The rows of plants in the distance finally gave Kristen an idea. They were obviously cultivated so that meant she was close to the mansion. She had not noticed anything during her wild ride earlier that morning and had followed blindly when the governor led the way to the swamp. If she walked towards the fields, she should eventually find her way back to the main house. She hoped it would be the same mansion she had left earlier.

The horse seemed to want to go in the same direction so Kristen let him, walking wearily beside him. Her mud-covered dress made it hard to breathe and hard to walk since her skirts kept tangling in her legs. Her stomach growled, making her wish she hadn't skipped breakfast. She estimated the time to be nearly one o'clock in the afternoon, judging from the high sun in the sky. It took nearly two more hours to make it back to the mansion. Nothing had ever looked so good.

Once in sight of the stables, Kristen let go of the reins and the horse took off at a fast trot.

"Glad *you* feel better." The blisters on her feet from the stylish boots made every step agonizing.

She nearly collapsed on the back steps. A middle-aged black woman wearing a full gingham skirt caught her. The woman's dark-black face made it difficult to determine where her hair started and her skin left off.

"Mz. Kristen! What happened?"

Wanting nothing more than to fall into this capable looking woman's arms, Kristen nearly sobbed out her story.

"That governor slapped you?"

Kristen nodded. "What could he have been thinking?"

The woman's eyes narrowed. Kristen wondered if she'd said something wrong, but what?

Silence.

"Let Lila just get you out of these wet clothes, for now," Lila said acting as if there hadn't been strained silence between them a moment ago. "Just get on up to your room while I send your maid up to help you get undressed."

"Thank you." Kristen grabbed her hand and squeezed. *Lila? Thanks for telling me who you are.* "And could you send up something to eat?" She did not think she would be able to climb the wide staircase in her exhausted condition. *One step at a time.* She trudged up the stairs, tracking mud on the thick, red carpet, too tired to care.

In the room she shared with her "husband," she pulled off her shoes. The maid, Missy, came in and helped her out of her dirty clothes.

Down to just a thin chemise, Kristen threw herself across the wide bed and closed her eyes, asleep in seconds.

"**W**here are you taking that dress?" Jeffrey asked on his way up the stairs.

"I's taking it down to be washed, master." Missy held Kristen's ruined gown out for Jeffrey to see.

His eyes ran up and down the gown, a frown furrowing his brows. Mud covered the back of the gown, the bodice lace ripped, buttons were missing, and the hem had come out.

His mind painted a picture of all the things that could have made Kristen's gown look this way, along with a picture of the governor. He found that for once he *did* care. Maybe the shared soul-searing kiss, or maybe watching her engage with so many men in too short a time had caused him to care. Jeffrey wanted his wife to feel as much pain as he felt because of what she had done. His meeting with the army could be delayed for a few hours while he taught his wife a lesson she would never forget.

Seven

*T*he sight of his wife sleeping so innocently across their bed fanned the flame of both Jeffrey's anger and his desire. Kristen's russet hair spread across the cream brocade comforter like fire. Her pale skin, dusted with a faint sprinkling of freckles, displayed a red handprint across one cheek, her full lips, bruised and slightly open in peaceful sleep. The one hand curled under her chin like a child belied an act of violence, he could only guess. Or was it?

Long, bare legs tempted Jeffrey's very soul. His eyes moved to where the thin material ended near the top of her thighs. One breast had escaped the low-cut chemise, a dark-pink nipple half-visible above the lace.

With an involuntary groan, Jeffrey clenched his fist. He hung onto his rage at what he imagined had brought his wife's lips to their swollen state. Desire arose in him and a primal need to claim his wife.

With slow deliberate movements, he undressed without taking his eyes off his wife's sleeping form. *I'm going to show her what it means to tease a man and then leave with another.* By the time he stood naked beside the bed he anger burned almost beyond control.

Something must have aroused his wife. Her eyes flew open. Up and down his entire body she stared, stopping just below his belly. The shy smile that lit up her face made her appear even more beautiful.

Jeffrey could stand it no longer. With rough hands, he took his wife by the shoulders. Slow and deliberate, he ripped her chemise down the middle. It parted in his hands as if made of paper. She gasped but did not move. Her nipples hardened at their sudden freedom. Jeffrey made the mistake of looking down at her breasts and lost himself.

*A*wakening to the strange man standing over her took Kristen's breath away. When he tore the flimsy chemise from her body, she flinched. Instinct urged her to turn away, yet she knew she had a duty to her husband at this time, in this place. If she acted otherwise, he would surely lock her up in a place she could never escape. *I have to act as his wife.*

With shaking hands, Kristen reached for Jeffrey. The memory of their earlier kiss burned her mind with its intensity. She pulled him toward her. Jeffrey did not resist.

Their lips met. The fire ignited.

*W*hatever Jeffrey might have planned for his wife left his mind. The feel of her familiar, yet unfamiliar lips on his, tasting, extracting pieces of both his mind and his soul erased whatever he had shared with his wife for the past three years. His weakness found strength in the power of his wife's need. Unable to hold himself back, he pushed Kristen's legs apart. His trembling hand found her wet center. It seemed to clutch at him, making him suck in a sharp breath. Never had she welcomed him like this before. That knowledge pushed him over the edge. He had to be inside or he would surely die of the wanting. Rolling on top of her lush body, Jeffrey pushed inside her waiting depths. Like dying and coming to life at the same time, the rhythm as old as time itself took over and together they rocked in perfect harmony.

His wife arched up and Jeffrey lost control. He buried himself in her warm body and let go. He whispered her name like a magic spell. *Could she save him?*

*T*he world returned to its usual form when Kristen felt Jeffrey's release spill into her. Never before had she experienced anything like what they had just shared. How did mere humans survive such glory? Surely, a person could die of such pleasure. No wonder the gods of myth had come down to make love with humans. For moments like what they had just shared, Kristen could see giving up eternity.

"I love you," she whispered, stroking his sweat-soaked hair away from his forehead.

Jeffrey stiffened. He rolled away as if she had struck him

"What's wrong?" Kristen said, alarmed at his change of behavior.

"What's wrong?" Jumping out of the bed he stood naked over her. "What are you trying to do to me? Do you think I don't know where you learned your new tricks in bed?" Jeffrey picked up his pants and pulled them on his sweating body. Kristen watched in appreciation.

"Did the governor teach you some new tricks this morning on your ride?" he said, his voice thick with disgust.

Kristen sat up. "I have no idea what you're talking about."

Jeffrey laughed. The sound held no humor. It grated on Kristen's nerves.

"I saw your dress." His eyes narrowed. "You tried to get it washed before I could see it, didn't you?"

"I fell in the mud!" Kristen said, her own anger rising to the surface. How could he be so cruel after what they had just shared together? *What kind of man am I married to?*

"Really?" Jeffrey sneered. "And what happened once you were on your back?"

"The governor tried to rape me, if you must know!"

For a split second the smile left his face and he looked unsure. Then it was back. He shook his head. "Is that what you call it now?"

"Yes, that's exactly what I call it!" Kristen shouted. How could he not believe her? "And I don't care if you believe me or not. It's the truth."

Jeffrey picked up his shirt. Giving Kristen one last look, he turned and walked out, the door slamming behind him.

Furious, Kristen threw every pillow she could reach at the closed door.

Eight

Kristen was still fuming when someone knocked at the door. "Yes?" *It couldn't be Jeffrey. He wouldn't knock.*
A timid voice called out. "Here's your lunch, ma'am."

"Come in." At least she could finally eat. Jeffrey had left her with an appetite that mere food could never satisfy, but it was a start.

"I broughts you your favorite," Missy said balancing a silver tray in one hand as she opened the door. "Kidney and liver pie."

"Liver?" Kristen's voice cracked her empty stomach roiling. "Kidney?"

"Lila sent it up. She said you'd be needing your strength for the ball tonight." Missy gave a wisp of a smile. "You want I should help you dress again?"

"Don't you usually?" Kristen tried not to breathe in the rich smell of the pie Missy set down on a nearby table. The aroma made her nauseous. *Am I allergic to liver?*

"I've been in training to be a lady's maid since Violet done been sold."

"Really?" Kristen tried to keep the horror out of her voice. Sold? How could any society condone the buying and selling of other human beings, especially in a country that wrote in its constitution that "all men are created equal." *Maybe some people are just more equal than others.*

"Yep," Missy said, warming to her subject. "Ever since she

took up with Jeremiah and done got herself pregnant, you say you ain't gonna stand for that kind of slave being your personal maid."

Apparently gossip lived in the nineteenth century, too. Kristen could not imagine selling a woman for becoming pregnant by a man she probably loved. Now the child would never know its father. How cruel. How could she have done such a thing?

Wait a minute. I did no such thing. The Kristen who lives in this time and by the rules of this century made that decision. Now I have to live by it. Or do I?

"Tell me, Missy. Does Jeremiah love Violet?"

"Sure enough, ma'am. Violet cried her eyes out when she found out she was going to be sold. I heard Jeremiah done the same."

Kristen shook her head. What kind of place was this? "Where's Violet now?" she asked the slave.

Missy's eyes widened. "She's with the governor now. You knows that."

"Yes, of course. I must've forgotten for a moment." Kristen took a deep breath. How was she going to get Violet back from that monster? She would have to go to Jeffrey.

"Maybe I can get those two back together again."

"You are?" Missy's eyes widened even further.

"Why not?" Kristen tried to sound sure. Which man did she take her chances with? The one who tried to rape her, or the one who succeeded in raping her so Missy seemed to consider this with a great deal of doubt. "I'll be back in an hour to help you dress for the Governor's Ball." She backed toward the door.

"The Governor's Ball?" *How could this be happening to me? When am I going to awaken from this nightmare? Not all of it's been a nightmare*, a small voice reminded her. "Yes, I'm sure I'll need your help." *More than you'll ever know.*

"Sho nuff, ma'am." With that, Missy closed the door.

Kristen looked over at the steaming pie and realized that at the rate she was going, she wouldn't need a corset to fit into her clothes. Pulling on a heavy-silk wrap she found in the chest at the end of the bed, she left the room. *I need to find out exactly where I am on a map and what year it is.* She knew very little about the Civil War,

42

but she knew it started in the spring of 1861 and that the South would be destroyed. Hopefully, her location would not be in the path of General Sherman's famous march through the South.

*L*eaving her room and the kidney pie behind, Kristen crept down the stairs. She did not want to run into Jeffrey or anyone else for that matter, but where to look first? She could not start asking questions. Everyone in the house would think she had lost her mind if she asked the year and month again. She also wondered if she had any brothers or sisters.

Another thing occurred to her. *I have no accent.* Of course, she did not have an accent because she had not lived in the South. Strange though, in this time, why did no one notice that she did not have the required drawl? Questions like these, required answers soon.

On her way downstairs, she thought of the perfect place to find the answers to all her questions. This big place should have a library. Did not people of this century keep their histories in their Bibles? Hopefully, she could find one in the library.

Creeping down the long hallway, Kristen peeked in door after door until she finally came to a room filled with books. Her luck held—nobody occupied the room.

Staring up at the twelve-foot-high shelves of books, Kristen gaped at the vast selection. Leather-bound copies of numerous classics caught her eye—Ivanhoe, Cervantes' Classic, Man of La Mancha, and more than a few books in languages she did not recognize. *Who's read all of these?* Somehow, she doubted that her alter ego read extensively. Kristen the first, she decided to call the woman whose body she now occupied. It did occur to her that if she were in this body, there was a possibility that the other soul was in *her* body. Now that would have been fun to watch, a spoiled Southern belle in the body of a medical student/housecleaner. If the other Kristen were in her body now, there would be no job or medical school to go back to, that she was sure of.

The Bible was easy to spot. It was so big it sat on a brass and wood stand off to one side of the room. Kristen pulled up one of the delicate looking Louis IV chairs and opened the book. Just as she thought, the first page was a family tree. This first page was dedicated to Kristen's family. To her surprise, her maiden name had been Bassett. If she remembered correctly, her grandmother had said that their family had come from France in the beginning. They had come from a proud, old French family by the name of Bassett. That meant Kristen the first, in this time period, could have been in her own family tree.

Moving her finger down the row of names she saw the name Margaret, Leona, and two more names Kristen recognized from her own family tree. What did it mean? Was it true? Had she been regressed in time to one of her previous lives? Does that mean a person's soul or spirit comes through the same family bloodline? An old Bible verse came to mind, something about the sins of the fathers being visited upon the sons. That would make sense if you were born to your own children in an unending circle.

Just thinking about it made her headache. Enough about regressions, she needed cold, hard facts. What year and month did she live in now? Whose life had she been dropped into at this particular moment in time? And why was she here instead of Kristen the first at this particular moment in time?

Kristen's date of birth was listed as September 2, 1843, her place of birth, Philadelphia—her parents, Jean-Paul and Yvette Bassett hailing from Montreal, Canada.

So, that explained why she had no accent. She came from the North. That might prove a little difficult once the war started. Maybe she should start her drawl now so she fit in. Looking down the list further, Kristen noticed a brother and a sister. Both died while still young.

"Good, that means I won't have any more surprises," Kristen said to the empty room.

Well, time to get dressed for the Ball. Now that'll be fun. A room full of people she supposedly knew, a husband who thought she had slept with the governor, the host of the ball who had tried to rape her. At least she would not be bored in this time zone.

Nine

Kristen rode in the carriage alone while Jeffrey sat up top with the groom and a footman. It would have been nice to have company but Jeffrey seemed to be in no mood for close quarters with her, so she sat alone.

She imagined riding in the carriage would be uncomfortable, but the navy-blue velvet seats were soft, with plenty of room to stretch out. The springs on the carriage and its wooden wheels, did not provide a bounce free ride on the dirt road.

The matching curtains over the widows could be tied back with gold cords, providing privacy or opportunities to watch people as the coach moved. Kristen pushed back the curtains to watch the passing countryside. The ride stopped.

"Wow!" A gleaming, white mansion stood at the end of a long lane of live oaks, spreading their graceful branches overhead. Four, wide, Greek columns supported the two-story structure, with tall windows and a gleaming double door of dark wood. The mansion looked like something out of a movie. Gone With the Wind came to mind. Kristen smiled—her mouth half open. She gave herself a reality check. Even if the locations reminded her of a movie, the buildings, furniture, and people were current for the time period. A time period she did not belong to but needed to fit in with for the time being. The fixtures here were not well-preserved relics from the past, but fresh and new. She was just a visitor, the one out of time and place.

Lighted lanterns hung everywhere, lining the circular drive and adding a fairytale ambiance to the house. Kristen noted candles burning inside the wide entrance at the open double doors. Men in dark suits extended their arms to assist brightly-dressed women as they exited their carriages in front of the mansion. She twisted her fingers, waiting to depart the carriage.

When the carriage door opened, she saw Jeffery for the first time since their afternoon of intimacy. Kristen extended her gloved hand for his hand despite the growing warmth in her cheeks.

He helped her from the carriage. His neatly-combed raven hair accented his intense gray eyes, which appeared to penetrate Kristen's soul. She tried to read that compelling expression but he gave nothing away. She dropped her gaze hoping her husband would interpret it as shyness, rather than mortification.

Offering his arm, Jeffrey led her up the wide stairs of the mansion into the bright, interior lights. The heavy scent of exotic flowers almost overwhelmed the mouth-watering odors of the spicy food spread out on tables lining the room. A sixteen-piece orchestra permeated the room with music, while dread took hold of Kristen's emotions. She had no idea how to dance in this era.

Jeffrey led her up the steps to a distinguished looking older gentleman wearing a smile that leaned toward being a lustful sneer. She recognized the governor, the man who had tried to rape her earlier. Kristen almost flinched when the monster held out his hand to her.

"Good evening, Mr. and Mrs. O'Connor," the governor's wife said smiling. She stood only five-feet tall, and almost as wide, but her face held a fading beauty emphasized by her good-natured smile. The governor stood next to his wife, still leering at Kristen.

"Mrs. Gustave," Jeffery said bending over and kissing her hand. "Your beauty ripens with each passing year."

His tenderness with the older woman made Kristen want to weep with frustration. *Why couldn't he act the same way toward me?*

"Jeffrey O'Connor, you lie so convincingly that I almost believe you." Mrs. Gustave winked at the handsome man still holding her hand.

The governor took Kristen's hand and brought it to his full lips.

Kristen looked up and found herself gazing into the eager eyes of the man who had abused her only hours earlier that day. Her cheeks burned with the memory. She wanted to snatch her hand back, but the thick fingers of the governor held her fingers firmly. She smiled and acted as if she were just meeting the disgusting man for the first time.

"You look lovely this evening," the governor said, his voice nearly a whisper as he bent over her gloved hand. "I hope we can have another look at those nesting birds."

Kristen had had enough. She yanked her hand out of the governor's grasp, thankful that she could not feel his flesh through her silk gloves. "I don't think I'll have time for that." She ground her teeth together, her voice tight despite her polite words.

"Oh, but I think you will." The governor gave her a sly wink.

She wanted to tell the lecherous old man to go to hell, but was pulled away by an iron grasp on her opposite arm. Jeffrey led her toward the ballroom, tucking the hand the governor had just defiled safely under his arm.

Grateful to be rescued, she smiled up at her husband. He greeted her with a steely look she would not have wished on anyone.

The sound of music drew her attention away from her scowling husband and toward the large ballroom, about the size of a modern football field. Floor-to-ceiling multiple-paned windows lined the walls, opened to allow the fresh evening breezes into the room filled with people.

Chandeliers sparkled, and lights danced across the ceiling painted with delicate, winged cherubs wearing sweet smiles. The chubby angels intensified the otherworldliness of the room. Intricate patterns of inlaid wood gleamed across the vast expanse of the ballroom floor.

Long tables covered with snowy-white tablecloths that hung to the floor were covered with platters of hors d'oeuvres, finger sandwiches and mounds of ripe fruits. A magnificent swan-shaped ice sculpture sat in the center, surrounded by shrimp, crab, and local crawfish.

Just the sight of the mouth-watering food drove Kristen to distraction. She could not remember the last time she had eaten and she now stood in front of a table filled with her favorite foods — enough to feed an army. She mused and cringed over being here in this time and the place.

Kristen stood in the candlelight, bathed in the romantic sounds of a live orchestra, on the arm of the most compelling man she'd ever met. Like Cinderella, she wondered when she would be whisked back to her old life, without her handsome prince.

The aroma of a rich, floral perfume floated over Kristen like a cloud. She looked up to see a tiny blonde drift toward them, wrapped in a swath of silvery silk that caressed her every delicate curve.

"Jeffrey. Kristen," the blond said through pouty, red lips.

She heard her name in the woman's greeting, but she sensed that politeness stimulated the acknowledgement, not interest.

"I've saved you a dance," the blond said, her longing gaze looking up at Kristen's husband.

I'm sure you saved him more than that. Kristen kept her smile in place but she felt her hands clenched into fists.

Jeffrey's interested return gaze caused Kristen's heart to contract. Of course he would be attracted to her. What man wouldn't be? Even she recognized the vision of femininity the woman projected.

Jeffrey smiled. "I would be delighted, Angela. Your wish is my command."

Peering down at her own deep-scarlet water-silk-taffeta gown, she suddenly felt out of place. Next to this elegant woman, she was like a large-udder cow. She could not get used to the style of dress and the constant battle to keep her full breasts from overwhelming the bodice of the gown. She would not be surprised if Jeffrey sent her home alone while he gave Angela the attention Kristen craved with every ounce of her being.

Saving herself the inevitable rejection, Kristen looked down at her hand on his arm and reluctantly left the warmth and security of his presence. "I think I need something to drink."

Jeffrey looked at Kristen, his eyes questioning. "I'll get you something." When she slid her eyes to the floor, he turned to Angela. "A Sherry for you?"

Angela smiled, tilting her head sideways. "You *are* such a gentleman," she drawled. The moment Jeffrey disappeared from sight, Angela turned to Kristen. "If you don't want your husband, the least you can do is to give him a divorce so he can find happiness with someone else."

Kristen's shock at the woman's boldness caused her to snap back to the woman's face. Her smile had been replaced by a pitying look.

"I know you're only hanging onto him for appearances sake," Angela said. "When everyone knows that you'd rather have a man with political ambitions."

Oh my God! She thinks I want the governor. How could anyone think I'd want that lecherous old man when I'm married to a man like Jeffrey?

Kristen finally gathered her wits about her. "You have no idea what you're talking about! I happen to love my husband very much." She knew this to be true the instant she said it. She had fallen in love with Jeffrey, the baffling man she'd married in this life. Dream or no dream, she had fallen completely, head-over-heels for a man who seemed to want her body but nothing else from her.

"Oh please, Kristen, spare me." Angela shook her head. "You're just playing with him, and a man like Jeffrey deserves better."

"Like you?" Kristen said, surprising herself. Never in her life had she been good at confrontation, and now here she was, butting heads with a woman like Angela. Scenes from her high school years, watching the mean girls take what they wanted came rushing back to her. Channeling those characters, she glared at the woman before her. "I happen to want Jeffrey."

Angela gave an indelicate snort. "Of course. And obviously Jeffrey wants you." She pursed her lips. "Look, Kristen. You can have any man in the county, including our esteemed host." She looked pointedly in the direction of the governor. "Now you and I have been friends for a long time. And since my husband had the good sense to pass away before his advanced age became a burden to me, I'd like to have yours."

"You've got to be kidding!" Kristen could not help but smile at the woman's candor. "Why would I want to divorce my husband?"

"Because you don't want children, and I'd like to start a family." Her large, blue eyes narrowed. "And I happen to know that Jeffrey would like children of his own, too."

Kristen could not believe what she was hearing. The women of the twentieth century considered themselves to be direct. They could take lessons from this delicate Southern belle. She could only imagine how Angela knew that Jeffrey wanted children.

Angela turned away from Kristen and toward Jeffrey who made his way back to the women with two crystalline-stemmed glasses, filled with a dark-red liquid in each hand.

"Well I'm not giving him up," Kristen said through clenched teeth.

"And I don't think you're going to have a choice in the matter, my dear friend." A bright smile lit up her face as Jeffrey came to stand in front of her.

"Oh, my goodness, you are one sweet man."

Jeffrey smiled at Angela, handing her one of the glasses. She licked her full lips before taking a small sip.

Appearing transfixed for a moment, Jeffrey smiled. "It was my pleasure, ma'am."

Kristen felt her heart plummet. Obviously these two had shared more than a "dance," and Angela had the power to push her right out of her husband's life. *What man in his right mind can resist the charms of such a woman?*

"Would your wife be willing to give you up for just one dance?"

Jeffrey turned to Kristen. She could not read his icy, gray eyes, but she could guess what he wanted. Biting down on her lip until she tasted blood, Kristen finally said, "Whatever Jeffrey wants is fine with me." *And I'm sure it's not me.*

Watching in dismay as her husband led the other woman out onto the center of the dance floor and took her into his strong arms, made Kristen want to cry.

Angela put her tiny gloved hand on Jeffrey's shoulder, and he grasped her right hand firmly in his left, she smiled up at him and they began to gracefully move to the romantic waltz the orchestra played.

Tall and wide-shouldered in his soft-gray uniform, Jeffrey held his partner as if she were the most precious thing in his world. They moved as if they had been together their whole lives. Angela, a vision in shimmery silver with her golden hair cascading across her creamy-white shoulders, danced as if her feet never touched the ground. They looked like the perfect couple, and at that moment of utter defeat, Kristen wanted nothing more than to wake up from the nightmare she had found herself in.

The other dancers, as if feeling the magic of the couple swaying in their midst, cleared the floor to give Jeffrey and Angela room, until only the two of them were left. A scene plucked out of a fairytale that crushed Kristen.

Something hard clutched at Kristen's heart as the song finally ended and Jeffrey led Angela off the dance floor. *How could she, as a wife, compete with this temptress who wanted her husband? Could she make him care for her again, before it was too late and he cast her aside for another?*

51

Ten

Jeffrey tried not to laugh at Angela's description of her husband's last days, but she had a wicked sense of humor. Angela took a morose subject — death — and could create such a humorous story.

Sweeping his partner in wide circles around the nearly empty dance floor, the music swelled around them.

"All I wanted to do was to make the man happy." Angela gave him a half-smile and a wide-eyed glance. "I'd just put on the nightgown I bought in Paris. He took one look at me, clutched his chest, and fell straight over onto the floor." She shook her head and frowned. Her golden hair shimmered around her shoulders. "I guess his desire drove him right over the edge."

"And you weren't expecting it?" Jeffrey raised an eyebrow.

With a coquettish pout, Angela shook her head. "Should I have?"

"I think that a woman like you should always be aware that her charms can be fatal."

"Not always, darlin'." Angela smiled and pressed up against him. "Sometimes they can be just what a man needs."

Certain that she might be what he needed, Jeffrey sighed. At least with a woman like Angela he knew exactly where he stood, unlike his wife, whose mood had changed in the last few days, leaving him questioning everything about their relationship.

His mind turned again to the last few hours he spent with Kristen. Desiring to teach her a lesson had only succeeded in breaking open the wound he kept hidden from everyone, especially his wife.

What he could use was a woman who could heal him...a woman like Angela. *There'll be no complications.* Angela's needs seemed simple enough. She only wanted one thing, and unfortunately Jeffrey knew that it would not be him. Kristen had the power to truly heal him of the bitterness eating away at his insides, but his wife only knew how to take.

Unable to resist, Jeffrey searched the room. Kristen stood in her scarlet dress. How appropriate that she should be wearing the color of passion when only that afternoon she had shown him more passion than in all the years of their marriage. She had come alive under him in a way he never thought possible. She had always been a skilled lover, but this afternoon had been different. Kristen had finally let go for the first time. His wife had let herself go—she had trusted him. And how had he reacted in the presence of her new trust? He rejected her.

With this sudden realization, Jeffrey blinked in surprise. He needed to know what that difference meant.

"Jeffrey O'Connor," Angela said. "You're not paying any attention to me. And here we are—such a lovely couple that everyone has left the dance floor to us."

With a look around, Jeffrey saw that it was true. They were the only couple sweeping across the gleaming wood floor, the orchestra playing the last notes of the waltz.

Jeffrey smiled at the lovely woman in his arms. "They're looking at you, my dear. Only you."

*A*ngela's laughter rang out across the room like the delicate tolling of a bell. It cut right through to the center of Kristen's heart, watching the striking couple enjoy a private joke between them. Unable to subject herself to any more misery, she turned and ran from the room.

Outside on the wide porch, Kristen hid behind a palm, using the shelter of its fronds to hide the tears threatening for some time to spill over. *What's happening to me? I don't even know this man or where I'm at for that matter, and I'm already a mess. If this is a dream, it's got to be the most realistic dream ever. One afternoon with the man and I've already lost him to another woman. I still have a perfect dating record. Twenty-eight and single and I can't even hold onto a man in my dreams.*

"Waiting for someone?"

Kristen turned to see the governor standing in front of her. While he did make a dashing figure in his suit and tails with his salt and pepper hair nearly to his shoulders, Kristen shuddered at the sight of him.

The governor wore an air of authority, stroking his trimmed Van Dyke beard. His gaze ran up and down her body, finally landing on her eyes. Kristen had no idea what her predecessor had seen in this man despite his good looks. She found him abhorrent.

"I wasn't waiting for anyone." She refused to take a step back from the man crowding her personal space. "I just needed some fresh air."

The governor chuckled. "Are you sure you didn't need to get away from the sight of the lovely Angela Beaumont and your husband? They do make quite a striking pair, don't they?"

Kristen clenched her fists into the folds of her dress. "I hadn't noticed."

The governor took a step closer, closing the space between them. He took Kristen into his arms, pushing her up against the wall. "But not as striking a pair as we make."

"Let go of me!" For the second time that day, Kristen struggled to free herself from the man's arms.

"Come now, my dear. I think we both know that you want it as badly as I do. Remember when we met in Charleston two weeks ago? You were the most skilled lover I've ever had the pleasure of being with."

"I told you to let go of me!" Kristen tried to push him away but he overpowered her. Digging his fingers into her upper arms, he bent down over her with his mouth as if to devour her breasts. Pinned against the unyielding wall, she found herself helpless to get away. The more she tried to push him off, the tighter he gripped her bare arms. Struggling worked against her, making the already low neckline of her gown slipped farther down. His rough beard scratched her breasts. One broke free of its flimsy constraints, causing the governor's breathing to grow louder as his mouth sought her nipple.

A familiar voice called out from behind the governor's back. "I can see that you're enjoying my wife's company, but I need to take her home now."

The governor lifted his head from Kristen's breasts but still held onto her so tightly she could not get away. "You think I'm the first to taste your wife's charms?" he said licking his lips.

"I said, let her go." Jeffrey's words were quiet but demanding at the same time.

The governor gave a short laugh, releasing her and pushing himself away. "Fine time for you to be worrying about a woman like this." He left Kristen standing in shock, trying to pull her dress up to cover herself.

Straightening his tie, the governor bowed at Kristen. "Thank you for your time, ma'am."

"Go to hell." Kristen slapped the governor across his face, surprising herself. If someone had told her she would ever have the nerve to strike a man, she would have laughed at him or her. Maybe the time and space she found herself in made her feel bolder than before. Or maybe the man standing before her now gave her the courage to act in ways she had never considered. She wanted Jeffrey to see her as more than Kristen the first had been, not something less.

Chuckling, the governor turned and left Kristen standing alone with her husband.

She lifted the front of the gown back over her breasts and stared up at Jeffrey. "I have no idea what that man was thinking — so much for the gallant Southern man."

Jeffrey stood in silence before his wife.

Kristen tried again. "I only came out for some fresh air —"

"Don't even try," Jeffrey said, his voice deadly calm. "I know exactly why you were out here with him. If this wasn't what I expected of you, I would have called him out." He shook his head in disgust. "Could you at least limit your games with men who aren't our friends?"

56

To her mortification, tears flooded her eyes. "But I most certainly did not encourage that man! Why can't you believe me?"

Jeffrey gave a short humorless laugh that hit Kristen like a blow. "I stopped believing in you a long time ago." He ran his eyes up and down her. "Now fix your dress so we can leave."

Kristen gave a final tug to her dress, which had barely covered her before the seam ripped. Hanging limply, the red silk exposed a great deal more of her breasts to the cool evening air. She almost smiled at the warm heat of lust that came into Jeffery's eyes as he stared down at her nearly naked breasts.

After a full minute Jeffrey shook as if to wake himself, took off his jacket, and laid it across her bare shoulders. His hand brushed against Kristen's bare flesh, sending a jolt of electricity through her body. Time seemed suspended for a moment as he struggled to contain a combination of anger and lust before pulling her forward.

Keeping a firm grip on her, Jeffrey took long strides across the side yard, causing Kristen to stumble in the dark across the raised-stone paths. He led her to the front of the brightly lit mansion. A row of polished, wooden carriages lined the circular driveway. Their carriage stood third from the front of the line. He pulled the door so hard, the silk curtains swung madly. She caught a glance of the driver. If the man suspected anything amiss at the early departure of his master's wife, his dark face showed nothing.

Lifting Kristen off the ground, Jeffrey nearly threw her onto the velvet-covered seat. The door slammed shut, leaving her alone in the dark carriage. She heard Jeffrey climb onto the carriage to sit with the driver. Unable to understand their muffled voices, but she did hear the driver laugh. She fumed at her husband's refusal to join her inside the carriage and the obvious humor he showed the driver. Kristen sunk down into the seat. "Now I really *am* Cinderella."

She vowed to keep her distance from the man who intrigued and confused her even as she breathed in his scent from the jacket she held tight to her body.

"At least I don't have to live the rest of my life in this crazy dream." Married to the man of her dreams, but only in a dream.

Kristen guessed she would wake up any time now, lying on the couch of the television studio with only memories of her time as a Southern Belle. Unfortunately, she now knew real passion and understood that no man in her waking world would ever compare to what she felt for Jeffrey.

Tears streamed down her face, full of regret for ever letting herself get volunteered for this past-life regression. Kristen did not even believe in regression and past lives and yet she was experiencing something. *It's just a fantasy, but it feels more real than my current life.*

The carriage finally came to a stop at the O'Connor mansion. This place felt like home to her. The door opened and the smiling face of the driver greeted her, instead of her husband. Disappointment cut to the bone.

"Ma'am?" The driver held out his white-gloved hand.

Kristen wiped her eyes and lifted her chin. "Thank you, George."

Walking through the house alone, Kristen vowed to keep her distance from Jeffrey and bide her time until she would thankfully wake up in her own time.

Eleven

*T*ossing and turning all night, memories of Jeffrey's hands touching her body haunted Kristen. Coming fully awake but still in another time and place, she needed to know everything about her life—or rather her former life with Jeffrey. Why did he hate her and how could she heal the rift between them?

She pulled her head off the pillow and gazed across the room. "The diary!" Pleased that she had a place to start, Kristen smiled. "I need to read the rest of the diary, and then I'll have the answers I need."

Determined to get to the root of Jeffrey's intense distrust of her, or of her former self, Kristen jumped out of bed and pulled the precious book from the pocket of her robe where she had hidden it. Pale moonlight shone through a space between the heavy draperies, the only light in the room. Although she could see to move around the room, she needed more light to read. She plumped up the pillows behind her head and then found the matches to light the oil lamp on the table beside her bed. She opened up the diary and started to read.

Two hours later, with the light of the morning sun coming through the drapes and her mind exhausted, Kristen closed the book and sighed. The diary covered the last five years of the life of the woman whose body she now occupied. While it seemed impossible, she had to believe the truth of everything written in the book. The key excerpts were:

"*I've never been happier in my life. Phillip is surely the most handsome man in all of Boston. I watch as other women stare at us as we walk through the park. They turn and whisper among themselves and I'm sure they're just jealous because I have him and they don't. If my father could only see the sweetness in him, how he tells me how beautiful I am and how he simply can't live without me. I'm sure Daddy wouldn't care for the liberties that Phillip takes when we're alone, but honestly, what does it matter? I'm certain he's going to ask for my hand in marriage, and then we'll marry within weeks because he's due to go out to sea again at the month's end. I do love him so!*

I can't believe Daddy said no! What am I going to do? I can't love any other man and now I feel that Phillip is growing tired of waiting. Daddy says that there are at least two women in different ports who claim to have given birth to children by him.

I asked Phillip about these horrible lies and he assured me that even if it were true, he's finally found his true love and that we were destined to be together forever. How could a lowly barmaid ever hope to keep a man like him happy when he could be with a true lady?

I pointed out to Phillip that one of the women who had purported to have given birth to a son by him, was hardly a barmaid, and in fact was from a family almost as old and illustrious as mine. He assured me that since the woman was married she had someone to care for the child, which probably wasn't his anyway. I then had to hold him in my arms as he wept like a child. How could I not believe in the goodness of this man?

Now Daddy is insisting that the rumors are true and that he's found a good man for me to marry. I can't believe him! I will never be happy with anyone but Phillip! He's the only one I can ever love completely. If my father doesn't allow me to marry him, I'll vow to never be true to any man my father forces me to marry.

I'm now married to Jeffrey O'Connor, the man my father said would make a good husband, and it appears that he eagerly wants to prove my father right. Jeffrey does anything I ask of him except to leave me alone. I want nothing to do with the man. His touch makes me cringe. His very presence makes me want to run from the room screaming.

Jeffrey, of course, makes my father very happy. I'm sure Daddy did something to have Phillip leave town sooner than his duties as an officer compelled him to. The only reason I agreed to marry Jeffrey is because I found myself in the family way, with Phillip on duty in another city. I sent my love letters every day, which I'm sure he never received, otherwise he would have come to my aid immediately and demanded we marry.

I only allowed Jeffery into my bed to disguise my condition. I could never bear the shame of having a child without a husband. Not with the shame it would bring to my father, though he does deserve to suffer for what he's put me through.

I told Jeffrey that I was with child and he seemed surprised that it happened so early. I had thought him an ignorant man, but maybe not. The only thing I have to keep me from going completely mad with grief is the thought that I'm carrying Phillip's child. I'm sure that once I get word to him, I can stop this sham of a marriage and be with the one I love.

It's been a month since I've written because I've lost the one thing I could have ever loved. I awoke feeling something wrong and by evening I was bleeding. The doctor said that it was for the best since a miscarriage usually means that something was wrong with the child. He also told my husband that the miscarriage could have been worse since I was nearly four months along. I could see Jeffrey doing the math in his head and I started to laugh. When he confronted me, I told him that he wasn't the first and that he certainly wouldn't be the last. I said that I'd found my true love and that if I couldn't be with him, then I'd never be true to any man, and that I'd never bear him a child, and that I'd wait for Phillip to come back to me. I thought that he'd strike me, but he only walked out of the room. I despise my husband more every day. Soon I'll find a way to get back to Phillip and live the life I was supposed to be living before my father ruined everything for me."

The diary ended with the author's anticipation of a rendezvous with the governor. Kristen knew how that had ended. Apparently, her past self wanted nothing to do with her husband whom she blamed, along with her father, for keeping her from her "true love."

"No wonder all of my relationships have been doomed." Kristen shook her head thinking about her most recent relationship with Brandon, a lobbyist for a large insurance company who had lied and cheated on her constantly. "Karma, baby, karma."

Kristen put her hand on her flat stomach. "I wonder if I've messed up your plans. She thought back to the previous afternoon's episode. "You might have a child for your husband after all." Birth control had not been an issue since her final break up with Brandon six months ago, so she had not bothered. It was not like she had time for even a one-night-stand with her seventy-two-hour-shifts-at-a-time schedule at the hospital.

What would happen when she went back to her time leaving this body to its original owner? If she were pregnant, would she try to get rid of it? Kristen guessed that such a procedure was possible in this time, though she could not imagine they would be safe.

"But it's not my body." Kristen had to remind herself. Her only goal at the moment was to win back the love of her hus-band — something she probably never had. Then what would happen when she left? If she did manage to get Jeffrey to trust her, would he be devastated when the real Kristen came back in all her hateful glory? Not to mention Kristen's loss when she found herself back in her own loveless world without the only man she would probably ever want.

She tried to go back to sleep, but the sun already shone brightly through the part in the curtains. Another strange day in paradise... Her last thought before drifting off to sleep.

A dream teased at the edges of her consciousness, a dream of her former life at the hospital. While making rounds, she came across an elderly woman lying in one of the critical care rooms. The woman looked familiar, but Kristen could not make out any of the words on the chart hanging at the end of the bed. A flash of light caught her eye. The old woman wore an antique locket around her neck. It had a purple stone at the center and sent a violet light sparkling around the room.

Kristen reached for the locket but woke with a start. *That was strange.* She could not shake the feeling that she should have know the woman and what the locket meant to her. A knock at the door brought her to full consciousness.

Hoping it would be Jeffrey, she sat up and ran her hands through her thick hair, though surely beyond repair after a night of tossing and turning.

"Come in."

Greeted by the sight of her grinning maid. "Morning, ma'am," Missy said holding a silver serving tray. "I broughts you the hot chocolate you likes for breakfast."

Smiling at the young girl in an attempt to hide her disappointment, Kristen sighed. "Good morning, Missy. Thank you so much. Yes, I do love hot chocolate in the morning." *Actually, I hate hot cocoa and I'm dying for some coffee strong enough to help me cope with this crazy world, but how do I ask you without making you think I'm crazy?*

"I know this is going to sound strange," Kristen said watching Missy bring the tray over to the table next to the window and set it down. "But I've decided that I'd rather have coffee in the morning instead. So why don't you have the cocoa and then see about getting me some coffee. Black is fine, okay?"

Wrapping the silk robe she tossed on the foot of the bed around herself, Kristen sat down on the brocade chair and turned to Missy. The maid's jaw had gone slack and her eyes were wide open.

"Oh no, Missy, I guess that wouldn't be right." Kristen stuttered to find a way forward, realizing that she had just crossed a huge line.

Missy recovered first. "Oh, that's okay, ma'am. I don't like that stuff anyway."

Certain that the young girl lied, Kristen took a deep breath. "Well then, I'll just have to drink it."

Missy nodded and poured the steaming hot chocolate into a delicate, floral teacup. Kristen hoped she would be able to function without her morning jolt of caffeine.

She nibbled on a piece of delicious buttered toast, watching Missy open a bureau drawer. The girl carefully pulled out a dress of rose and moss green plaid. She placed it at the foot of the bed then picked out a set of lacy white undergarments and another torturous corset, which she despised.

Kristen did not mind the hour it took to bathe, have Missy dress her, and do up her hair. Today would be the first day in her quest to win back the love and respect of her husband. Jeffrey had no idea how determined she could be once she set her mind to something.

Husband, what a nice sounding word! I can't say it's ever held much appeal for me...until now, that is.

Finally dressed, Kristen swirled in front of a full-length mirror and admired the luxurious clothes she wore. She had to admit that she had never looked more feminine, and it suited her far better than the hospital scrubs she spent the majority of her time in. She had no real plan for getting her husband to fall in love with her, but these clothes would certainly help.

"Why did we ever stop dressing like this?"

"Sorry, ma'am?"

"Because we don't have wonderful maids like you, Missy." Kristen said taking Missy's hands and squeezing them. "Thank you so much."

Her wide eyes seemed to be stuck open for almost a minute. Finally, Missy blinked. "You has always had house maids."

"I know, Missy." Kristen smiled. "Is Mr. O'Connor at breakfast?"

Missy frowned. "I saws him this morning, but he was in an awful hurry 'bout something."

Feeling her heart squeeze in dread, Kristen turned and started toward the door.

"But I ain't finished with your hair yet." Missy held up the brush she had been using on Kristen, along with a handful of jeweled pins.

"It's fine." She hurried from the room. "I have something very important to do today."

Twelve

Kristen hurried through the hallway, breathless by the time she reached the wide arched stairway. She watched the stairway across the black and white checkered floor one-story below in case Jeffrey was going up to her room. Kristen did not see anyone on the staircase in front of her until she collided with the housekeeper, on her way up with a load of dishes. The tray hit the stairs and tumbled down with a series of loud crashes, the teapot and silver scattering over the carpeted stairs until they hit the marble floor below.

"Oh, Lila. I'm so sorry." Kristen dropped down to help pick up the pieces.

Lila stood back with her hands on her wide hips, shaking her head. "What in the world are you doing, child? You ain't supposed to be helping no slave."

"I'm not?" Kristen froze at the chill that ran up her arms.

"No you ain't," Lila repeated. She cocked her head to one side and stared at her mistress. "Something is certainly different about you, Miss Kristen. I feels it deep down in my bones, and those old bones ain't never lied to me before."

The stress of pretending to be someone she else for the past two days overwhelmed Kristen. Tears formed at the edges of her eyes. She fought to control her emotions, but the warmth in the older woman's eyes broke her down.

"I'm not the same — and I have no idea how to explain it."

Lila nodded. "Best you come into the kitchen where's you can tell me all about it. My grandmother, back in where's my people come from, knew all about these sort of things. I never believed most of what she told me, but seeing you lately makes me wonder if I might be wrong."

Feeling relief wash over her, Kristen followed Lila into the empty room where a young slave girl brought in a fresh sterling tea pot and the accompanying porcelain teacups.

"You all gets out!" Lila said with a wave of her hand. The girl dropped the tray back down on the table in surprise and stood staring at Kristen. "I said gets!"

The girl turned and ran from the room.

Lila motioned to one of the chairs at the table. "Take a seat while I gets you some tea." Disappearing from the room for a moment, Lila came back with a teapot from the kitchen, made from brown porcelain with more than a few chips on the rim.

Kristen sat down and watched in silence as Lila poured a cup of black tea from the pot. She wondered how much she could say to the older woman without seeming like a crazed person. A shudder ran up her spine at the thought of being in one of the mental institutions of the time.

"Soon as you finish, I'm gonna read the leaves and see what's going on with you."

"Really?" Kristen had not expected to have her fortune read today.

"My grandmamma taughts me how to read the leaves, so just drink it down so's I can sees what I need to see."

Kristen took nervous sips from the tea, which tasted like a combination of fresh rosemary and old dirt. Anxious to find out what the leaves might show, Kristen drank the scalding tea as quickly as possible.

"Good," Lila said taking the cup from Kristen. Peering into the cup and making clucking sounds with her tongue, Lila nodded.

"Well?" Kristen could not see how anyone could make sense of wet tea leaves stuck to the bottom of a teacup, but Lila seemed to see something worth contemplating.

"I sees that you are a healer," Lila finally said.

Kristen's heart seemed to stop beating for a moment.

Lila continued. "I sees that you have come here to fix what

is wrong with your life. You are here to heal your life in a future time."

"The tea leaves are telling you all that?" Kristen said, her eyes wide with surprise.

Smiling, Lila pointed at her heart. "Some things I sees from the leaves, and some things I sees from right inside here. And I knows for a fact that you've made some terrible decisions in this life, and now you's wants to fix them."

"Oh." The idea of the housekeeper knowing about Kristen's situation so surprised her she could not think of anything to say. Making bad decisions had been a way of life for her since her teenage years. Rebellious against her parents who refused to let her do whatever she wanted, including date a boy ten years older than her sixteen years. The boy had died of a drug overdose in the bed of his female band mate, and she ended up spending a year homebound with only her college studies providing her any relief. The whole ordeal had given her enough wisdom to know that she did not want to be an accountant like her father, but rather a healer like her mother — a nurse. Unfortunately, she had acquired a jaded view on love, which led to a series of one-night-stands with not even one lasting relationship.

How could the crazy dream she found herself living, help her with anything she had done in her past? Working to become a doctor seemed to be the only successful part of her current life.

Lila nodded as if reading Kristen's thoughts. "Sometimes we makes mistakes so bad that it hangs on to us all through the lives we live afterwards." Lila peered into Kristen's eyes. "And you need to make sure you gets this life right, or you'll never find happiness in the life you done come from."

"But what mistake did I make?" *Not counting the ones in my own time.*

"I's can't tell you, Miss Kristen," Lila said covering Kristen's cold hand with her own large, warm one. "You will know the right thing to do when the time comes. You just have to trust yourself."

"Like that's worked out well for me," Kristen muttered to herself.

Lila lifted an eyebrow and shook her head. "It don't matter

what's done happened before, only what you's doing right now."

"But I thought you said that I came here to fix the past?"

"And you's gonna do it right now, 'cause it's only right now that counts."

"You sound like one of those New Age gurus," Kristen said.

"Ain't know nothing new about ages, they's always coming and going. You needs to worry about the here and now."

"Right. I got it." Kristen closed her eyes and took a deep breath. "I'm guessing from the diary I read, that I've messed things up with my husband."

"That ain't gonna be too easy, since Mr. Jeffrey done left to put those Yankees back in their early graves this morning."

"What? Oh my god, no."

Lila shook her head. "It's just more of mens foolishness, having to go fight each other 'cause they all have to be right about everything."

"What did you hear exactly?" Kristen said breathlessly.

"That those damn Yankees were firing on a fort down in South Carolina and causing all kinds of trouble."

"Fort Sumter?" Kristen sucked in sharply. "Then this must be April of 1861 —"

"Sure enough is, Miss Kristen. But I figures General Lee is going to send those Yankees packing right quick."

Kristen sighed. "Actually, the North is going to win."

Lila looked at Kristen sharply. "That is never gonna happen, Miss Kristen. Our boys is gonna woop some Yankee ass, and that's all there is to it." She wiped her hands together and then put them on her waist. "And I don't knows how you could think no different."

Kristen just shook her head, too sick to say anything to the contrary.

"In your times, you knows what happens."

"I do," Kristen answered. "And it's not pretty." She eyed the woman before her carefully. "So you don't think I'm crazy?"

Lila threw back her head and laughed. "I done thought you were 'till just three days ago, now I think you're finally making some sense. You's is certainly a different woman from the one who came to this house after marryin' Mr. Jeffrey."

"Do you think I'll have a chance to mend things with Mr. Jeffrey?"

"If you wants to, I suppose you can. God always gives us chances to make things right."

"I think you're right, Lila. And I'm going to need your help."

"What's you got in mind, child?"

"Well, I'm going to need some clothes." She saw Lila raise her eyebrows. Kristen laughed and looked down at the low-cut silk gown she wore. "Actually, I need some men's clothes."

"What's you saying, child? Why you want to put on men's clothes and hide all the woman parts that Mr. Jeffrey done married you for?"

"Did you know that I'm a doctor?" Kristen said.

Lila's eyes narrowed. "If you say so."

"Well, here's what I think." Kristen stood and paced the room. "I think that I came to this time as a doctor, so that I can fix what's wrong with my life in this time. And to do that, I need to follow Jeffrey, and I'll need to disguise myself as a man."

"That might be all well and good but you can't go 'round wearing men's clothes, no matter what you say you is. And you can *not* go following Mr. Jeffrey to no war. War is about killing, and you's going to get yourself killed, or something entirely worse if any men find out you's a woman."

From the look on Lila's face, Kristen understood her meaning completely. "But I have to go, don't you see? I can't waste this chance I've been given." Kristen stopped pacing. She put her hands on Lila's shoulders, staring into the housekeeper's eyes. "Did you say that I came here to fix my life?"

Lila shook her head. "You's spinning a tale worse than Mr. Jeffrey used to do when he was a boy. I just pray that the good Lord is watching over you in this craziness."

Smiling, Kristen hugged her new-found friend. "I knew you'd help. Now I'm going to need a shirt, pants, and some boots for riding—just as fast as you can find them."

"Don't matter what kinds of clothes I get for you, they still ain't gonna hide the fact that you's a woman."

They both looked down at Kristen's full breasts. "Hmm, you do have a point, but I think I can take care of that." She looked up at Lila. "Just hurry, I might not have that much time."

"Mr. Jeffrey is gonna kill me when he finds out that I helped you with this nonsense."

Paying no attention, Kristen reached up and started pulling at the pins holding up her intricate hairdo. "And I'm going to have to cut my hair."

"Oh, no, Miss Kristen. Mr. Jeffrey will kill me for sure if I goes and cuts your hair." Lila held a hand up to her gaping mouth.

"Well, then I'll just have to do it myself." Kristen looked around the kitchen for a pair of scissors. With the scissors in her hand, she grabbed a handful of her thick hair and started the scissors chewing through it before she could change her mind. Once she had cut through it, she held it out to Lila.

"There. Now you'll have to help me."

Her eyes went from one side of Kristen's head to the other. Lila clucked her tongue. "Lord, child, you is surely going to get yourself killed—either by Mr. Jeffrey or those damn Yankees. I just don't know which."

Kristen gritted her teeth, watching Lila cut the rest of her hair off. She only spoke once to tell Lila to cut it shorter. Finally, Lila held up a mirror for her mistress.

Staring in horror, Kristen put her hand up to her hair now one inch from her scalp all the way around her head. "I look like a boy."

Lila gave a snort. "Honey, you ain't never gonna look like no boy with that figure."

"Right." Kristen put the mirror down. Feeling the lightness of her shorn head, she did not need to see that she had lost her favorite part of herself. *Somehow, I don't think that the previous owner of this body is going to be very happy with me for doing this.*

"Guess I'm going to have to bind my breasts up tight if I'm going to pass for a man."

Lila shook her head. "And you're also gonna have to learn to ride a horse a whole lot better than you done yesterday."

Kristen could not help but laugh. "That might be the hardest part of this whole thing." *What do I have to lose?* If she wanted her dream man, then she would have to go after him. She would also have a chance to use her medical training skills on a real field of battle. She could not decide if she felt excited or terrified, but she had taken over control, no longer waiting for others to mold her life. She would be the one casting the die of her future.

"One more thing, Miss Kristen," Lila said turning and pulling open a tiny drawer nearly hidden in the wide cupboards of the kitchen. Taking out a black, velvet bag, Lila opened it and pulled out a delicate locket made of gold with a deep-purple stone set in the center that sparkled in the sunlit room.

Taking the locket from Lila's outstretched hand, Kristen felt its warmth. Opening the thin locket, Kristen saw a black and white photo of a beautiful, dark-haired woman.

"She was your momma," Lila said, her dark eyes growing moist. "She sure was a pretty thing."

"I can see that." Kristen felt her own eyes start to tear up looking at a woman who certainly did look like she could be related. In fact, she looked just like herself.

"Wear it to bring you luck."

Kristen laughed through her tears. "I'm sure it will." She lifted the locket over her head, placing it around her neck.

"Thank you for everything." She moved into Lila's arms to hug and be absorbed in a tight return embrace.

Thirteen

Slow down! I mean whoa!" Kristen yanked hard on the reins, no longer worried about hurting the stubborn beast she sometimes admired and most of the time loathed. She again pulled back as hard as she could and leaned back as far as she dared in the saddle. The black stallion slowed and shook his head.

"I'll let up when you decide to behave."

Diablo came to a reluctant stop. Kristen took a deep breath and looked around. She knew the ocean needed to stay on her right to find her way to Charleston, even with her pronounced lack of direction. "My car may have been a piece of crap, but at least it came with a GPS and didn't try to buck me off."

The horse flicked an ear in response.

She figured finding a coastal city could not be that hard. She knew Jeffrey had to catch a train in Charleston in three days, so she just needed to catch up to him. "Since you're the fastest beast in the stable, I expect you to catch him."

Her mount snorted and shook his head as if offended that she might think he could not catch the gentle mare Jeffrey rode.

"Or catch your favorite gal." As much as Kristen had not wanted to ever ride the black beast, Lila had convinced her that Diablo loved and would follow the gray mare Jeffrey rode.

Daylight started to fade, which meant she should stop for the night. She could not take another minute in the saddle anyway.

Her tired arms needed a break from controlling Diablo, and her rear end needed a break on something softer than a saddle.

She lead the horse to a nearby patch of thick, green grass. She pulled the bridle over Diablo's head and let the bit slide out of his mouth as she had been taught by the stable boy. Diablo did not bite, but maybe he waited for the right moment.

She left the big horse's halter on, tying its long rope to a nearby tree to give him some freedom. Pulling a stiff-haired brush from one of the saddlebags, Kristen ran a brush down the stallion's back while he grazed on the thick grass at his feet. Diablo rolled his eyes at her. She stood her ground with him more, her fear of the big animal diminishing.

"I think you're more bark than bite." She offered him a carrot. Diablo took it, biting it first in half and then chewing on the rest as he gazed at her with his dark, liquid eyes.

"That's right. I know you're starting to love me." Diablo nickered and pushed Kristen's hand with his nose. Kristen rubbed the horse's neck, marveling at the power of the stallion. His skin quivered at her touch.

"Here's the part I wish I could skip." If she did not want Diablo to go lame from picking up a rock and riding hard on it all day, she had to check her mount's hooves. Holding the strange metal tool that looked like a fork with only one prong on the end, she took a deep breath and started her least favorite chore.

Kristen ran her shaking hands down Diablo's leg to let him know that she meant to help him out. "Please don't let there be anything in your hoof," she said under her breath with a groan. After digging out one particularly large stone from Diablo's front hoof, the horse nuzzled her shoulder.

Smiling in relief at having gone all around her horse and finishing successfully, she let out the breath she had been holding.

"No problem, big guy. It's the least I can do after you carried me around all day." She patted him on his rear. "That couldn't have been easy."

After eight hours of riding she needed to start a fire, but her tired body collapsed against the saddle she had just taken off instead.

"I have no idea how I'm going to get it back on you," Kristen said staring up into the horse's wide, brown eyes. He nickered at her and bent his head to the bright green grass at his feet that grew beside the small stream.

She nibbled on the ham and cheese sandwich Lila had packed for her, nothing had ever tasted so good. When she started on her apple, Diablo leaned his long neck over her shoulder, his nose close enough to touch the apple. He gave a loud snort.

"I just gave you a carrot," Kristen said laughing at the beast. "Okay, here. You can have the rest." She held it up. "I'm too tired to eat it anyway."

Lying back against the saddle, her warm, wool cloak tugged all around her, she gazed up at the stars twinkling in the dark sky. A bright half-moon outlined the trees and shed enough light to see.

Her eyes closed and Kristen's mind conjured up Jeffrey's coal-black hair and blue-gray eyes that twinkled so nicely, the same way the stars did in the darkened night sky. The remembered touch of his hands on her skin awakened feelings she had never felt before. The soreness faded from her tired thighs, replaced by warm thoughts of her husband that made her moan out loud, the only sound in the quiet evening.

Diablo whinnied, bringing her fully awake. "Sorry, boy." She laughed. Who could hear her out in the middle of nowhere? Her thoughts once again turned to Jeffrey and she wondered if she could ever make him love her. "Damn that man!"

"Pardon, me?"

Kristen sat up straight, wishing she had taken the small pistol Lila had offered her. Her heart felt as if it would beat a tattoo right out of her chest. Visions of rape and murder ran through her head. *This would be a great time to wake up.*

Heavy footsteps crunched through the small thicket. Kristen stared into the darkness. The half-moon had disappeared behind some clouds, leaving the night nearly black.

"Who's out there?" Kristen hoped her voice didn't sound as shaky to the intruder as it did to her.

"If it were anyone else but your husband, you'd be dead by now."

"Jeffrey?"

Finally he stepped into view, his gray uniform barely visible in the darkness.

"Kristen O'Connor, what in God's name are you doing out here?"

She found her courage and answered. "Following you."

"I can see that." He led his gray mare to the patch of grass next to Diablo. He patted the stallion on the nose. Diablo nickered and rubbed his nose on Jeffrey's sleeve. Seeing to his own mount, he unsaddled, brushed, and examined his horse's feet, then he turned to Kristen.

Standing over her, he shook his head. "Why, again, are you following me?"

Kristen pulled the wool cloak tighter around herself as a protection from her husband's wrath. "I could help with the wounded."

"You faint at the sight of blood, and now I'm going to have to ride with you all the way back to the house. I don't want to have to ride Melly into the ground, but I can't see any other way of getting to town on time." Jeffrey took off his hat and rubbed his hair with both hands.

"I will not faint at the sight of blood," Kristen said.

"Since when?"

A thousand comebacks crowded Kristen's mind but she knew she could not say any of them. "Just trust me. I won't faint at the sight of blood."

Clenching his jaw, Jeffrey took a deep breath. "This is by far the stupidest thing you've ever done, Kristen. What would possess you to follow me into a war zone?"

"You can't stop me." *I know I'm not being rational, but I have to be with him.*

Jeffrey glared at his wife. She stared right back at him. Finally, he spoke. "What the hell did you do to your hair?"

Kristen put a hand up to her closely cropped hair. "I did it to keep from being mistaken for a woman."

"Well, it's working."

"Thanks," Kristen shot back, but felt awful at her husband's casual assessment of her haircut.

"Let's just get some sleep." Jeffrey picked up his blankets and spread them on the ground a few feet away.

She lay back down on her own wool blanket, covering herself with her long, black cloak. She felt the hard ground beneath her and wondered if she would be able to sleep, but sleep found her before she finished forming the thought in her exhausted mind.

*J*effrey wished he could still the thoughts churning through his mind. As if he didn't have enough to worry about the war ripping apart his country, now his wife behaved in ways he would never have believed possible. Following him because she wanted to help? Because she wanted to save lives? He now knew for certain that his wife's thought process had become irrational. The Kristen he knew only thought about herself.

Sighing, he closed his eyes and tried to sleep. For the moment he could do nothing about Kristen, except find someone to take her back home where she would be safe. He had to get to Virginia, where General Lee trained his troops to fight against their brothers from the North.

Jeffrey vowed to send Kristen home before something happened to her. He had no illusions about the horrors of war. She would not be safe from the soldiers of either side if anyone recognized her as a woman, no matter how she dressed. War could be hell, especially for women.

She does seem different — besides the short hair. Something else has changed.

He knew this could not be the case because on the outside, she looked as she always had, well, except for her hair — cut short like a boy's. Giving it more thought, he found that he did not dislike the short hair as much as he would have imagined, and even thought that it suited her, somehow.

When he finally drifted off, Jeffrey dreamed about fighting men in blue coats, followed by men in gray coats, and finally his wife. He woke up with a start. He found himself looking into Kristen's deep-green eyes. During his sleep he had moved closer to her, as if while lost in his dreams he had forgotten that he no longer wanted anything to do with her. The woman he had imagined before they'd married did not exist. This woman played games with men, and tore him apart.

Only inches away, the yearning in her eyes drew him like a magnet. A look of passion mixed with a fear of rejection reflected in those moss-green depths. An irresistible urge to kiss her came over him. He fought it. *She'll use it against me just as she has nearly every day of our three miserable years together.* Her sleep tousled hair and full lips almost won.

Using every ounce of his willpower, Jeffrey sat up. "Time to get going." He could not keep the gruffness out of his voice, vowing not to let himself be tempted by his beautiful wife again. "We have a train to catch in Charleston."

"You mean I'm going with you?" Kristen's eyes lit up in a way that almost had Jeffrey fooled.

Never again. He reminded himself of another time, and another man he had caught her with. "No, you're going home. War is no place for a lady." Even as he said it, he groaned inwardly.

My wife is anything but a lady. I know that she will not want to endure any real hardships. How she managed to ride this far makes me wonder again if I really knew her at all.

"Actually, I don't believe I'm going back," she said.

Her eyes challenged Jeffrey in a way he would not have thought possible. She never did say outright what she wanted, but somehow always managed to have him doing exactly what she wanted. She didn't usually confront him by being upfront and honest. A new approach for her.

He blinked in surprise. "Kristen, what makes you think you have the skills to help men wounded or even dying on the battlefield?"

Her green eyes narrowed into slits, which reminded him of a cougar he had cornered once. "I'll be of far more help on the battlefield that you can even imagine." She took a deep breath and opened her mouth as if to say more, but closed it instead looking at him with a steady gaze.

"Kristen…" He tried again, his patience wearing thin. "I order you to go back home." He got up from his makeshift bed and turned away from her toward the horses. Their heads remained down, grazing on the new spring grass. With his back to her, he continued. "I'm going to saddle your horse, and you're going to get on him and ride as quickly as you can back to the house."

"I'm not going anywhere without you," Kristen said. "I can help whether you believe me or not. If you try to force me to go back, I'll just ride this horse all the way to Virginia where I'm sure I can find a doctor who needs my skills."

Jeffrey turned with a laugh. "Your skills? You mean dressing up and charming men at parties?"

Still smiling he noticed the look on her face. Something had changed but he could not quite put his finger on what troubled him. Her eyes told him that she *could* rise to the occasion with a confidence that surprised him. For a second he believed that Kristen actually *did* have the courage to face a battlefield full of wounded men. What had happened to her?

With a sigh, he finished saddling Diablo. "I guess there's nothing I can do if you're that determined." Though he said it, he felt confident she would lose her bravado at the first sign of blood. Grown men had been known to do the same. Jeffrey had seen some of the horrors of war when he had fought under Jackson. She would not have the stomach for the war in store for them all.

"Have it your way." He cinched up the girth on Diablo's saddle. The big horse turned his head as if to bite Jeffrey. He smiled and patted the horse's neck.

Once he'd saddled his own horse, Jeffrey helped Kristen up. Together they headed north to Charleston where they would board a train, along with their horses and ride to Virginia. Jeffrey hoped to find someone he could trust to get Kristen back home safely.

Fourteen

Kristen had not eaten except for a hard biscuit and some cheese from her saddlebag. Her empty stomach grumble in protest by the time they stopped around noon to rest the horses. Her sore behind had reached a new level of discomfort she had not thought possible. She almost collapsed on the ground when she dismounted. Her stomach, back, and legs too weak to hold her upright, rebelled at the idea of riding any further.

She stifled a groan and tried to catch her breath. She wanted Jeffrey to think she could handle the journey. *Of course I can!*

"We'll stop here and eat." Jeffrey dismounted his horse.

He did it with an ease that made Kristen want to slap him. Too tired to form words, she limped behind him slowly, willing her legs to keep working. When her big horse spotted the water, he nudged her from behind. She almost fell flat on her face.

"Just when I thought you were starting to respect me." Kristen whispered at her mount. She steadied herself, yanked on the reins in an attempt for control, then led a submissive Diablo to the stream to stand beside Jeffrey's gray who already drank in loud slurps.

"Are you sure you can make it?" Jeffrey pulled a wax paper bundle from his saddle bag.

"I'm sure." Kristen willed her voice to be strong. She tried to stand up straighter to prove her point and put her hand on Diablo's big rump to steady herself. He moved away causing her to slip and fall to the ground in a heap.

"I can see that." Jeffrey raised his eyebrows, offering her a hand up.

She glowered at him. He rode every day, she did not. He would not be sore or tired. Yet she could barely get herself back on her feet, walk over to a rock and watch while Jeffery busied himself building a small fire pit with a circle of river rocks. He filled it with branches of cottonwood and some moss, and with a flint, he soon had a crackling fire going.

A small, tin coffee pot, filled with water from the steam soon wafted with the aroma of freshly-brewed coffee. Kristen stared into the fire and felt her mouth water in anticipation. Although this coffee would not be her usual trendy, over-priced brand of brew, no coffee had ever smelled this good.

"Would you like some?" He motioned to the pot.

She turned and found herself looking into Jeffrey's eyes. In the bright sunshine, they appeared more gray than blue and even more appealing, if that were possible. She couldn't read his feelings.

"That would be wonderful."

Without a word he took a tin cup, wrapped it in a piece of cloth, and tipped the small pot into the cup. He handed it to her.

She took it with shaking hands. Fatigue threatened every part of her body but did not stop the electric shock when their hands touched.

"Thank you," she said, and meant it. As she had anticipated when she brought the steaming cup to her lips, no coffee had ever tasted this good. "So much better than a drive-through," Kristen said under her breath, the warmth spreading through her exhausted body.

Seeing Jeffrey's frown, she smiled at him. "You make excellent coffee."

"Are you hungry?"

Unable to help herself, she gave a vigorous nod. *And not just food.* Her eyes wandered up his tall form, starting at the black leather boots that reached his knees and traveling up to the form-fitting gray trousers with the stripe down the side. Her eyes reached his chest, covered with a rough, cotton shirt open at the neck, then to his determined chin, pursed lips, and long aquiline nose. Finally, her gaze found his steel gray eyes.

"I still have some biscuits, cheese, and dried fruit that Lila packed for me," Kristen whispered. *Where did my voice go?*

Draining his own coffee, Jeffrey nodded. "I'll make us some dinner."

He fried up some bacon, which they put between the biscuits and cheese. Kristen felt satisfied that at least one of her needs had been met.

"Time to get moving again," Jeffrey said.

She flinched. The thought of getting back onto the saddle, astride the huge beast might be more than she could handle.

Jeffrey chuckled. "You can still change your mind and head home."

"And have you be right?" Kristen narrowed her eyes and tried to straighten her back, which refused to cooperate. "I'll be just fine."

"I can see that," He said dryly, watching her try to stand. "Let me help you."

The moment he took her arm a bolt of electricity shot straight through Kristen, making her gasp.

"Are you okay?"

She blushed. "Of course I am."

"Kristen, you aren't going to make it," Jeffrey said.

The caring tone in his voice almost undid her. Steeling herself against the weakness in her body that threatened to undo her, she shook her head and walked over to her horse. She took up the reins and slid them over his head. After guiding him to a large rock, she mounted her horse, settling herself into the saddle.

Turning back now would get her nowhere. Obviously, she had come back in time to complete a mission of some sort and she would not quit on the second day, not after all she had gone through.

"I'll be fine." She dug her heels into her mount. "And if we're going to catch this train, we'd better get going."

An unreadable look passed over Jeffrey's face. He clucked to his horse and off they went at a brisk pace.

After an hour of riding, she did not feel any less pain in her thighs and back until they went numb, which she took as a good sign. Taking in the countryside as they rode, she marveled at the live oaks spreading their massive branches over the dirt road they traveled. All around them magnolias and dogwoods bloomed. The hot, moist air, made her clothes moist, soaked her horse, and made her stick to the saddle. She wondered if she would ever be dry again.

When she wasn't fantasizing about the man riding in front of her, Kristen imagined jumping into one of the cool ponds they passed. She even imagined the cold water washing away the constant stream of sweat working its way down her back.

She could not help thinking about all the things she had taken for granted—running water, an air-conditioned car, soft leather, adjustable seats instead of the hard saddle that caused her to ache. Consumed with her own dreary thoughts, she almost let her horse run into Jeffrey's gray when he suddenly stopped. The horse had more sense, and came to an equally quick stop, almost throwing her over his neck. Diablo then moved up alongside Jeffrey's gray. Her leg pressed up against her husband's lean form.

She jerked the reins to the side. Diablo sidestepped with a snort and a jerk of his head, almost pulling the reins out of her hands.

"We can stop here for the night," Jeffrey said frowning at her antics.

"Sounds good to me." She said as she struggled to get her horse back under control. Diablo appeared too tired to put up much of a fight and put his head down to follow his mare into a shaded glen. There did not appear to be any water nearby, but the branches of the trees gave shade and privacy of a sort. "Do you know what time it is?"

Looking up at the sun he said, "Not quite six. We've made good time, so far. And you look as though you could use a rest."

"That's an understatement." Kristen tried to laugh but nearly choked on the pollen being kicked up by the horses walking through the long grass sprinkled with wildflowers.

"Guess I'm allergic," Kristen said in between sneezes.

Jeffrey frowned again. "You've never been allergic to anything before."

Kristen caught her breath. *Can that be true? Have my allergies somehow made it through time to plague me, even now? How do I answer Jeffrey without him thinking that I'm lying?* She shrugged her shoulders hoping he would forget.

He dismounted. "I chose this place because of the lake."

"Lake?" Kristen could hardly hold her excitement in. She looked around. "But there's nothing here."

The heat shimmered in waves blurring everything as far as Kristen could see. Tired she could hardly keep her eyes open.

"The lake is behind those trees." Jeffrey motioned with his head as he pulled the saddle off his horse. "Why don't you take a look? I'll take care of your horse."

"A lake," Kristen said breathlessly. Never had those words sounded so good. How wonderful it would feel to sink her hot, sweaty body into cool, clean water. She swung one aching leg off her horse, then slid down the saddle and started walking toward the clump of willow trees he had indicated.

"Watch for snakes." Jeffrey called out after her.

"Sure." Kristen walked away in a half daze. She couldn't wait to get into the water and cool off. Besides, snakes do not swim, she thought.

Walking through the long grass and into the cool shade of the willow and live oaks, she finally saw the cool, dark-green waters of the small lake. Never had a body of water looked so inviting.

With a quick look around for privacy, Kristen smiled and unbuttoned her rough cotton shirt. Almost white, it was brown in places from sweat and dirt of just one day of riding. She could not believe how filthy riding a horse and sleeping on the ground could be. Shrugging off her shirt, she threw it onto the grassy bank. *I'll wash it after I wash myself.* Too hot to think at the moment.

Next, she unwound the length of cotton cloth from around her chest. It functioned quite well as a makeshift sports bra. The air felt moist against her skin. Two flies buzzed around her as she unbuttoned the stiff, cotton trousers she wore. Next came the locket. Kristen undid the latch and placed the locket carefully in the pocket of the shirt she had just removed, buttoning it closed for safety.

Due to the now burst blisters on both thighs, Kristen's pants stuck to her trembling legs. She took a deep breath and yanked them down, stifling a cry. Next came her "granny-pants."

"If I have to stay here much longer, I'm going to change women's underclothes."

The freedom of standing naked in the hot summer air felt wonderful. A slight breeze caused her to shiver in delight.

"Well, here goes." She walked into the still water. The deeper she went, the better it felt. Two days of sweat and grime washed off of her skin. She waded in until her feet didn't reach the bottom and she had to move her arms and legs to keep her head above water.

She flipped onto her back and gave a lazy kick, closing her eyes to the rays of the sun sinking lower in the sky. Birds twittered to each other in the tree branches over her head, the air filled with soothing sounds. Despite the long ride, Kristen felt as if she had entered paradise. She only needed a soft bed to dive into when she got out and life would be just about perfect. She pushed aside the thought of her "husband" sleeping in that soft bed beside her.

The birds chatter stilled. *Uh oh.* She frowned, scanning the clear blue sky. She turned to look at the branches of the willows where they dipped into the water. Nothing seemed to be out of the ordinary until a ripple on the water caught her eye.

Coming toward her, swimming gracefully along the surface of the water, a snake headed straight for her. She eyed the head, close enough to see its tongue flicking in and out of its thin mouth.

Stay calm and don't move.

The snake's gray and brown body closed the distance. Kristen wanted to dive under the water, but she did not know if the snake could do the same. She gave way to her primal instinct and screamed.

Fifteen

A terrified **scream** split the air. Jeffrey's heart skipped a beat. He dropped the brush he had been using to untangle Diablo's gleaming black mane and pushed his way through the thick bushes and branches surrounding the small lake. Kristen's thrashing about turned the water white with foam in her effort to evade something that he could not see. An explanation for her panic caught his eye. A snake moved gracefully across the water toward her.

"Don't move!" Jeffrey pulled his pistol from its holster.

"Are you kidding?" Kristen thrashed some more. "There's a snake coming right at me!"

"I said," Jeffrey shouted back at her, "to hold still!"

U sing **all** of the control she could muster, Kristen stopped thrashing, her eyes pinned on the snake who also seemed to hesitate in response to her sudden stillness. Her legs sank and she found herself standing on the muddy bottom of the lake, her toes sinking into the ooze. She stared at Jeffrey, praying he would do something, though she had no idea what. All she could think about was running out of the water as quickly as possible, even though she knew she could not outrun the snake who had seemed to come to his wits and was moving toward her again.

Just as the snake lifted up to strike, a shot rang out. The snake flew through the air and landed next to her. She screamed again, then fainted.

Jeffrey threw his gun to the ground and waded into the water. He caught Kristen as she fell, and pulled her out of the water. The mud sucked at his boots, straining his legs, but he finally made it to shore holding his wife's limp body. He'd seen and felt her naked body before, nothing new, but somehow it felt different. He lay her down in the soft grass next to the fire he had built.

Kristen's eyes snapped open. "The snake!"

"Dead." Jeffrey used every ounce of his willpower to keep his eyes on her face. Never had she looked more appealing as she did at the moment, with her hair plastered to her head and her eyes wild with fear. *All I want to do is protect you.*

"Thank you." Kristen closed her eyes, then opened them again. "I'm naked!"

Jeffrey chuckled. "And alive."

"Yes, thank you." Kristen fluttered her hands against her chest, as if unsure what to hide from his searing gaze. Surely, he had seen her naked before, since they were married. She needed to act natural about being naked in front of her husband, a man she had only met two days ago, although she felt very uncomfortable.

Steeling herself against her own flushed cheeks, Kristen stared into Jeffrey's eyes. She would not be the first to look away. Expecting nature to take its course, he surprised her by breaking eye contact first. He stood and turned back to the lake, stooped and picked up his gun.

Lying in the grass, watching the last of the sun set below

the trees, she tried to slow her breathing. Was it the near-death experience that had her heart fluttering in her chest, or the look in her husband's eyes? She had no idea.

Just keep breathing.

Gradually, her heart stopped its wild rhythm and her breathing returned to normal.

It's time to find my clothes and get dressed.

Kristen sat up and looked around.

What if Jeffrey had missed? Would she find herself back on a couch in a television studio with an audience watching her? Was part of her back on the couch talking? Was she saying everything to the psychic at the same time she said it to Jeffrey in this time? Was she actually losing her mind? She had no idea what was real anymore.

Kristen realized that she felt insecure about Jeffrey seeing her naked and running off. The vision of him hurrying away from her did nothing for her self-esteem. Could the new haircut be the problem? Or something worse that she did not even want to contemplate? She wondered about the quality of their sex life. Who knew what people did in this time period?

Nothing she could do about it now. She picked her way with care through the long grass in case the dead snake had an angry mate, or cousin, or whatever snakes had for relatives. She found her clothes, stiffening as they dried. Holding her shirt up to her nose, Kristen groaned. "What I'd give for some laundry soap."

"I'm not going to see any in this lifetime," Kristen mumbled and then smiled at her pun. She picked up her underclothes and started sloshing them around in the lake water, then wrung them out. She hoped that her clothes would dry quickly in the heat, if not the humidity.

After washing her underclothes, Kristen pulled them on and re-wrapped the piece of cloth around her chest like a tube top. Semi-dressed so her husband would not run off in horror at her nakedness, again. She then washed her pants and shirt and left them on a branch to dry.

"Not bad." She did a mock pose. "A very modest and slightly uncomfortable bathing suit."

A delicious smell wafted across her nose. Her stomach

rumbled. The two-day trip had certainly been good for her waistline. She did not feel as if she had eaten a full meal in days.

I've probably lost some weight.

When she made her way back to camp, she found Jeffrey seated on a large rock by the crackling fire. His handsome face glowed from the heat as he held a stick of meat over the fire.

"I had no idea you were a gourmet cook," Kristen said, smiling and taking a seat next to him. She did and said what she thought a wife would do and say.

Jeffrey grinned, turning the stick with the meat sizzling as it cooked the fat dripping into the fire.

"Where did you get fresh meat?"

"It's the snake," Jeffrey replied his eyes still on the meat.

"What!" Kristen pulled back as Jeffrey moved the stick of meat towards her. "That's disgusting. I'm not going to eat that thing."

Jeffrey turned, a grin on his face. Then he looked at Kristen's apparel and his mouth fell open.

"What?"

"Where are your clothes?" Jeffrey sputtered, nearly dropping the stick of meat into the fire.

"It's like a bathing suit," Kristen said with a grin, proud of her ingenuity.

"Kristen," Jeffrey said, "to a man, you're not wearing anything." He took a deep breath. "Trust me on this."

Kristen looked down at herself. To her horror, the wet cotton wrapped around her chest appeared transparent. Her breasts outlined perfectly through the cloth, with nothing left to the imagination. Concerned that her lower anatomy and underwear might be equally exposed, she could not summon the courage to look down any lower.

"Oh.," She swallowed hard. "I washed my shirt and trousers and wanted to let them dry before I put them back on. Besides, we are married."

The look on Jeffrey's face said otherwise. "Kristen, we may be married, but not for much longer. You asked for a divorce, if I happen to make it back alive."

Kristen stared into the fire. She really could not say much on the subject, since her life here in this century may not last long.

Jeffrey continued. "I'm sorry that I broke my promise to you this afternoon. It won't happen again. I know you don't want any children, and I don't plan on giving you any." He stopped and seemed to gather himself. "I have no idea why you're following me into this war, unless it's to torment me even more than you have for the past three years." He laughed sharply, devoid of any humor. "Of course, it could be to meet up with a man you'll find worthy of your attention. A general perhaps?"

Again, Kristen could think of nothing to say. Falling in love with Jeffrey *would break her heart.*

The safe thing would be to concentrate on my work just as I have for the past six years. At least with the promise of a war, I will have plenty to do.

She shuddered at the thought.

All I know about the Civil War, is that tens of thousands of men died. The war will happen, that is guaranteed. How I am able to handle that kind of carnage is an open question. It will be like working in the Emergency Room non-stop for years.

"I'm not out to find a new husband," Kristen said. "I really do want to help wherever I can with the wounded during the war, and there will be more than you can imagine."

Jeffrey frowned. "This war, if it even happens, is only going to last a couple of months at most."

"I'm afraid not," Kristen said, trying to keep the sadness out of her voice. "And the South is probably going to lose." She had to be careful how much she said. She did not want Jeffrey to think her a full-fledged crazy person.

He did not seem to notice his wife's certainty. "The South has superior troops, *and* we have General Robert E. Lee. The North has yet to find a general who isn't completely incompetent. Back in September, Lincoln's general McClellan refused to attack, even when his spies told him that the union army outnumbered Lee's troops three to one. General Lee managed to fool McClellan by setting up logs as cannons." Jeffrey grinned.

"Lincoln had to give McClellan an ultimatum. The war will

start February 22, or McClellan would be replaced." Warming to his subject, Jeffrey continued. "Then, McClellan refused to listen to Lincoln's plan on marching back to Bull Run. McClellan said that it was too dangerous. He wanted to surprise Lee by traveling down the Chesapeake and attacking from the east."

"When McClellan finally got his men moving on February 27th, the boats he'd had built to carry his troops wouldn't fit through the canal."

Kristen laughed in spite of her herself. She could easily picture the look on the face of the great Union general when he first realized the fatal mistake that his men had made, by making boats too big for the canal.

"So how can you think that the South can't win against that kind of leadership?" Jeffrey asked. "If Lincoln had been able to persuade General Lee to head his army, then maybe the South would have never had a chance, especially considering that the North has us outmanned, and the ability to manufacture weapons. The North has factories, while the South has tobacco and cotton."

Kristen heard the conviction in Jeffrey's arguments and she felt different living in the time of the Civil War than she had learning about it in school. She remembered very little about the war from history, except that in spite of the huge numbers of men who had died, the end result of the war had freed the slaves. No matter what he thought, the South would lose the war.

Another thought occurred to her. What if she somehow managed to change history? Kristen knew enough about the history of the Civil War to know that General Stonewall Jackson would be wounded by one of his own men. Not fatally, but the great man ended up dying of pneumonia due to complications from the amputation of his arm. What might happen if she saved his life? She knew more about infection than any doctor in the 1860's. Could she make a difference? Should she even try?

She had not thought about the long-term consequences of her actions in the war. Staying with Jeffrey mattered more than anything to her. Could her husband in this life be the reason she had come to this painful time in American history?

"I wish you were right," Kristen said with a sigh, "But don't you think it would be better to have our country stay in one piece?"

Jeffrey shook his head. "The government is trying to take away the rights of the states. How can one government know what each state needs and wants? This country is too big to be run from one place by one man and a few representatives making the decisions for all of us."

"I totally agree," Kristen said. "And it's only going to get worse."

Jeffrey twirled the stick still holding the snake over the fire.

Kristen had to admit that the smell of the roasting reptile made her mouth water.

"I've never known you to be interested in politics."

Kristen looked away from the fire. "I didn't used to care, but I've become more interested lately, especially when I see how it can affect our lives so deeply."

Jeffrey pulled the meat out of the fire and held it up to Kristen. "Here, why don't you have the first bite?"

Feeling her stomach grumble, Kristen took the stick out of Jeffrey's hand and took a small bite. It burned her lips but tasted wonderful.

"Who knew something so scary could taste good."

Smiling, Jeffrey took the stick as Kristen held it out to him. Their eyes met for a long moment. She could not help regretting that their marriage appeared to be coming to an end before she even had a chance to experience it.

"My clothes must be dry by now." She forced her eyes away from the man sitting next to her. She needed the armor of her clothes before she did something stupid, like throwing herself at the man she loved and face his rejection again.

Sixteen

Finally reaching Charleston, Jeffrey made arrangements to have his horse put on the train to follow him to Virginia. The Andersons would take Diablo home along with Kristen. The crowded train carried both soldiers being transported to the war, and civilians trying to get out of the way. The war raged in Virginia, where General Lee fought to capture the nation's Capital, Washington D.C.

"I'll be serving under General Lee," he said down to Kristen, boarding the train with one foot on the step, the other hanging in the air. "The fighting will be fierce and there will be casualties, which means it's no place for a lady."

"I didn't know you considered me a lady," Kristen said with a grin.

Jeffrey smiled in spite of himself. "You certainly don't dress like one." He paused, the smile leaving his face. "Or act like one."

"I didn't know you cared."

"I care because you're my wife—that is until the Yankees make you a widow." Jeffrey took a deep breath. "Kristen, I know we've had our difficulties, but war is no place for a woman. You won't last a day with what you'll be seeing."

"It's what I need to do."

Jeffrey shook his head. "I have yet to see war settle anything—at least not for long. Anyway, General Lee asked for me, so I'm going. The war hasn't come to the place where we need to ask our women to join us."

The train whistle blew. Jeffrey turned to Kristen. "I want you to be safe." His gray eyes darkened. "I've made arrangements for you to return home with the Andersons. Please do as I say and forget this crazy idea that you could help care for the injured. You have no skills in that direction, and you'll only end up getting in the way."

Kristen's mouth opened as if she wanted to say something but then she closed it and looked up at him, her face blank.

"Until fainting four days ago, your idea of helping someone was allowing them to sell you a new gown. I don't know what's come over you, but I expect that you'll be back to your old self before you get back home."

"I'm happy to see that you find my lack of compassion so amusing."

"Then you'll go back with the Andersons without causing them any problem?"

Kristen said nothing.

"Kristen..."

"Aren't you about to miss your train?"

The conductor waved his hand toward the crowd of men still clinging to their sweethearts. Jeffrey wanted to grab Kristen, but did not act on the impulse. As much as his wife had changed over the last few days, he feared her selfish actions would prevail. He had tired of her schemes and vowed never again to fall into her consummate acting traps.

"Kristen, if you don't go home with the Andersons, I won't be accountable for what I do when I get home." Jeffrey climbed the rest of the steps to the train.

Kristen merely smiled and waved as the train pulled away.

The moment Jeffrey turned away and disappeared into the train car, Kristen ran. She nearly knocked over a few well-dressed ladies who looked at her in disgust. The air grew hotter from the train's engines blowing black smoke into the fresh air. The train's whistle gave a screech, drowning out the shouts of goodbye and any other parting words couples might have tried to say to each other.

She only had one chance, so she grabbed a handrail and

leaped onto the stairs as the train gathered speed. Safe aboard the train and gasping for air, she watched the boarding platform grow smaller and disappear into the distance.

Now that she had made it onto the train, she only had to stay out of Jeffrey's sight for the next two days. The money she'd stolen from his pants pocket while he slept might come in handy, if caught without a ticket or if she wanted to eat after that little camping trip. She thought about the snake that almost killed her and then the taste of eating it. *I swear if I ever make it back to my own time, I'll take myself out to the nicest restaurant in Seattle and eat everything on the menu.*

Kristen's instincts kept telling her that she had come back to this time because of Jeffrey. She had to stay as close to him as possible in order to fulfill whatever her mission might be. Once she arrived on the battlefield it would be too dangerous to send her home, and he would just have to deal with her presence. She would help care for the wounded and show her husband that she really had changed, more than he would ever know.

Seventeen

Kristen sat on a board bench, crowded with men in what looked to be home-made uniforms of either butternut yellow or gray. One of the men had a hollow diamond above three chevrons on his sleeve. The other men's sleeves were bare of any sort of identifying rank. She assumed the man with the chevrons would be the sergeant. He had a thick gray-streaked beard and the biggest cigar she had ever seen dangled from his mouth. The other men laughed and ribbed each other. They shared strips of dried beef that reminded her of jerky.

Between abusing each other and telling ribald jokes, the men looked Kristen up and down, as if trying to decide how she would do as a soldier. The youngest of the four grinned, his teeth slightly protruding, which added charm to his freckled face.

"Going up north to fight?" He gave her a shy grin.

Kristen shook her head and lowered her voice. "I'll be joining up with the medical corps." She hoped she used the right term.

"You don't sound like a Southerner." The sergeant chomped on his cigar, his eyes narrowing.

"I don't?" Kristen drew out her vowels in what she hoped would pass as an acceptable imitation of a Southern accent. *Please drop it.*

"Hmm." He pulled a large newspaper wrapped bundle from the seat beside him and opened it. Inside was a large sandwich. He took a bite.

The young soldier next to Kristen eyed her with interest.

"You don't look old enough to fight in no war."

She turned away trying to shrink into the hard, wooden seat.

"In fact, you don't even look much like a man at all." The soldier lost all shyness and leered. "You is far too pretty."

Smelling the whiskey on his breath, Kristen tried to lean away. He came in for a closer smell.

"In fact, you smell just like a girl I used to know back home." His nose hovered inches from her neck. "If I didn't know better, I'd say you *was* a girl." He made a clumsy move toward the front of her shirt when a hand grabbed him from behind. Someone lifted the young soldier clear off his seat.

"I think you'd better leave this young man alone."

The soldier's face turned red. He choked out a protest as he hung an inch above his seat.

Kristen looked up to see Jeffrey glaring down at her.

The sergeant opened his mouth in apparent protest at the treatment of one of his men, but the large bite he had just taken from his sandwich lodged in his throat. He tried to swallow but no air could get past the ham, cheese and thick bread. His eyes grew wide, attempting to cough.

"He's choking to death!" Kristen leaped from her seat and tried to fight her way through the tangle of soldiers' feet.

Jeffrey dropped the young soldier he held and grabbed Kristen's arm instead. "Let's go."

Kristen struggled to get away from his iron grip. "Can't you see that he's choking to death?"

"No, he's not." Jeffrey tugged on her arm.

"Not him. *Him!*" Kristen pointed to the sergeant whose face had turned gray. Breaking free of Jeffrey's grip, she rushed to the side of the sergeant and pushed the soldier away who had been pounding on the big man's back.

"Get out of my way." Kristen used a voice the soldier recognized as someone in authority because he held his hands up and backed away. The sergeant now doubled over in his seat had his head nearly on the floor. She leaned over her patient and wrapped her arms around his middle. Balling her hands into a tight fist, she pulled up sharply. Nothing happened. She repeated her move and gave it as much force as she could muster.

A piece of the partially-chewed sandwich flew out of the man's throat. It hit Jeffrey's boot where he stood transfixed by what she had just done.

Kristen finally let go of the sergeant, who slumped forward without her support. The soldier Jeffrey had been holding, grabbed his sergeant and settled him back into his seat.

"Kristen, we need to go, *now*," Jeffrey said in almost a whisper.

She looked up at him and nodded.

Following the excitement of the choking incident, the soldiers gathered around their exhausted leader. They paid no attention to Kristen as Jeffrey led her down the aisle, where he stopped at one of the doors, opened it, and sat Kristen down on the upholstered seat.

"How did you know I was on the train?" Kristen found it hard not to smile.

"Because *I* didn't have *my* ticket."

"Oh."

Jeffrey took a deep breath, glaring at her. "Why are you on this train?"

"I've already told you," she said with patience. "I'm going to help with the wounded."

Jeffrey gave a short laugh. "Kristen, I don't know why you think you will be any help at all, considering you can't stand the sight of blood. All you're going to do is get in the way and cause me more grief."

"I've changed." She raised her chin.

"Changed?" Jeffrey swiped a hand down his face. "Kristen, you've never cared for any living soul in all your life, except yourself. Now I'm supposed to believe you want to give up your life of shopping, gossip, and parties to live in a tent to care for men who have been shot to pieces?" He shook his head. "The odor alone will drive you back home with your tail between your legs."

"I can help." Kristen stuck out her chin. "And your army is going to need me."

"The last thing the Confederacy needs is a helpless, hysterical woman during a time of war."

"You think you know me, but you don't!" Kristen did not like losing her temper but could not help it.

Jeffrey gave a snort. "Kristen, I know you better than you know yourself. You don't have the stomach for the injuries you're going to have to see in this war. All you're going to do is get in the way of people who know what they're doing."

"Jeffrey O'Connor, I'm going with you no matter what you say." Kristen slapped the wall next to her. "And there's nothing you can do to stop me!"

Jeffrey's mouth opened, but a knock on the door silenced his original thought. "In!" He called out. A man in uniform hesitated at the doorway.

"I'll get something to eat," Jeffrey said, his eyes narrowing. He stepped in front of the confused soldier who looked first at Kristen and then quickly moved back.

He left the room and pulled the door closed behind him.

*K*risten chuckled and leaned back in the cushioned seat. *I'm going to show that stubborn husband of mine that he doesn't know me at all.* Once he saw that she really did know something about medicine, he would have to admit that she was right about coming along. Maybe she would discover the reason she had been brought back to this period of time. Then she would be able to make it back to her own time. Unfortunately, if she returned, it would be without Jeffrey. She did not want to think about such a loss. She closed her eyes and was soon sound asleep.

Eighteen

Everywhere Kristen looked in Richmond, Virginia bustled with activity. Soldiers performed drills and target practice. Laughter came from the tent circles scattered across the lawns of the city parks, as if the war would be one big party. Soldiers crowded the train station, with varying shades of gray disembarking onto the loading platform.

"Doesn't look like much of a war," Kristen said.

"Still no place for a lady."

She grinned up at Jeffrey. "I thought you said I wasn't a lady."

"You don't look like one in that outfit."

Looking down at her wrinkled shirt and trousers, Kristen shrugged her shoulders. "Dressed like this, at least I'll be safe from the men."

"Damn," Jeffrey said, muttering the curse under his breath.

"I know you think I'll get sick at the first sight of blood —"

"I know you'll collapse the first time you have to do any actual work." Jeffrey rolled his eyes. "Since you refuse to listen to me, you'll just have to find out for yourself."

She sensed a tangible air of anticipation amongst the soldiers. No one yet knew the horrors that the war would soon bring. *I can't believe I'm standing here in Richmond, right where the first battle of the Civil War begins!*

A young man in a gray uniform with two stripes on his sleeve came to a halt in front of Jeffrey and gave him a sharp salute.

He looked like a boy to Kristen, his blond mustache almost

105

too faint to be seen.

"Captain O'Connor, sir."

"Yes?"

"First Sergeant Randall, sir."

"Go ahead, Sergeant Randall."

"I'm going to show you to your tent, sir, serve, and introduce you to your company."

"Very good, Sergeant." Jeffrey took a deep breath and turned to Kristen. "You'll be staying in my tent, Private Bissett."

Kristen tried to look the part of a serious soldier. She nodded, relieved that Jeffrey could not send her back to the plantation. She followed Jeffrey and the young sergeant.

The tent was half the size of the bathroom back at the plantation. Several cotton bales stacked against one wall made the bed with a dingy pillow and a single blanket tucked neatly into place. Kristen found herself staring at the cotton bales. She tried to imagine two people sharing such a tiny space.

"I'll need another cot brought in for my assistant," Jeffrey said.

"The private can sleep in my tent." Sergeant Randall took Kristen's arm. "You'll be wanting your privacy, sir."

It took a minute for Jeffrey to answer. Kristen felt her heart constrict in fear. She could not believe that Randall would make such a suggestion. Surely her husband would not let her sleep in a tent filled with soldiers as her punishment...would he?

"Private Bissett will be staying with me," Jeffrey said.

The embarrassed look that passed over the sergeant's face almost made Kristen laugh. Jeffrey's look kept her humor at bay, daring her say something. She had no intention of sleeping in a tent full of noisy soldiers.

"That will be all, Sergeant."

With a sharp salute, the sergeant left them alone in the small tent. Jeffrey's penetrating stare made the tent feel even smaller.

"I can see that you're making a big sacrifice for me," Kristen said.

Jeffrey frowned. "This is hardly going to be fun and games for me. I'll give you until the first wounded men are brought in. Then you'll be anxious to get on the first train bound for home."

Kristen raised her chin. "I'll stay as long as you do."

106

Jeffrey laughed. "I've made arrangements for you to work in the medical unit, if you're still serious about helping with the wounded." He stopped and took a deep breath. "But I'd recommend that you keep up the pretense of being a man." He sounded pained at his own words. Clearing his throat, he continued. "I'll treat you as such, so as not to arouse any suspicions."

"That shouldn't be too hard for you," Kristen said.

Jeffrey's only reaction, a pair of raised eyebrows. *Sure, now that you find me less appealing with my boyish hair. I guess I'll have to just live in close quarters with you while you ignore me. Okay, I'll do the same to you, but it sure won't be easy.*

"I'll walk you over to the medical tent," Jeffrey said, sounding anxious to be rid of her.

"I could probably find it on my own."

He ignored her comment, opened the tent flap, and looked outside. "I'll walk you over and introduce you to Dr. Vogler."

Kristen followed Jeffrey. Hundreds of soldiers readied for the upcoming battle. She raised an eyebrow at the very few soldiers in uniforms, or even any semblance of a uniform. Most of the men did not even have proper guns, at least not as far as she could tell. The rifles she *saw* looked like old-fashioned flintlocks, which dated back to the turn of the century. The camaraderie of men gathered together for a common goal and confident of their ability to win the upcoming war seemed to dominate the atmosphere of the camp.

The summer sun beamed upon the energetic men, making the air grow warmer. Her heart sank at their talk of how quickly they would send those damn Yankees running home, as well as a discussion about the superiority of the Southern generals. The prewar bravado rang high, the men drilling with enthusiasm and bragging they would all be home in time for the fall harvest.

Jeffrey stopped at a large tent where a red-haired giant barked orders at the top of his voice.

"Dr. Vogler?"

The huge man turned, and upon seeing Jeffrey, aimed a fierce glare toward him. "Are you a physician?"

"No, sir," Jeffrey said with ease. "But I brought you an assistant."

Dr. Vogler turned his piercing, blue eyes toward Kristen.

"He's not much more than a boy." He turned away and barked an order to a young woman who smiled despite the doctor's harsh tone. "Nurse, show this boy where the bandages are, and have him start folding."

The nurse patted down the apron tied around her waist. With a brisk wave, she led Kristen through the long tent to a covered hallway.

Kristen hurried to keep up with the woman's long stride.

With a slight frown, the nurse looked Kristen up and down. "Why are you dressed as a man?"

Taken aback by the woman's instant recognition, Kristen blushed. "How did you know?"

"My name is Mrs. Bitterman. I've been a nurse for ten years, and a nun before that. There are many women dressed as men to fight in this war." Mrs. Bitterman shrugged her wide shoulders. "I take it you aren't a very good shot. You want to help, so you chose medicine."

"I've had some training in it," Kristen said.

Mrs. Bitterman sighed. "I'm sure it's neither adequate nor up-to-date." She walked through another tent. "We'll start you out folding bandages. In that capacity you won't be able to hurt anyone with your lack of skills."

Protest died on Kristen's lips when she realized she could say nothing to dispute the words of nurse Bitterman. She would just have to show the nurse that she did indeed know something about medicine. Even if she had another year of residency to complete, Kristen knew that she had more knowledge and more experience than anyone else in this time.

The nurse stopped at a table where they kept the shredded clothes. Kristen touched the pile, marveling at the rough texture of the raw, unbleached cotton.

"We don't have much in the way of medical supplies," Nurse Bitterman said, "but at least we do have bandages." She picked up one of the lengths of material and started ripping it apart fiercely. "These need to be torn into long strips."

Kristen nodded.

The older woman gave Kristen a long look. "You plan on continuing your charade as a man?"

"I think it would be better."

Nurse Bitterman nodded. "It would make you more useful. Dr. Vogler won't feel too badly about using you as a man. He would as a woman."

"You're not going to tell him?"

"If I did that, I'd have to turn in more than a dozen women that followed their husbands and sweethearts into this war." She sighed. "Until the real battle starts, everyone thinks this is going to be nothing more than an adventure to brag about to their grandchildren someday." Her eyes filled with sadness. "War is never anything different than men trying to kill each other for reasons they can't remember. Just staying alive becomes the main goal of everyone in the end."

"Sounds like you've seen your fair share of war."

Shaking her head, Nurse Bitterman frowned. "I just know human nature."

Kristen didn't get a chance to ask any more questions. Left alone, she ripped the cotton material into strips, and folded each neatly into a pile beside her. Several ladies from counseling came in to help. They wore fashionable tresses that resembled the men's gray uniforms, as if they too were part of the Confederate Army.

The women's chatter fascinated Kristen. They talked of their children, their husbands, beans, and the price of bacon having doubled. One of the younger women, a lovely delicate blonde, flirted with her until she was informed by her older, more experienced companions that Kristen was a woman. This caused a great deal of laughter as the ladies began telling stories of four other women they knew who also dressed as men to fight in the war. Her new friends promised to keep her secret, assuring her that the South would indeed win the war, and that everything would get back to normal in just a few short months.

By the end of the day, Kristen's hands were so red and tired she did not think she would have enough strength left in her arms to lift a fork at dinner. When she left the plantation, she had not envisioned tearing bandages.

Patience. The war will start soon enough, and then there'll be plenty of real work to do.

Nineteeen

Once finished, Kristen was sent back to her tent. Campfires blazed all around as she made her way through the crowds of men milling around. Some grumbled over their lack of uniforms, but most seemed excited to be doing something important. Many of the men looked as if they had just left childhood. Some faces had not yet seen a razor, and many might not need to use one for another few years. *Or maybe never*, the tiny voice in her head cautioned.

Twice she lifted the flap of the wrong tent, only to be greeted by rough voices of men laughing at her mistake. Finally, she found the tent she had left that morning. She recognized Jeffrey's dark form bent over a small table with only the glow of a single candle. He had a map spread before him, and made notations with a piece of charcoal pencil.

She entered and Jeffrey looked up. "Ready to go home?"

The wariness dropped away and anger took over. "I'm fine, thank you."

Jeffrey shrugged. "I guess I lost my bet."

"I believe you did," Kristen said, firmly. Even in the semi darkness of the tent, she could make out her husband's lean form. The muscles in his long legs seemed flexed against his officer-grade trousers, tucked into gleaming black boots. He worked without his uniform coat in a revealing white shirt with rolled up sleeves, due in part to the stuffy heat of the still night. His black, curly hair made a sharp contrast with the paleness of the shirt leading her gaze up and down his lean body.

Thoughts she never before imagined shook Kristen with their power. She looked around the tent, trying to diminish the intense emotion. She noticed another cot in the tent. A thin brown woolen blanket covered it, and a flat gray pillow lay on top. The small space between the two beds shrank the living and working area. Her imagination drifted to the sight of the two cots that if place together could become part of one large bed. Heat rose in her cheeks, imagining what it would be like to live so close to Jeffrey, night after night.

He turned—his eyes followed Kristen's gaze. He raised one dark eyebrow. "As you can see, your cot has arrived."

The blush on her cheeks deepened. The space felt too small to hold all the emotions consuming her. She backed up to the tent opening without turning around and gasped. "I think I need some air."

Once outside, Kristen looked up at the darkening sky and breathed in the sweet summer air. Even in her exhaustion, she felt revived merely by being near Jeffrey. She trembled. *How can I ever live like this?* With him so close she only thought about running her hands over his body, breathing in his scent, and tasting the sweat of his skin after making love. Everything about her husband rattled her until she could think about nothing else.

A soldier stopped in front of Kristen, his hands holding a tray. "Capt. O'Connor requested dinner be brought to his tent."

Kristen recognized the voice. She took the tray from the sergeant's outstretched hands.

"Thank you, Sergeant Randall." The aroma coming from the two bowls filled Kristen's nose. Her stomach grumbled.

She would have to go back into the tent and face him. She could handle his presence now. He was only a man after all. Kristen stepped back inside.

Jeffrey did not look up from his map.

"Sergeant Randall sent dinner," she said.

After a moment, Jeffrey looked up and frowned. He folded the map and placed it on the table. "Are you sure you can eat this food?"

Kristen's stomach rumbled again. "I'm hungry enough to eat my own cooking."

When Jeffrey opened his mouth in surprise, Kristen knew she had said the wrong thing again. "I...I mean if I cooked." Kristen put the tray down on the table and hoped it would distract him.

"Hah! I'm not sure you've ever cooked anything in your life." Jeffrey grinned.

"Of course." Kristen blew out a relieved sigh.

The rich smell of stew wafted up from the two, large, earthenware bowls resting on the pewter tray. A loaf of dark, warm bread and a crock of butter sat next to the stew. Jeffrey cut the bread and handed Kristen a slice. Her teeth sank into the thick bread releasing its yeasty flavor. She thought her moan was only imagined until she noticed Jeffrey staring at her

"It's really good." She swallowed it quick.

Jeffrey arched a brow. "I've never known you to like anything but those little sandwiches cut into triangles. You told me that only crude people would eat anything with the crust on it."

"I've changed." Kristen reached for another slice. Never had she enjoyed food more.

"I can see that." Jeffrey pushed a bowl of stew toward her. "I'm not sure why, but officers are generally given better rations than the other men."

Kristen picked up one of the huge pewter spoons. Whatever was in the stew, it smelled delicious. She took a bite. It tasted better than anything she had ever tasted before. The meat reminded her of beef with something added to it. The vegetables were still on the crunchy side, yet she chewed them with relish.

"This is wonderful! What is it?"

Taking a bite, Jeffrey nodded. "Probably venison."

"You mean I'm eating Bambi?" Kristen dropped her spoon. She'd never eaten anything more exotic than turkey and pressed turkey at that.

"What's Bambi?"

"Just a story about a deer that I heard as a child."

Jeffrey frowned. "It's best not to name something you might have to eat later."

Kristen laughed, nearly spitting out her food. She looked up into Jeffrey's eyes and noticed they twinkled.

"I just hope tomorrow's dinner isn't rabbit."

Jeffrey's spoon slid back into his bowl, considering his wife. "And if it is?"

Kristen grinned. "Because I know a rabbit named Thumper from the same story."

Jeffrey laughed, and Kristen joined him. A feeling of genuine warmth floated through her that had nothing to do with the humor she found in her situation. A man who could make her laugh, might be able to reach the places she had kept hidden from everyone her whole life.

To cover her newfound emotions, she ate the rest of her dinner in silence. Never had she felt more satisfied by a meal. When they both finished, Jeffrey picked up the tray and set it outside the tent.

Just like in a five-star hotel. Kristen mused looking at Jeffrey's back. The muscles stretched underneath his shirt, leading her thoughts back to the afternoon they had shared only a few days before. "I have got to get myself under control," Kristen whispered under her breath. How could she spend night after night in this tiny tent with a husband who ruled her thoughts like a general? "I just can't let him know how I feel," Kristen murmured.

Jeffrey did not seem to notice her distress as he came back into the tent and picked up his map again. He spread it on the table and leaned over it.

"What are you studying?" Kristen leaned over his shoulder.

"Where the Yankees will attack first."

Kristen tried to remember where the first battle of the Civil War had been fought, but at the time such information had not seemed important. She vowed never again to consider any fact unnecessary.

"Any ideas?"

"Not a one." Jeffrey rubbed his forehead.

The light of the solitary candle seemed better suited to romance than for reading a map. The tiny candlelight brought a fuzzy glow to Jeffrey's lean, slightly whiskered jaw. The effect made Kristen want to rub her finger over the stubble.

She could hardly believe the recent flow of her thoughts. Surely adolescent boys were not this emotional. Perhaps it

114

would be better if she just went to bed for the night. Dr. Vogler had promised another busy day of making bandages. Fatigue finally overtook Kristen's lustful thoughts.

"I'm going to bed now," she said. "See you in the morning."

Jeffrey continued to be absorbed in his map, giving Kristen nothing more than a grunt. She turned toward her cot and started unbuttoning her shirt, thinking how pleasant a hot bath would be right now, or better yet a cold shower. She could probably strip naked and he would not even notice. Her thoughts shocked her, but she could not seem to control them. That one afternoon in bed with him showed her how good life could be with a man who totally enthralled you. Who was she kidding? She wanted to make love to her husband for the rest of her life, but so far, she could not be sure she would get even one more chance. Wearing only her undergarments, she slid into the blankets of the narrow bed. The muggy, hot air forced her to kick off the thin blanket. She tried to plump up the gray pillow. After several minutes of frustration, she finally found herself slipping into a sleep borne from exhaustion.

*J*effrey turned from the map and stared down at his beautiful wife. How he longed to comfort her while lying beside her on the narrow cot. Her short hair lent to an air of innocence he would not have believed his wife possessed. He knew now that a woman could look like an angel and be quite the opposite. He learned his lesson the hard way and had no desire to experience it again.

Pushing back his chair, he blew out the tiny flame of his candle, causing smoke to rise. He had no idea when or where the Yankees would come to fight the Southerners on the battlefield. He hoped General Lee had a crystal ball.

Stripping off his clothes, Jeffrey lay on top of his own cot and stared up at the cramped interior of the tent. It took every ounce of his will not to turn and watch Kristen. She lay nearly naked, her long legs now tangled in the scratchy wool blanket. Taking her in her sleep would have removed his worries about the war, but doing so would give her enough ammunition to crush him emotionally. He closed his eyes with an effort, willing himself to sleep. He could only fight one battle at a time.

Twenty

The next morning, Kristen awoke feeling as though she had not slept at all. The shock of waking up in such a strange place faded slowly. She gazed at the empty cot, barely an arms-reach away.

Getting up from her cot, she walked over to the door of the tent and lifted the flap open. She concluded that her husband wanted to be away from her.

What time is it? Bathed in semi darkness, she heard the crows cawing out a morning ritual.

A steaming pot of coffee sat on the table and a single, empty cup sat beside it. The aroma of the coffee increased her need for the welcome caffeine. She slipped into her clothes, ignoring the previous day's dirt and sweat. After drinking two cups of coffee, she felt human again. She stood up from the folding, wooden chair and lifted the tent flap to look outside again. The sun rise bathed the sky with golden light and the air smelled of bacon.

Soldiers sat or stood around individual campfires, drinking coffee and eating their breakfast. It amazed her that many of the soldiers brought their own food with them, or stole it from local farmers.

Not an early morning person, Kristen almost gagged at the thick wave of grease smoke passing over her. She held her breath and made her way to the hospital tent. Some of the soldiers sat quietly, some sang, and one played a harmonica filling the air

117

with haunting music.

She rushed past row after row of gray-white tents, erected in orderly lines across the grassy field. The walk gave her a chance to stretch her legs. Every muscle in her body ached with the need to be moving again. One night of sleeping on the cot had her wondering how many more nights of such torture she could endure. Even the ground tempted her.

She reached the hospital tent just as the sun's light brightened the entire sky. Kristen found everything in chaos. Nurse Bitterman barked orders at young nurses, who ran around in circles. Some of the people living nearby brought their children to the camp hospital to see the doctors on duty. While waiting, one farmer complained of missing hogs and chickens since the soldiers had come to town. A rooster crowed from a tent in the middle of the camp. It left no doubt in her mind as to the validity of the farmer's claim.

Two soldiers carried a young woman in a sweat-soaked nightgown inside the tent. They laid her down gently on a cot, each grasping a small pillow to give the woman comfort. The woman herself looked too weak to do anything but lie on the bed and moan. Only her distended stomach showed any movement. It rippled with labor pains gripping the woman's tired body.

"Private Bissett," nurse Bitterman yelled out. "Get me some whiskey for Mrs. James."

"Whiskey?" Kristen could not believe what she heard.

Dr. Vogler turned away from the moaning woman to glare at Kristen. She noticed the woman's ghostly-white complexion, paler than the cotton nightgown she wore. The poor woman appeared to have not a drop of blood left in her. Kristen looked down at the cot where the woman laid soaked in blood.

Kristen looked at the doctor. She saw his bloodshot eyes and his bright red cheeks. She nearly jumped when he growled at her. The smell of whiskey on his breath nearly choked her and his walk had stagger to it.

"I said, get the patient some whiskey."

She turned and searched the tent for anything that looked like a whiskey bottle. Hidden behind the doctor's desk, she spied a brown bottle. Kristen grabbed it and pulled out the cork.

"Is this it?" She held the bottle up for all to see. The overpowering smell attesting to the fact.

"Give it to her," the doctor shouted, then vomited on the woman's cot.

Kristen looked down in horror at the doctor's filthy hands. He was about to plunge them into the woman's birth canal.

"You can't do that!" Kristen shouted, nearly dropping the whiskey bottle in her haste to grab the doctor's arms.

"Private Bissett!" The doctor shouted in disbelief. "What do you think you're doing?"

"You've got to sterilize your hands or you'll cause an infection! And, you're drunk!" She dared the doctor to argue.

Dr. Vogler stared at Kristen as if she'd lost her mind.

"I know it sounds crazy." Shaking her finger at him, she said, "You're going to have to trust me on this."

"Trust you?" Dr. Vogler's eyes widened in disbelief. "You know nothing about being a doctor. I spent two years in medical school, and you mean to tell me how to do my job?"

Two years? Kristen could not believe what she heard. It took only two years to get a medical degree? She spent twice as much time on just her anatomy courses. How could she explain germs to this man with his dirty hands?

"Why don't I try to turn the baby." Kristen said in as calm a voice as she could manage. "My hands are much smaller than yours, Doctor." She held out her slender hands in front of the doctor's face but he did not answer. He had passed out in the nearby chair and snored loudly. At least she would not have to explain to him what she was about to do.

She rushed to a bucket of water and the bar of soap lying next to it. The soap smelled strongly of lye, so she assumed it would kill any germs she might have on her hands. The water stung the blisters she already had on her hands but she continued scrubbing, including her arms.

The woman giving birth gave a weak scream. She looked around the room in terror.

"I've helped many women give birth before," Kristen whispered into the woman's ear. She moved underneath the bedclothes of the exhausted woman and slid her hands into the slippery opening. She felt one tiny foot.

The woman moaned at another contraction hitting her hard.

Kristen pulled her hand out so the opening could clamp down. She waited until the contraction subsided and then slipped her hand back inside. Even without a fetal monitor she could tell the baby was under duress, but to perform her first C-section under these circumstances, the risk for the mother and child were high. If she allowed the mother to attempt this any longer, she and the baby would not survive.

"How long has she been in labor?" Kristen said to the pale-faced young man who appeared to be the husband.

"Going on two days now, ma'am," he said in a shaky voice.

"Too long," Kristen muttered under her breath.

To her surprise, the patient sat up on the cot and glared at her through red-rimmed eyes. "Too long for who?" She panted, glaring at her.

Despite the situation, Kristen found herself smiling. "Too long for you to endure, but don't worry. We're going to get you taken care of right now." She turned to Nurse Bitterman. "Get the laudanum and give it to her."

"How much?"

Kristen turned away from the patient, taking the nurse with her. "Enough to knock her out. I'm going to do a cesarean."

"Not here?" The nurse looked at her as if she had lost her mind.

"It's the only way to save the mother and the baby," Kristen said. She hoped her voice was not trembling.

The nurse stared at her in disbelief. "You can't!"

Kristen took the nurse by the arm, leading her away from the patient. "If I don't operate immediately, this woman will die — and so will her child."

"We need to wait for Dr. Vogler." The nurse cast a furtive glance at the unconscious doctor.

"And how long until the good doctor will work his way into consciousness again?" Kristen said.

Without another word, Nurse Bitterman marched to the table and a locked chest that stored the few medical supplies maintained by the hospital. Carefully, as if it were gold, the nurse poured some of the contents of a dark gray bottle onto a square of cloth. She walked back to the moaning woman on the cot, and laid the cloth over the woman's mouth. After only one inhale, the woman became as still as if she had just died.

Nurse Bitterman looked over at Kristen. "Now you can operate," she said. Her eyes held a challenge.

Kristen did not wish to confront anyone, but she had to either operate or let this woman die. The young soldier still holding his wife's hand, broke the temporary silence. "You've got to save her."

The boy looked to be no more than sixteen-years-old. The way he clung to his wife's hand told Kristen how much the woman meant to him.

"I'll need the instruments that the good doctor uses," Kristen barely managed to whisper. The enormity of her actions weighed on her mind. *Seven years of medical training and assisting in at least a dozen cesareans, I know what to do – but should I?*

Nurse Bitterman handed her a tray of surgical tools. Kristen took a deep breath. "I'll need them sterilized."

She saw the look of incomprehension on the woman's face. "I'll need them washed as quickly as you can," Kristen said.

Nodding, the nurse hurried over to the bucket where Kristen had washed her hands earlier. She returned quickly handing Kristen the tray of still wet instruments.

Kristen had the knowledge to perform the operation, but did she have the guts to do it without all the latest equipment and a senior staff member looking over her shoulder? This was far different – in a crude tent with only her own knowledge to guide her.

She drew the patient's nightgown all the way up to her neck. The woman's stomach had grown still and her breathing shallow. She had to start right now or it would be too late.

"Give me a bucket of water and some soap," Kristen said, surprised to find herself sounding like one of her instructors.

"And a needle and thread which needs to be washed also."

The nurse returned in seconds. The father's eyes wide open as she washed the patient's stomach area carefully, then drew a scalpel across the skin below the belly button. The line became red with fresh blood.

"I'll need you to swab behind me."

Nurse Bitterman nodded, already working to keep the area clear.

The operation would take a steady hand, and it pleased her to see her hands not shaking at all. The wound she inflicted bled more than she had hoped. *I'll have to work fast.*

One last cut with the knife, then she put it on the tray. Using her fingers, Kristen felt through the tissue and blood to define the firm form of the child within the uterus. With both hands she drew the baby out, lifting it clear of the mother's body with the afterbirth still connected. The nurse cut the cord without being asked.

The child was not breathing. Kristen massaged the baby's stomach, ignoring the outstretched arms of Nurse Bitterman.

"You're going to have to slap him!" The nurse glared at her.

"We don't do that anymore," Kristen said pressing harder on the baby's stomach. She willed the child to start breathing. No sound came from the infant.

The nurse grabbed the baby away from Kristen and placed him on the table. She turned him over and slapped him sharply on the back. The baby let out an enraged cry.

Kristen breathed a sigh of relief and noticed Nurse Bitterman wore a slight smile.

The father, who had been staring in amazement and horror the entire time, finally found his voice. "I have a boy?"

Turning her attention back to the mother, Kristen nodded. She needed to concentrate on sewing up the wound she had inflicted. Layer by layer, she closed and stitched each opening she had made with the knife until finished.

Kristen looked down at the mother. "I hope she makes it." There was nothing more she could do for the woman.

"What time is it?" She turned to Nurse Bitterman.

Busy cleaning up the baby, the nurse motioned toward the doctor's desk. Kristen saw a tiny clock that read nearly 5 o'clock. She had been working since dawn. Exhausted, she fell into a wooden folding chair. Her hands shook.

The nurse took the baby to his groggy mother returning to consciousness. The mother gave her screaming baby a weak smile and then moved her nightgown out of the way so the infant could nurse. The father beamed, gazing at his newborn son.

The scene brought tears to Kristen's eyes. The father hardly more than a boy himself, already a soldier fighting in the war. She wondered if he would live to see his son grow up. She wiped her stray hairs out of her eyes and lifted the tent flap for a breath of fresh air, hoping it would revive her.

Loud voices coming from inside the tent interrupted her thoughts. She recognized the doctor's voice and closed her eyes. She didn't look forward to hearing from Dr. Vogler, now that he had sobered up enough to check on his patient. *How am I going to explain doing a major operation?*

Kristen could barely make herself go back inside the tent and face what should have been a celebration instead of a dressing down by an incompetent fool of a doctor.

Twenty One

Nurse Bitterman gave Kristen a nod as if to say that she had at least one friend. She gave a weak smile in return, then braced herself for Dr. Vogler's wrath.

"Did you kill that woman?" The doctor's voice boomed inside the tent. He shook himself and tried to rise from the chair where he had been sleeping.

"No, but you surely would have," Kristen said.

The doctor glared down at her, his face as red as his hair. His narrowed pale-blue eyes made him look even more dangerous. "You've got no business taking care of my patients." The intoxicated man lifted the thin blanket that covered the woman.

The new mother wore a contented smile on her face. Kristen could not see how she could endure the pain without any modern-day painkillers, but the tiny woman had a contented look on her face as she watched her new son sleep.

"You cut the baby out?" Dr. Voigt Vogler's deep voice boomed, waking the baby. At the child's cry, the mother gave the doctor an angry glare. Dr. Vogler let the blanket fall back down.

"I had to do it. The baby was stressed," Kristen said. "The mother was so exhausted—she couldn't deliver the child."

"What?" The doctor shouted back, his face growing even redder. Kristen feared the man might have a heart attack.

Nurse Bitterman surprised her by coming to her defense.

"I watched the lad work, Doctor, and he did a fine job. I don't know where he got his medical training, but he certainly knows what he's doing."

It looked as if the staring contest might have gone on indefinitely, if a high-ranking officer had not stepped inside. Kristen looked up and thought she imagined the man. Standing in the tent's doorway, she recognized the man from her history books.

"So, what seems to be the problem?"

"You're Robert E. Lee," Kristen whispered.

The general turned and looked at her. "And who might you be, young man?"

"K...K...Kristen—I mean Kevin Bissett, sir." She found herself tongue-tied in front of the famous General Lee.

"You're a doctor?"

Dr. Vogler broke away from the staring contest with nurse Bitterman. "He most certainly is not! I'm the only doctor here!"

The general raised an eyebrow and stroked his beard. His gaze fell on the new mother, totally engrossed with her new baby.

The father of the child came to attention immediately. "General Lee, sir!" He barked out with a sharp salute.

"At ease, soldier." The general walked over to the baby and ran a finger over the boy's cheek. "I see you've just become a father."

"That's right, sir." The soldier looked over at Kristen. "This young doctor had to operate on my wife, and take the baby right out of her belly." He said this as if re-living the experience, his face turning pale

"That's very interesting," Lee said turning his attention again to Kristen. "So are you a doctor?"

She took a deep breath. "Well...I've been in training." She tried to keep the hesitation out of her voice.

The general nodded. "Sounds as if you've been trained well. We're going to need all the good doctors we can get once this war starts."

"What!" Dr. Vogler's face turned beet red. "I'm in charge of this hospital—"

"And you're no doubt happy to see another competent doctor

on your staff." Lee smiled at the doctor.

Vogler stared open-mouthed at the general for a moment, then he turned to Kristen. "Welcome to the hospital," he said with a nervous glance toward the general. Clearly Lee's steady gaze had sobered in him up.

"Thank you." Kristen smiled back. She knew this would be the beginning of their own personal battle, but at least she would now be able to do something besides make bandages.

"Why don't I take the young doctor to get something to eat," Nurse Bitterman said.

At the mention of food, Kristen realized how late in the day it was, and she had not eaten since dawn. She was famished.

She looked at Lee and saw him engrossed in conversation with Dr. Vogler. She wanted to say goodbye, but thought better than to press her luck with her new boss. Vogler reminded her of a boss in the 21st century. A doctor who was also secure in his godliness because he saved lives

"Quite a day we've had so far," Nurse Bitterman said when they walked outside.

"Now that's an understatement." Kristen sighed. She looked at the nurse and they both laughed.

"You've made yourself a powerful friend and a powerful enemy, all in the same day."

Kristen made a flatulent sound with her lips. "I take it you're referring to Dr. Vogler as the enemy."

Nurse Bitterman nodded. "But you've also made a good friend in General Lee. He's a man who's very much admired by everyone."

"I can see that." Meeting a figure from history had been a thrill Kristen had not anticipated. She rubbed her arms where goosebumps formed.

Most of the camp had settled down for the night. A few troops were still up doing target practice.

"Doesn't it ever stop?" Kristen nodded to a line of men they passed who wore tired expressions under the gunpowder soot covering their faces.

"Those are Captain O'Connor's sharpshooters. I've heard

they're going to be the best trained troops that Lee has. Capt. O'Connor has them practicing day in and day out." Nurse Bitterman shrugged.

"Jeffrey?"

"You know Captain O'Connor?" The nurse stared at Kristen.

"He's my husband." Kristen decided to give an honest answer.

Nurse Bitterman gave her a knowing look. "He's a man worth following into battle."

She smiled and her face grew warm. The two women entered Nurse Bitterman's tent. A delicious odor came from a small table, holding a tray with a whole roasted chicken surrounded by tiny white potatoes, carrots, green beans, and pearl onions. Kristen's eyes grew wide at the sight of such gourmet food. Even the silverware was real silver, and China showed a tiny rosebud design around the edges. Three candles in matching China candle holders stood nearby.

"Well," Nurse Bitterman said smiling. "I helped deliver the mayor's wife's baby, and my dinner has been like this every night when I come back from the hospital."

"It must've been quite a delivery." Kristen sat in one of the chairs. Nurse Bitterman sat in the office chair.

"It was." The nurse bowed her head in prayer. Kristen did likewise. "Eat all you want." The nurse waved at the food.

The delicious meal, along with the red wine sent a warm glow throughout Kristen's tired body. She could not remember ever eating a better meal. The freshness of the food and the kindness of the nurse, contributed to the entire experience. She almost licked the plate when she finished eating. She drained her glass of wine and noticed they had emptied the entire bottle.

"That was wonderful."

Nurse Bitterman smiled. "I don't know how long the mayor's wife is going to treat me to her marvelous cooking, but I'm certainly going to enjoy it while it's here."

"Heh heh...I would too." Kristen pushed her plate away. "So tell me about the delivery of the mayor's wife's baby."

Pushing her own empty plate aside, Nurse Bitterman took

in a long breath. "All I did was give her a liquid that I told her was birthing medicine." A wicked gleam came into the nurse's eyes. "It was, of course, whiskey, milk, and a little chocolate. It made giving birth for the woman a whole lot easier. Not that it would've been that hard, mind you. That woman was born to give birth, but she was also a staunch believer in the use of no liquor, and swore to never let a drop pass her lips. Until her last child, I guess she hadn't tasted any. Which was probably why it hit her so hard when I gave her some of my birthing medicine."

Kristen slapped her thigh. "Hah! So, how long was your labor?"

Nurse Bitterman frowned. "I'd say about two hours, and I guarantee that woman hadn't had as much fun making that child as she did giving birth to it."

Kristen's eyes widened. "Weren't you a nun?"

Chuckling, the nurse shrugged her shoulders. "I've learned a lot since I left the convent and was married."

"Where's your husband?" Kristen just realized that only one narrow cot occupied the neat tent.

"I'm afraid I outlasted him." Her eyes got moist at the corners. "He was a good man," Bitterman said in a faraway voice. "Andy was a mighty good husband." The nurse got up from her chair and brushed off her uniform. "And you have a good man you need to be seeing to."

Just thinking about Jeffrey sent warmth through her body, not unlike the two glasses of wine she shared with dinner. "I guess I better be getting back."

Bitterman took Kristen's hand and nodded with a sly grin on her face. "He's a good man. You need to hold onto him."

"I will," she whispered. Whether from the wine, exhaustion, or thoughts of him, she could not say, but she felt lightheaded. She had finally met the man she had been looking for her entire life, and she would do everything possible to win back his love.

Twenty Two

Walking back through the orderly lines of pale, gray tents glowing under the moonlit sky, Kristen found herself enchanted by the songs the men sang while sitting around the campfire. Some sang Irish folk songs of heartbreak and betrayal, while others sang rowdy army songs about the girls they left behind. One fire had an intense game of cards going with one man winning. The other four accused him of cheating and called him vile names all in the spirit of good fun.

Knowing what she did about the Civil War, Kristen found it hard to believe that one out of three of these men would not survive the next four years of their lives. They would never return to their homes and farms in the warmth of the South, or see the wives and sweethearts they left behind.

A deep chill ran down her spine at the realization that Jeffrey was also one of those soldiers. Would he die in the war? Had she spent her whole life looking for the man of her dreams, only to come up empty?

Pushing aside those thoughts, she reached the tent she shared with Jeffrey. The faint glow of a candle told her that he was inside. She hugged herself against a different kind of chill washing over her body.

Kristen grabbed the tent flap and stepped inside. Again, he had the map spread across the table. He did not say anything at her entrance, but when she sat down across from him at the table he looked up.

Kristen smiled. "So how was your day?"

Lifting one arched eyebrow, he said, "Not as interesting as yours, apparently." Jeffrey took a deep breath. "Kristen, I've found you a dress." He motioned to her cot where a plain, cotton dress and petticoats lay across the bed. "You're to dress as a woman and behave accordingly, beginning right now."

"Excuse me?"

Jeffrey leaned across the table, his blue eyes like steel in the candlelight. "I heard that you interfered with Dr. Vogler's work and nearly killed a woman."

Kristen noted that a muscle twitched near his eye.

"I trusted you to do what you were told to do in the hospital. You claim to want to help, but so far all you've done is get in the way, and make the doctor in charge of this army very, very angry."

"But I— "

"You've no experience in medicine, except taking it yourself," Jeffrey said. "Now is it true that you actually cut the woman open with a knife?"

"Actually, it was a scalpel."

"It's true?" Jeffrey held his face only inches from hers.

She leaned back. "I know what I'm doing!"

"How could you?"

Kristen leapt to her feet, knocking her chair over. She stood over Jeffrey. "I've had nearly seven years of medical training, which is about five more than Dr. Vogler has. Yet you want me to stand by and watch him kill a woman and her child, just so I won't cause any problems for you?" Even as she said it, Kristen knew she was now in for far more trouble than she had been in before.

Jeffrey pushed back his chair. He stared at her as if she lost her mind. Then he began to laugh. He laughed until tears ran down his cheeks. Finally, he caught his breath. "And when did you go to medical school, Kristen? I've known you since we were both children. When did you sneak in seven years of medical training?"

"When I…" She could not think of anything to say, so she said the first thing that popped into her head. "I read books for seven years, and I watch the surgery channel."

His eyes went wide in disbelief. For once he looked as if he did not know what to say. He finally found his voice. "You never went near the slave quarters!"

"You don't know everything about me." Kristen took a breath. "In fact, I'd bet you know absolutely nothing about me. Nothing at all!"

"This is getting ridiculous." He shook his head. "I know far more about you and the way you think than you do yourself." He ran both hands through his thick hair, making it stand up from his head. His blue eyes appeared cold and unyielding. "I forbid you to go back to the hospital tents. You're to leave Dr. Vogler alone. You're not to step foot within one hundred yards of anyone having anything to do with medicine!"

"You can't order me around!"

"I'm your husband!" Jeffrey slapped his chest. "That gives me a God-given right to tell you what to do, and you will obey!"

She had read about men's attitudes toward women in the nineteenth century, but this experience with them brought what she had read to life. Kristen did not remember ever being so mad at anyone in her life. *How can he even think I'll blindly obey him?*

"I'll do what I feel is best," she said in a low voice.

"You don't know what's best."

Her whole body trembled. *I've never known a more stubborn man?* That counted all the doctors and surgeons she'd met in the last seven years of medical school and her residency. Yet Jeffrey O'Connor could hold his own with any of the most arrogant men she had ever worked with, thus far.

"I will do as I wish," Kristen said, her face only inches away from Jeffrey's.

Peering down his nose at her, he glared back. "Kristen, for as long as I've known you, you've done exactly as you pleased. Where has that gotten you? Every decision you've ever made has been wrong, and every idea you come up with has been a mistake." He paused as if trying to catch his breath and hold his temper. "Very shortly, war is going to take place. You have no idea what war is like, and I'm very sure that you're not going to like this one. You'll be running for home when you finally see men kill each other, to die alone in muddy fields, whimpering for their mothers. I fought in the Mexican war. I know what I'm talking about.

"So, until you go running for home with your pretty tail between your legs, keep out of the way of real men and women trying to do their jobs as best they can. They don't need you interfering with their work!"

To Kristen's horror, her throat started to constrict. Her eyes welled up. Before she could stop herself, she sobbed. Embarrassed, she flung herself down onto her cot and knocked the dress onto the ground. She had never been filled with so many conflicting emotions. *I can't tell him I'm qualified to practice medicine.* She could not tell him either that her motives were not selfish. She certainly could not tell him that she was not the same wife he had married.

Faced with an endless list of things she could not say, she put the thin pillow over her eyes. After an exhausting day of surgery, she just wanted to sleep.

*J*effrey looked down at Kristen's sobbing form on the tiny cot. *What in the world did I say that upset her so much?* He knew she had no interest in medicine. At least now she had an excuse to leave the hospital, and she would not have to see any more blood. While she thought she wanted to work in a hospital, he knew she would faint at the sight of blood. For a woman who fainted at the sight of blood her entire life, how could she think she could work in an army hospital where she would see more blood than she could imagine? He could not comprehend her way of thinking. Of course, she must obey her husband. All wives knew that—love, honor, and obey. She said those very words to him just three, short years ago.

Kristen had never once stood up to him, and now she shouted back at him as if his equal. With every fight in the past, she had nodded in agreement at everything he said and then went off to do whatever she pleased. *Who is this new person she's become?* She stood her ground, unafraid of incurring his wrath.

Not knowing what else to do, Jeffrey took his weeping wife into his arms and held her as he would a child. At first, she fought him but finally settled into his arms, sobbing into his shirt until it was soaked.

When Kristen's sobs abated, he noticed how good she felt. He held his arms around her slender waist, one hand stroking her back until she drew back from him. Her deep-green eyes, soft with tears, begged for his understanding. What she wanted he did not know, but he vowed to listen. Silently, Jeffrey pleaded with his eyes for her to understand. Yes, he loved her, but he could not let her get close to him again. He feared the pain she would cause him. He didn't believe they could salvage their relationship and he felt she knew that too.

"I'm sorry," Jeffrey found himself saying.

"There are so many things I can't tell you — "

"Shhh..."

"But I need to tell you."

"I don't need to hear them."

She sighed. "You wouldn't believe me anyway."

Jeffrey lost himself in Kristen's deep-green eyes. Memories of the afternoon they shared came crashing back on him. Aware of just how soft she felt in his arms. Desire swept through him, making him weak.

Kristen must have sensed it. A slight smile crossed her mouth. Tentatively, she raised her lips toward his. He steeled himself against the fire that threatened to rage through his body.

Kristen pressed herself against his chest, moving even closer. His mouth crashed into the soft lips she offered. He lost control and his emotions ignited. Their tongues touched. In a frenzy he tore at her clothes. Closer, he wanted to get closer. He needed to feel her soft skin against his own. She alone held the power to put out the fire raging in his mind, body, and soul.

Never had he felt such an urgent need to have his wife. He had lusted after her before their marriage. Afterward, he found enjoyment in her soft, feminine body, even as she extracted a piece of his soul every time she gave in to him. However, this was different. Just like the time he had taken his wife on that afternoon, he prepared for her scorn. He received a soft look instead. The walls around his heart began to crumble while something precious took its place. A surge of energy swept over him that seemed like hope, something

Jeffrey hadn't felt for a very long time. He decided to act on it before he had time to doubt it.

Kristen lost every button on the cotton shirt she had worn for the past few days. Next, she lost the button holding the soft corduroy trousers. Her undergarments came next, Jeffrey's hands exploring every inch of the body he should have known well. However, it seemed completely different to him now.

Fitting them both on the single cot would be tricky. Jeffrey carefully laid Kristen down, stood over her and admired her, his body blazed with inner heat. His knees went weak when she lifted her arms up to him. Grabbing at his own clothes with even less care than he had hers, Jeffrey soon stood naked in the nearly dark tent. He stroked her legs while his hand shook.

"I wish you'd hurry," Kristen whispered in a strangled voice.

That was all it took. Jeffrey could hold back no longer. Shocked by Kristen's words, he had to follow through. With one hand on either side of her, he lowered his body onto hers. Every inch of his sensitized skin felt her creamy soft skin ignite with a heat equal to his own. Her arms reached up and encircled his neck, pulling his mouth down. A tongue parted his lips before they had a chance to part on their own. Her hips moved upward, pressing tightly into him. A moan escaped his lips.

He had known her for most of his life. She married him at nineteen years of age. However, he would swear on a Bible, that the woman lying underneath him, urging him on, could not be that woman. Not until the heat came to an end for both of them did he hear a voice call out.

"Excuse me?" Sergeant Randall stood in the tent doorway — his eyes wide in disbelief.

Jeffrey shot a hand out on the floor to balance the cot, but it toppled over anyway. Kristen landed in a naked heap on top of him, giggling.

He threw the blanket over her naked body, then he pushed the cot upright and turned to Sergeant Randall. "Don't you knock?"

"I did, sir. I heard her screaming and thought you needed assistance." He looked straight ahead. "I wasn't aware that you're entertaining a young lady." As the young sergeant mumbled a few more words, his face grew a rich shade of scarlet.

"Would you mind leaving us?" Jeffrey placed a hand on a naked hip.

"Certainly, sir." Sergeant Randall turned, lifted the tent flap, and was gone.

Jeffrey shook his head. He looked down at Kristen. She broke out in a fit of laughter.

"Can I assume that our discussion is over?"

Is he serious? Kristen stared in disbelief. Jeffrey called that a discussion? Coyly, she sat up, letting the blankets slip off from her chest to settle around her hips. "I think it is."

Jeffrey frowned. "Then you'll obey me and stay away from the hospital tent?"

Kristen said nothing. She knew he took her silence as acquiescence to his demands. He would soon learn not to assume anything with her, *ever*.

"Good," he said bending down to pick up his pants. "I'm trying to look after your best interests." He pulled on his pants and started looking for a shirt. "I have to see what Sergeant Randall wanted. I'll be back soon." He buttoned his shirt, then put on his socks and his boots.

Too bad you don't have a mirror. Kristen gave him a sweet smile, her eyes fixed on the large red mark on his neck. There could be no question what everyone would think about the mark, and he did not know it was there. She had no desire to bring it to his attention. Not after the way he demanded that she obey him.

Just before Jeffrey left, he turned. He looked as though he wanted to kiss her. "Goodbye." He left the tent.

Kristen threw her pillow at the tent flap. It bounced against the canvas then sailed through the open-air. Male voices grumbled outside the tent. The pillow came back through the same opening and landed on the floor. She could not help but laugh out loud, hoping Jeffrey would hear her. The man definitely needed to loosen up.

Kristen did not know when she had felt more satisfied. She hugged herself as she re-lived the event she had just shared with her husband.

Now, if she could only take a long hot bath, life would be just about perfect. She lay back down on the cot and fell asleep, dreaming of Jeffrey and content that he would fall in love with her again.

Twenty Three

Kristen **did not** have a chance to talk to her husband. General Beauregard's plan to stop the Union moved the troops northward to Maryland. Never had there been so many soldiers in one place. All the tents lined up in orderly rows had looked rather impressive, but to see everything packed up and moving seemed like total chaos. She tried her best to stay out of everyone's way.

The tent she now shared with Amy, a girl who helped out at the hospital, had been torn down by Sergeant Randall and loaded onto a wagon. The grassy field where they camped now nothing more than a mud pile as hundreds of horses pulling wagons and cannons churned it apart.

Amy told the story of her life as they walked along, following the wagons. Nearby soldiers started singing songs. Everyone seemed to know the words, singing along as they marched. Tears welled up in Kristen's eyes at the joy and hope on the men's young faces. While Amy talked, Kristen thought about the chaos to come and how so many young-soldiers' dreams would be crushed.

"I met Hank at the local school," Amy said. "He was the oldest boy in the class. He was twelve and I was ten. I didn't like him too well at first because he was always making fun of me."

Kristen smiled. To her new friend, the war had become a wonderful adventure. Too soon, Amy would discover the hardships and sorrow war caused.

"He said my freckles look like dirt." Amy grinned. "I told my mama and she said, that if a boy makes fun of you that's just his way of saying he likes you."

"Wise mother." Kristen nodded.

"So…the next day I told Hank that making fun of me was because he liked me. You should've seen how red his face got!"

Kristen threw back her head and laughed. Several of the soldiers nearby turned and stared. One of them winked at her.

Amy continued her story. "After that, Hank didn't dare say a mean word to me because he didn't want the other boys in the class to think he liked me."

"But he did like you, right?"

"Of course." Amy grinned. "He started courting me the day I turned fourteen."

It seemed a bit young to Kristen, but the short life expectancy in this century forced people to mature and marry younger. "And now you're married."

"For two years now," Amy said, a proud smile on her face.

"Two years?" Kristen could not believe it. "But you're so young."

"I'm eighteen." Amy looked down at her flat stomach. "It does seem an awfully long time to not have a baby yet."

Kristen could not even imagine. A blood curdling shout interrupted her thoughts, followed by a hoarse scream of pain from somewhere ahead. A crowd of men running after an unmanned horse cart came straight at her. She grabbed Amy by the arm to pull her out of the way. Amy's hesitation allowed the unmanned cart to hit her with a glancing blow, which sent both women onto the muddied ground.

Amy screamed in pain and held her right leg.

Kristen crawled to the crying girl, but had to wipe the mud from her own eyes first before she could pull Amy's hands away from her wounded leg. Soldiers surrounded them, peering down.

"Please move back!" Kristen waved her free hand. "I can't take care of her if you don't give me some room."

Her words fell on deaf ears. The men moved closer to see the commotion. One of them reached down and picked Amy up.

"Stop that!" Kristen pulled at his hands, but he lifted her up anyways.

"She's my wife."

Kristen looked into the warm, brown eyes of the soldier who appeared to be no more than sixteen. He wore a mustache which looked more like peach fuzz. He gazed down at his stricken wife in shock, and appeared about to cry.

"Hank?"

"Yes, ma'am."

Taking a deep breath, Kristen reasoned with the young husband. "You need to put Amy down for a minute so I can examine her."

"But I need to get her to a doctor," he said, his voice high, threatening to break. Amy moaned in his arms.

"Hank," Kristen said, her voice calm. "I can help her. Now set her down so I can see how badly her leg is injured. If a vein is severed, then Amy will need a tourniquet. If you go dragging her off, she might bleed to death."

He almost dropped his wife setting her down.

"Thank you." Kristen set to work.

Blood oozed from the wound. Pushing aside the long skirt, Kristen pulled up Amy's pantaloons. The blood seemed to originate in the shin. The wheels of the canon must have run over her lower leg. For once, she did not curse the mud. It had probably saved the young-girl's leg from being completely severed.

Feeling gingerly over the skin, she detected the break. Out of habit, Kristen talked as she worked. "Clean break to the tibia. Could be damage to the fibula, I can't tell yet. She's going to need her leg immobilized."

Kristen looked up to see Hank staring at her. He clearly did not understand what she said. She patted the man's arm. "Let's try to find a place where we can take her. I don't think the bleeding is too serious. I can bind her leg right here." Everywhere she looked, she saw mud and dirty uniforms from the soldiers walking past.

She set to work making a bandage from a piece of her dress lining. She hated to tear the dress, but the most sterile material available just happened to be under her dress. "I see a farmhouse ahead," Hank said.

"Good. Pick her up and let's get her inside."

Hank lifted his wife again. Mud covered Amy, except for her leg and its snowy white bandage.

Turning away from the mass of men and wagons, Kristen led the way toward a modest farmhouse. A white picket fence surrounded the two-story house. A dog barked from the wide front porch, while a child swung from a rope swing tied to a giant oak in the middle of the front yard.

When Kristen arrived at the front gate, the child jumped from the swing and ran to the front door. Seconds later, a woman appeared on the porch, her hands on her hips. "What can I do for you folks?"

Kristen smiled and waited for Hank to catch up to her while she held the gate open. "This girl has been run over by one of the wagons and needs medical attention. I wondered if we might use your home for a short time."

The woman's eyes fell on the young girl, the bandaged leg, the blood, and she frowned. "Bring her into the house."

The woman pointed to a sofa and motioned for Hank to put Amy down. She left the room and came back with bandages and hot water which she lay on the floor beside the stricken young woman.

Kristen got to work. Despite her concentration, she noted that Hank gritted his teeth and winced every time Amy groaned in pain. Once she had done all she could, Kristen wiped her sweating brow and patted Hank on the shoulder.

He took his wife's hand and stroked her cheek as she slept, unconscious from the pain.

Kristen walked outside to wash her hands at the pump. She pumped with twice the effort necessary to get the water flowing, which put her out of breath. Watching Hank with his wife made her long for her own husband. Her heartache awakened new thoughts of Jeffrey, so real she could smell him. When she heard his voice behind her, she almost screamed in surprise.

"What're you doing here?" She glared at him.

Jeffrey chuckled. "I thought I was marching my men into battle, but I think they're all going the wrong way."

Still angry about her friend's injury, she missed the humor of the situation. Instead, she wanted to throw herself into his arms.

His eyes ran over Amy's still form. "What happened?"

Hank jumped to attention upon seeing his commander. "She got run over by one of the cannons, sir."

"Her leg?" Jeffrey nodded toward her wrapped wound.

"Yes, sir."

"I heard a woman had been run down," Jeffrey said looking at Kristen.

"And you thought it was me?" Kristen said.

Jeffrey shook his head. "I'd be more afraid for the cannon." He turned back to Hank. "Let's get her to a doctor." He extended his arms forward. "Give me the girl while you get on my horse."

Hank, quick to obey, picked up his wife and handed her to Jeffrey. They went back outside into the yard. Hank leaped onto the big horse that stood by patiently. Amy groaned in Jeffrey's arms. He handed Amy up to her husband.

"Now get going, son." Jeffrey slapped the horse on the rear.

"But I can take care of her," Kristen said through gritted teeth.

"Kristen," Jeffrey said, "you're not a doctor. I know you want to help, but you're getting in the way."

Kristen opened her mouth to protest, but realized he would not believe anything she could say.

"Let's get back now." Jeffrey offered her his arm.

"Not so fast, mister!" She held up a hand, still angry at him for moving out of their tent. "I believe you owe me an explanation!"

"Really?"

"Yes. I thought last night meant something to you. When I woke up, you had moved out," Kristen whispered. She had to run to keep up with his long strides.

"Mrs. Campbell needed a place to sleep."

"And our tent was the only place you could find?"

He walked along in silence for a long time. "Kristen, last night was a mistake, and I'm sorry. It's difficult for a man to go without a woman." He paused, avoiding her eyes. "Whatever your sleeping arrangements, that won't happen again."

Grabbing his arm, she turned him around to face her. "But we're married, aren't we?"

Taking a deep breath, he looked just past her. "Kristen, you don't want me, you've made that abundantly clear. From now on, I'll respect your wishes."

"But—"

"When this war is over, we'll go our separate ways. Until then,

I'll stand by and protect you as best I can."

Stand by? I know he still loves me, but why does he put up a wall?

"I wish you'd consider going home," Jeffrey said in a defeated voice.

"No," Kristen said though she wondered if staying would have any effect on Jeffrey's heart. As things were now, she could not even practice medicine, but it didn't matter. "I'm going to stay and help wherever I can."

Jeffrey nodded, turned, and walked toward the sea of soldiers moving northward. He did not look back.

Kristen wanted to scream.

Twenty Four

*A*fter days of marching, Kristen wanted to settle in one place and rest her feet. They stopped and set the tents up in a Maryland field where they could draw water from a nearby creek.

Hank brought Amy back to the tent the two women shared with her leg tightly bound between two sticks and tightly wrapped with bandages. Hank found a long tree branch that forked at the top for Amy to use as a crooked crutch. Kristen asked him to find an old shirt which she wrapped in the curve of the branch for padding. The new crutch was a great success.

"I'll carry the buckets," Kristen said when Amy tried to pick up one of the buckets to fill from the small creek nearby.

Amy sighed. "I hate feeling helpless."

"You've done more than you should already, even without a broken leg." Kristen held her back. "Besides you're going to need your rest from now on."

Amy gave her a puzzled look.

"You're pregnant," Kristen said.

Amy nearly fell off her crutch. "I'm what?"

Laughing, Kristen took Amy's arm. "I said, you're pregnant. About three months, I'd say."

"But I haven't seen Hank in weeks." Amy stopped and gave a shy smile. "At least not in that way." She looked at Kristen. "How do you know for sure?"

145

"Amy, we've been friends for a week now, and we've been living together." She put her hand on Amy's nearly flat stomach. "You've been sick every morning, and you've grown about two sizes already." Kristen eyed the young girl's chest. "I guess all that sleeping out in the fresh air did it for you and Hank."

Tears formed in Amy's eyes. "I guess I wasn't paying much attention, with my leg and all."

Kristen hugged her friend. "I'm very happy for you."

"I can't wait to tell Hank." She grinned from ear-to-ear.

"I'm sure he'll be overjoyed." Even as she said it, Kristen remembered the war, the fatalities, and the losing side. Putting her thoughts aside, she let go of Amy and bent down to pick up the water buckets. Before she could lift them, a pair of strong hands took them from her. She looked up into blue-gray eyes.

For a second she found herself unable to move. Having only seen her husband for a few brief moments recently, his nearness overwhelmed her. Warmth flushed her cheeks and then moved downward, making her skin tingle. Jeffrey's open shirt because of the heat mesmerized Kristen. Her eyes followed the trail of buttons down his shirt until they stopped at the brass belt buckle. Embarrassed that Jeffery had seen her staring at him, she forced herself to look away.

"What're you doing here?" She hoped her voice sounded steady.

"I just wanted to see if you're all right," Jeffrey said in a soft voice.

Of course, I'm not. Kristen wanted to scream at him, but she bit her lip instead. She had her pride to consider, just as he did. "I'm fine."

"Amy's doing even better, I see," Jeffrey said walking away from the creek with the buckets. Despite the crutch, Amy nearly ran to find her husband.

"She's anxious to tell her husband the good news."

"Good news?"

"She's going to have a baby," Kristen said.

Jeffrey did not answer. She noticed a pained expression flit cross his face before he turned a calm face toward her. "I'm sure her husband is going to be very happy."

146

She shrugged. "As happy as he can be, considering the cir-cumstances."

His anger flared and he bit his lip. "The war will soon be over, and they can both go home and raise their child in peace."

Kristen took a moment to consider her husband's anger. He never had the chance to be happy for very long about his wife's pregnancy. The other Kristen had taken the joy away from him. *It was not my fault. But Jeffrey doesn't know that?* She wanted to kick herself.

Unconsciously, her hand slid over her own flat stomach. At least living in this time had been good for her waistline. Nothing fattening had been cooked recently. Of course, her favorite ice cream, Cherries Garcia, could not be found here.

"You're not worried, are you?" Jeffrey said.

"I hope not!" Kristen said without thinking. When she looked at his face, she regretted her words. *I said exactly the wrong thing.*

Now he thinks I don't want a child just because it would be his. How could I have said such a thoughtless thing? He doesn't know that I'm not really his wife, at least not in the way that he thinks. How can I give birth, not knowing when I'll be back in my own time?

"I mean I wouldn't want to have children until we finished with this war," she said. One look at Jeffrey's hardened eyes told Kristen she had not convinced him at all.

"I'll leave you here," Jeffrey said, his voice cold. He set the two buckets of water outside her tent.

Kristen watched her husband walk away, his back stiff and straight. "All I do is make things worse between us," she said un-der her breath. She carried the water inside, then cleaned the tent from top to bottom to ease her frustration.

147

Twenty Five

A my came back to the tent just as Kristen finished putting the pillows back on the cots.

"Hank's so excited!" Amy fell onto one of the made up cots and rubbed her stomach in wonder.

"I'm so happy for you," Kristen said smiling at her new friend. "He's going to make a wonderful father."

Amy looked troubled for a moment. "Hank's so light, you know, his blonde hair and all. Do you think the baby will look like his dad? I want our baby to be the spitting image of his dad."

The **Confederate** army camped outside Washington and waited on the Yankees' next move. Kristen left the ladies after dinner to go watch Jeffrey drill the sharpshooters, practicing in a nearby field. Approval shot through her, watching how her husband molded a ragtag group of farmers into skilled soldiers. He patiently showed them how to load the rifles, how to sit in trees, and how to use the branches for leverage while the men shot the cans on the ground.

The soldiers loved Jeffrey. They followed his commands, working hard to earn their commander's respect. One of the better shooters began challenging the other men, and soon money changed hands throughout the camp. One young private from South Carolina hit every tin can, no matter what the distance. Someone called for Jeffrey.

"Come on, Captain," one man shouted. "Show the young upstart how a real man shoots a gun."

Laughter followed, and more money exchanged hands. They passed a flask around — each taking a long drink from it.

"Tomorrow morning," Jeffrey said joining in the laughter. "I need my sleep."

A bearded man slipped in next to him. "The Captain needs a night with his pretty wife." He winked. "He wants to practice using his other gun."

Kristen blushed when she realized she had been observed. She stood beside a large oak tree where she thought no one would see her, but Jeffrey's face registered surprise and moved toward her. The laughter of the men increased.

"How long have you been there?"

"Not too long." The time had flown by. It had grown dark which meant she'd been watching for hours.

"This is probably not something a lady should be exposed to." Jeffrey stood there grinning.

"I found it fascinating," Kristen said. Jeffrey's nearness led her mind to places that made her blush. The day still hot and humid, made her wish she had worn pants and a shirt instead of a long heavy dress with miles of underclothes.

"Did you?" Jeffrey stepped closer and put his hand on the trunk of the tree over Kristen's shoulder.

He wore no jacket and his shirt had become unbuttoned nearly to his waist. His skin glowed with exertion and his face had a smudge of black powder. Kristen smelled the whiskey on his breath. His eyes appeared heavy with fatigue and the effects of the alcohol.

The men had gone back to their tents and their dinners, leaving them alone. The moon slid above the treetops, bringing silver light to the still night, like a casted spell. Not wanting to say anything to break that spell, Kristen waited. Blue eyes held hers, sending sparks throughout her body. Silent, Jeffery seemed content to gaze upon her with longing.

Unable to stand it any longer, Kristen lifted her face toward Jeffrey. When he did not move, she kissed him with all the pent up passion she'd felt for the last week. This might be her last chance to connect with the man she loved.

Jeffrey broke off the kiss and moved away shaking his head. A cold look came over his face. "Are you here to flirt with me? Or is this a new game of torture you've devised to pay me back for marrying you?"

"What?"

"Kristen, it's been a long time since you took a man to bed. Are you here looking for one of my men, so you can make a fool of me?"

"That's disgusting!" Kristen whispered, hoping no one could hear them.

"Is it?" Jeffrey held a cold smile on his face. "Remember the time you just had to accompany me to Savannah to look at Diablo before I bought him, and I found you in the stable with the man who sold me that damn horse."

Her jaw dropped. "You did?"

Jeffrey's eyes narrowed. "Don't tell me you don't remember?"

She did not remember because she was not there. She had to think fast. "I've changed since then." Her chin went up. She looked her husband straight in the eye. "I'm not the same girl that you married. Can't you tell?"

Jeffrey threw back his head and laughed. The sound grated on her nerves. More than anything she wanted to slap him across his smug face. She did not ask to come back in time, nor had she expected to inhabit the body of a woman with the morals of an alley cat. None of this was her fault, and now Jeffery laughed at her.

"I don't really care if you believe me or not!" Kristen said through clenched teeth. She turned and started back toward the camp. Fingers of steel grabbed her arm and spun her around to face her husband.

"Kristen, I can handle our relationship if it doesn't include you pretending you feel something for me." He gave a heavy sigh.

Kristen had an overwhelming desire to stroke his clenched jaw, to take away some of the pain she caused him.

"Just stay away from me, and my men." He stared at her for a second before letting go of her arm. "Please."

She wanted to cry.

How can I stay away from the man I love? The man who strips away all of my defenses and leaves me trembling in his wake? How am I supposed to resist those eyes and the passion we shared? I can't just walk away from the man who taught me what passion is, and or more importantly, what love is all about.

Kristen was willing to die for Jeffrey at a moment's notice. She could not see how she could keep from being drawn to him like a plant growing toward the light of the sun. He was her sun, her reason for waking up each morning. Her legs grew weak at the emotions he stirred, flowing through her body like warm ocean waves. She leaned against the wide trunk of the oak for support.

"I wish you'd go home," Jeffrey whispered, his face almost hidden in the shadows of the tree branches.

"I can't," she whispered.

Nodding, he turned and walked away.

She stayed against the oak, as if to draw strength from its massive trunk, a tear rolling down her cheek. She wanted to do as her husband asked, which meant leaving him alone.

Jeffrey's pain washed over her as if it were her own. With a heavy heart, she vowed to stay away from the man she loved to the core of her being. It didn't matter that she had not been the one to inflict the original pain. She was the cause of his current anguish.

I'll stay as far away from you as my heart will allow, and I'm going to ask for forgiveness if I have a moment of weakness.

Twenty Six

It took days for Jeffrey's mind to clear itself of the images of his wife. He drilled his men until their arms shook trying to hold their muskets and rifles steady. A few of his men protested, but none would dare do it in his presence.

Too preoccupied by thoughts of his wife, he lost a shooting contest for the first time in his life. Much money had changed hands that day, but he did not notice. He thought only of how different Kristen seemed, beginning with the day she fainted in the parlor.

That fainting spell took place nearly a month ago, and Jeffrey could not shake the feeling that somehow his wife really *was* different. What could have happened to her? Surely, a bump on the head could not turn a person's actions completely around, yet that was exactly what happened. Kristen had not been the same since that day in the parlor, and that concerned him. For too long his wife had played with his emotions, honing her skills over the years of their marriage, until she could hurt him with just a glance.

Jeffrey puzzled over the change in Kristen. It bothered him that he never knew what to expect any more.

What is she setting me up for now? This war is enough to deal with.

Shaking off those thoughts, Jeffrey focused again on his men. He had to concede they'd worked hard — beyond exhausted. Although he had been preparing his men for the upcoming battle, they might be too tired to fight it.

"Okay, that's enough for the evening. Stand down." Without

153

thinking, he glanced in the direction of the large oak where only last night she had watched him. Jeffrey recalled the kiss she had given, his knees grew weak again. Whatever change had come over his wife had increased her power over him. If she betrayed him again, he hoped a Yankee bullet would make sure he would not have to endure it for too long.

The young private who had just beaten Jeffrey in the shooting contest came up to stand beside him. "Maybe you would shoot better with your wife watching," he said grinning.

Jeffrey grimaced.

"This is the first time I haven't seen her watching our practice." The young boy chuckled.

"Really." Jeffrey wondered if that were true. Had his wife watched them more often than he even noticed?

"She seems to be your lucky charm." The private hurried off to join his fellow soldiers.

Left alone to consider what the young man said, he realized that he had not been aware of her presence. Why did she watch? The only rational reason—Kristen must have her eye on one of his men. Never before had she cared what he did, unless it interfered with something she herself wanted to do.

Sergeant Randall approached just as he reached the tent he now shared with another captain.

"Captain O'Connor, sir."

"Sergeant Randall?"

"General Beauregard wants to see all of his officers, sir."

Jeffrey took a deep breath. He nodded to his sergeant. "Tell them I'll be right there."

With a salute, Sergeant Randall turned on his heel and walked toward the main officer's tent.

Jeffrey could not help but admire the young man. Never had he seen a young lad more suited to his work. A poor farmer's son, Randall had been one of the first to enlist. His willingness to work hard and his shooting skills assured his success. Possibly, this war would bless a man like Randall, who without it would not do any better than his work-worn father with his forty acres of fertile land.

In General Beauregard's tent the men sat for dinner. Maryland's choice to remain sympathetic to the Southern cause of state's rights, as opposed to the federal government in Washington, DC, had helped in many ways determine what the rest of the nation would do. Good men had joined the Southern side—officers of character and honor. General Beauregard, being one of those men, became the officer that gave the order to fire on Fort Sumner.

General Lee, also at the meeting, had been the soldier with the best reputation in the country due to his heroism and planning during the Mexican war. Lee had also been in charge of capturing John Brown at Harper's ferry, setting the stage for the beginning of this current conflict. Lincoln had asked him to lead the Union Army, which left him torn, since his home state of Virginia seceded from the Union General Lee had always served. He decided to remain loyal to his home state.

Jeffery took his place at the long table where nearly thirty other officers sat and listened.

"We need to know what the Yankees are thinking," Beauregard said.

"How to get out of this." This boast from the group caused an eruption of laughter.

"That may be," Beauregard said. "They'll have to fight to save the Capitol. If we can take Washington, we can end this thing right here and now. Then we can all go back to our homes and loved ones, and live out our lives knowing we have the right to govern ourselves through our state officials."

General agreement ensued.

Asking for quiet, Beauregard spoke again. "Some of our ladies have volunteered to do some spying for us—several in fact. But the one we'll use is Mrs. O'Conner, Captain O'Connor's wife."

"What?" Jeffrey said unable to believe what he just heard.

General Beauregard stroked his goatee. His steely gaze fell on Jeffrey. "I take it you don't know about your wife's current status as a spy for the Army."

"No, sir, I didn't know," Jeffrey said, his voice tight. He could not imagine what Kristen might be thinking to volunteer for such dangerous work.

"Well, I'm very proud of your wife's bravery." Beauregard nodded, turned away, and started a discussion about obtaining more arms and ammunition. The talk soon turned to railroads and harbors that the Yankees had blockaded.

Jeffrey's mind focused only on his wife's stupidity. Kristen had found a surefire way to get herself killed. What could he do to prevent it?

After the meeting, Jeffrey marched straight into the tent his wife shared with Amy. Kristen had finally gone too far. He had no idea what had gotten into her, but he had to change her mind before she ended up in a Yankee prison. Any man with sense preferred death to prison. He could not even imagine what prison would be like for a woman. Dying would be the least of his wife's problems if she got caught spying.

Twenty Seven

Kristen thought about how it might be to run messages for the Army. Never had she done anything so daring, at least not since she had traveled to an earlier century. She had no idea if she would, or even could change history, but she had to stay away from Jeffrey — for his sake. Besides, any time now she would wake up on Diana's couch in that local television studio and be back in her own time. So why not live a little while she had the chance? At least she could walk away from this war knowing what to look for in a man. Her husband had shown her *that* much.

"You need to hold still," Amy said. She sat at Kristen's feet sewing a coded message into the hem of her skirt.

"I can't help it." Kristen tried not to squirm. "This is the most exciting thing I've ever done." She wanted to add something about going to medical school, but doing so would have been inappropriate. This opportunity would help her keep her promise to stay away from Jeffrey. When the ladies asked for a volunteer to spy against the Yankees, she shot her hand up. If captured, she doubted they tortured women prisoners. Southern men revered women, so she assumed that Northern men felt the same way. The worst that could happen would be for her to be locked up for a while. Maybe even for five years, but at least she wouldn't be executed.

Kristen's different accent had made her the best choice. She could pass as a Northerner quite easily because of it. Having grown up in the North as a child before her parents moved south to take over her grandfather's plantation meant Kristen was comfortable in both worlds.

"Now, are you sure you know who your contact is?" Amy smoothed out the hem of the skirt she had stitched back into place.

"Mrs. Rosie O'Neill Green."

Amy stood up, one hand going to her stomach, the other going to her back. The front of Amy's slim form showed no swelling, and the young girl glowed with happiness. "Kristen, you're so brave to be doing this."

"Not really." Kristen had no stake in this life. Jeffrey did not want her help, so she might as well do something to keep herself occupied until she woke up in her own time.

"Oh, yes you are," Amy said grinning. "You're also one of the craziest women I know. I can't believe you'd cut off all your beautiful hair to follow your husband into battle."

"It was pretty silly, now that I think about it," Kristen said feeling the back of her neck. Her hair had started to grow back already. The hat she had been given would make her look like her hair had been pinned up like any of the other Southern woman in town.

"No." Amy shook her head. "It was brave, and it shows how much you love your man."

Kristen tried to smile but her face felt as if it were frozen. Loving Jeffrey did not matter. He did not want her love, because the woman who had been his wife had killed all of his feelings toward her. Unfortunately, she could not tell him that he had a different wife now. She would never hurt him. How could she know what would happen when she woke up in her own time? Would that leave Jeffrey vulnerable to the woman who had hurt him?

She decided to keep her distance so he could concentrate on his men and this war. She did not want to be responsible for getting him hurt or killed.

"Nurse Bitterman is going to let you use her carriage."

Kristen nodded and smoothed out the lovely, yellow, silk gown she wore. The dress had lace at the neck, just enough to be modest yet let men wonder if they might be able to see the swell of her breasts. She looked enough like a rich Northern belle to pass in the wealthy company in which her contact moved.

"I guess I'm ready."

Amy nodded, her face serious. "You'll be careful?"

"How hard can it be to go to parties and listen to Northern officers who might have too much wine in them to have any good sense?"

"If you get caught—"

"I know," Kristen said adjusting her hat in the tiny mirror Amy held up for her. "I'll go to one of those horrible Yankee prisons."

Amy shook her head. "I don't think you're taking any of this seriously enough."

"Yes, I certainly *am*." She blew out a long breath. "It's just that I don't believe I'll get caught. How can I? No one suspects women of spying, and I've certainly never heard of anything happening to any woman spies during the Civil War."

Amy stared at her. "The Civil War?"

"Oh, I mean the upcoming battle of Northern aggression." Kristen really had to watch what she said.

The carriage waited outside the cabin. Sergeant Randall escorted her and helped Kristen into the elaborate coach. She felt a new respect for him as he let go of her hand.

"I hope you'll be careful, ma'am."

"I will, I promise. And now I'd like to ask for a favor."

The sergeant's eyebrows shot up. "Anything, ma'am, just ask."

"I don't want my husband to know what I'm doing."

The man frowned, his brown eyes crinkling. He looked like a schoolboy to her. She wondered how old he was.

"He should know, ma'am."

Kristen let it slide. "I don't want to worry him. I'll tell Jeffrey everything when I get back." She smiled at the handsome soldier. He did not look old enough to be soldiering. Not a single line on his face, just a dusting of freckles that made him appear even younger than she thought he might be.

"Sergeant Randall, if we don't find out where the Yankees are and what they're planning, we won't be prepared. It's important that I go. If my husband had been told, he surely would've tried to stop me. I couldn't let that happen." Kristen took a deep breath. "Jeffrey will learn everything when I get back. Until then, it would be best if he knew nothing."

The sergeant nodded and closed the carriage door.

Mrs. **Rosie** O'Neill Green's mansion seemed gracious to the extreme. Rich wood-paneled walls lined every room, while twelve-foot ceilings, painted with clouds, birds, and ivy, made the rooms appear to be outdoors instead of inside. The elegant home was filled with furniture that looked too delicate to hold adults. Kristen sat on the edge of a spindly-legged velvet chair, drinking tea with the lady of the house.

"I hope your trip to our fair city was pleasant."

Kristen smiled at Mrs. Green. If Southern women were known for their charm, this woman must be Southern to the bone, her pale blonde hair tucked neatly around her long, oval face. The blue eyes appeared to be as innocent as a newborn child. She wondered if she had the right house. "Very pleasant."

Mrs. Green smiled sweetly and then turned to her black servant. "You may leave us now."

The French doors in the parlor closed and Mrs. Green dropped her vacant look and turned to Kristen. "You can be assured we're alone and that no one can hear us."

Shocked at the instant change that came over her hostess, she could only nod.

"I've arranged for you to attend the ball tonight in honor of our brave, Union soldiers."

Kristen blinked in surprise.

"My dear, you don't look too well. Are you all right?"

Kristen gave her hostess a hard look. "Don't they know you have Southern sympathies?"

"What do I care about any of this boring war nonsense?" Mrs. Green smiled and blinked, her pale-blue eyes going vacant. She gave a most convincing act.

"You missed your call to the stage." Kristen felt an immediate bond with the older woman.

"You'll learn as well," Mrs. Green said. "With your beautiful face, all you have to do is smile and bat your eyes at whomever you're dancing with, and listen to every little thing they say."

"Hah!" Kristen grinned. "I'll do my best."

Mrs. Green turned serious. "This is dangerous business, you *do* understand that?"

"Perfectly." Acid roiled in Kristen's stomach.

She spent the rest of the day with her hostess, getting fitted for her ball gown. Two seamstresses worked until only minutes before the ball, sewing her into a flowing outfit of icy-green silk — just a shade darker than her eyes. Another slave did things with her hair she would not have thought possible. First, they pulled her short hair back and used elaborate pins to hold the pearls and diamonds. Then her attendants placed a hairpiece of real hair, the exact shade of her own auburn tresses on top.

Then, Mrs. Green's personal maid helped Kristen into her corset and petticoats of white silk. Her gown came next. Then something she had not yet experienced, a hoop to hold the yards of green silk away from her body in a wide circle. While the seamstresses finished their work, they had her walk around to observe its movement on her body. She thought her breasts might fall right out of the dress. The bodice was so tight that only a thin layer of transparent chiffon covered them. She blushed at the sight of herself in the mirror.

Mrs. Green nodded her approval. "Not a man alive is going to be able to concentrate when you're in his arms."

"Isn't this dress a little risqué?"

"My dear, when you distract a man, he'll not be able to control what he says. It'll take every bit of his willpower not to stare at your magnificent assets. Trust me on this." Mrs. Green dabbed perfume into the deep valley of her own cleavage. "I've heard about the plans of the Northern generals from these fools and from Mr. Lincoln himself."

"I can imagine," Kristen said.

The older woman patted her pale-blonde hair back into place. Her own gown, an icy-blue silk, matched her innocent, blue eyes. Kristen guessed her hostess to be somewhere in her early forties, but it was hard to tell exactly. Meeting the grown son of Mrs. Green might give her a clue, but the woman hardly looked more than a few years older than she.

"Your carriage is here," a young black male announced, entering the huge bedroom.

"We'll be down in a moment," Mrs. Green said. "Is my son ready?"

"Your son is in the carriage waiting for you," the man said, then turned and left the room.

"We must be going now, my dear," Mrs. Green said. "Just remember what I told you. Smile, dance, and most importantly, listen."

"I promise, I will."

"And use this." Mrs. Green handed her a lacy fan with delicate flowers and butterflies painted on one side. "I have found that running it down a man's chest can do wonders for making him forget himself."

Kristen's eyes went wide.

"We Southern women know how to get what we want," Mrs. Green said grinning wickedly at her. "How do you think I managed to marry so well—three different times?"

Both women were handed silk shawls by the maid and then escorted by a handsome, black groom to the carriage outside. Snow-white horses stood by, ready for the carriage painted a glossy black. When the groom opened the door, Kristen marveled at the red velvet lining the inside. The groom helped her into the coach. Since her wide hooped skirt surrounded her, she was unsure if she would even fit through the door. Once inside, she almost sat on a dark form already seated against the opposite door.

"I'm so sorry." She tried to control her skirts nearly burying the man who sat in the dark corner of the carriage.

"That's quite all right," said a deep voice, reminding her of a late-night jazz radio disc jockey. "I would gladly share my seat with a woman as lovely as you."

A tingle rode up her spine at the deep voice. Too dark to see what the man looked like, Kristen could only make out his wide shoulders and long, muscular legs.

In another flurry of silk, Mrs. Green joined her and the strange man inside the carriage. After arranging her wide skirts, Mrs. Green turned to her. "This is my son, Terrence."

"How very nice to meet you," Terrence said in his deep voice.

"Nice to meet you," Kristen said, finding it hard to keep her thoughts straight.

As if sensing her unease, Mrs. Green took over the conversation. "Terrence is an officer in the Union Army under Mr. Lincoln."

Kristen blinked hard in the gloom. How could that be? Her hostess helped the South, while her son fought for the Union.

Continuing as if nothing she had just said might be unusual, Mrs. Green smiled at her son. "He believes that keeping the nation whole is more important than individual State's rights."

"As my father would have believed."

Mrs. Green clucked her tongue. "Your father would not have felt that way. I knew your father as you never could, son. He believed that centralized power would hold our democracy together."

"Mother, I don't wish to argue in the presence of so lovely a woman as Miss Bissett."

"And I agree, son, which is the reason I support your decision."

Kristen did not know what to say.

"How long will you be staying with my mother?" Terrence said.

"Just a few days." Kristen's eyes became accustomed to the twilight of the carriage. She could just make out the features of the young man seated next to her. He had his mother's blonde hair, though a few shades darker. She noticed the young man wore a blue Union officer's uniform. The long coat tied at the waist with a dark-red sash ending in fringe. A red stripe ran down the wool pants, perfectly tailored for his long legs. Mrs. Green's son was a very appealing young man.

The carriage came to an abrupt stop after only a few minutes. Since Mrs. Green lived in town, many of the more elegant mansions were fairly close to each other.

"I'll look forward to a dance," Terrence said. He handed Kristen to the waiting coachman at the open door.

She found herself smiling. She had not enjoyed as much male attention in her entire life as she had in the past month. Maybe it was the clothes, which accented Kristen's feminine assets, with the uncomfortably tight-fitting clothes.

When she and Mrs. Green stepped through the double doors

of the brick mansion, crystal chandeliers lit the huge ballroom. A twenty piece orchestra played a waltz and women swirled around the room like bright flowers. Most of the men wore the navy blue uniform of the Union Army. It gave Kristen pause to realize where she now stood. *This is history, and I'm living it.* The music was light and cheery, the officers gallant, and the ladies sparkled. No one seemed to be suffering in this occupied city.

"May I have this dance?"

Kristen turned, smiled, and looked up into the face of a very handsome officer. She knew just enough about dancing to follow her partner. The men of this century danced as easily as men from her time played sports. The men danced as if they had been born to it, which was most likely the case. She wished that her own time reflected more of this slow, gentle time.

The evening passed in a blur of movement, light, and music. Kristen always had a partner. She smiled and listened to everything they said. It seemed every officer felt the need to give her a hint of what he knew. By the end of the evening, she had enough snippets of information to piece together one short message. The Union Army would gather at Bull Run Creek.

"How are you doing, dear?" Mrs. Green said.

Kristen turned away from her last partner, giving him one last smile. "It's been wonderful." The officer who had been her partner bowed and left the two women alone.

"Has your evening been fruitful?" Mrs. Green asked in a whisper.

Kristen nodded.

"Then we should be going home now."

"I can bring her home, mother." Both women turned to see Terrence standing in front of them.

"And, Miss Bissett has promised me a dance."

"Fine, son. If Kristen wants to stay, I can send the carriage back for the both of you."

Looking from mother to son, Kristen found herself nodding. This might be the only chance she had to be Cinderella. She was not yet ready to have the clock strike twelve.

Terrence kissed his mother's cheek and then turned to Kristen. He held out his arm and she slipped her gloved hand under his arm, joining the other dancers. Light on his feet, he held her tightly, whirling her around the room under the flickering lights of the chandeliers. Only once did she allow herself thoughts of Jeffrey. She imagined that her partner's hair was glossy black, his uniform more gray than blue. If she half closed her eyes, she could almost see Jeffrey instead of her partner. She nearly swooned in his arms for her imagination and lack of breath due to her corset, the imaginary transformation almost quite real.

Terrence took her into his arms, holding her close for a moment until her head stopped spinning. "Would you like to go outside for some fresh air?"

"That would be wonderful." She blinked and tried to bring the room back into focus.

With his arm around her waist, he led her out onto a wide porch. Lack of food and oxygen made Kristen lightheaded enough to faint. Terrence turned, pulling her into his strong arms. She leaned against him. At least she would not fall flat on her face this way, and it *did* feel good to have a man's arm around her – even if they belonged to the wrong man. The right man did not want her and she needed to stay away from him. Terrence drew her close. She pushed all thoughts of Jeffrey out of her mind.

Her partner jerked away from her.

Kristen wondered what she had done to make him draw back so quickly. Without the support of his arms, she nearly fell flat on her face. Terrence struggled with another man. She heard fists hitting flesh and bones cracking.

What's going on? Terrence dropped to the ground. She prepared to scream but a hand covered her open mouth. She resisted and bit down. A muffled cry made her want to laugh. She bit down again and tasted blood this time.

"Please stop struggling," an angry voice whispered in her ear.

Knowing it was useless to fight the strong arms that held her, Kristen stood still.

"Promise not to scream?"

She nodded.

The hand came off her mouth. She took a deep breath, as if to scream, and the hand snaked back over her mouth.

"Kristen, I really need your cooperation."

165

Even at a whisper, she recognized that voice. She nodded her head vigorously this time and the hand came off her mouth. "Jeffrey? What are you doing here?"

"Trying to rescue you."

"But I'm not in need of being rescued," she said spinning around to face her husband. In the pale light of the porch, she saw the face of the man she had come to love. The shadow of a beard shaded his strong jaw, making his eyes appear bluer. She hardly recognized the man before her, dressed in scruffy clothes that looked as if he'd slept in them for a week.

"You will be if we don't get away from here," Jeffrey whispered into her ear, sending chills down her neck. Why did the man have to affect her so strongly when she meant nothing to him?

Jeffrey pulled Kristen along behind him down a dark alley. Shadowy shapes filled the passage, scuttling out of the way with tiny squeaks and glowing eyes.

She tried to avoid stepping on any of the moving creatures and imagined tiny feet climbing up her stockings. Kristen did her best to keep up with Jeffrey's run through the darkness.

"Where are we going?" she said when Jeffrey finally came to a stop.

"Back to camp." He blinked and stared at her as if she were an idiot.

"But I haven't finished what I came here to do."

"And what might that be?" Jeffrey said. "Cast a spell over the whole Yankee army?"

Pleased with his evaluation of the situation, she grinned. Jeffrey made a snorting sound and pulled her along through the alleyway again.

"I demand to know where you're taking me!" Kristen stopped, digging the heels of her dancing pumps into the ground.

"I've already told you."

"I know, back to camp." She took a deep breath, then yanked her arm out of Jeffrey's grasp. "Well, if we're going back to camp, then I need to get my things from Mrs. Green."

"I can't let you do that."

"Why not?"

"Because if I'm seen by her son, I'll be sent to a Yankee prison."

Jeffrey cleared his throat. "Of course that would leave you free to carry on with him."

Kristen swore under her breath. Closing her eyes and praying for patience, she nodded. "I see your point. I'm sorry I didn't think of it sooner." She lifted her skirts. "I suppose if I can't go back for my clothes. I'll have to wear this."

Jeffrey appeared to hesitate. He gazed up and down at the gown and frowned. Kristen's cleavage left little to the imagination. His gaze darkened.

She smiled in triumph. "I can see that you haven't thought of everything." Looking down the deserted street, she said, "So, where's the carriage?"

"My horse is around the next corner."

"Your horse?" Kristen said, her voice rising.

"Kristen," Jeffrey said in a low voice. "You really need to be quiet. If the Yankees hear us—"

"I don't care!" Kristen whispered. "You cannot expect me to make an eight hour trip on a horse in this dress."

"You'll be fine."

"I will not!" Kristen put her hands on her hips and glared at her husband. "Do you have any idea what it's like to breath in one of these things? And you expect me to ride a horse?"

For the first time since she had met Jeffrey, he appeared to be at a loss for words. She might have felt sympathetic to his bewilderment if she were not so appalled. Riding a horse in a silk gown complete with petticoats would be impossible.

"Why don't I just go back into the party and I'll meet you at camp in a day or two."

Jeffrey stood silent for a moment. "Kristen, you are my wife, it's my job to protect you."

"From what?" She demanded her voice rising. "From men who want to dance? That's a laugh. You're the one who's in enemy territory. And if you get caught—"

The sounds of voices and footsteps interrupted her tirade. Jeffrey once again grabbed her arm and dragged her through the darkness. Running over the uneven bricks in dance shoes with narrow heels, she felt every pebble. They might have out run the men who chased after them, if something warm and furry had not attacked Kristen's leg. The creature bit down hard.

Unable to hold back a scream, she kicked at the tiny rodent attached to her leg. She tripped and fell headfirst onto the ground.

Jeffrey lifted her up. "Don't worry about me."

She cried out, batting her hands at the terrified animal clinging to her ankle. "If you're caught, you'll go to prison!"

"I'm not going to leave you," Jeffrey said.

Four soldiers surrounded the couple.

Twenty Eight

"**L**et go of her!"

Kristen turned, recognizing Terrence's voice. Her heart pounded a tattoo against her chest. What if Jeffrey had to spend the rest of the war, if not the rest of his life, in a Yankee prison?

"Take care of him," Terrence said.

Kristen watched in horror as one of the three soldiers yanked her out of Jeffrey's arms. Jeffrey rushed toward the men, but her captor pointed a gun at her head.

"Either let go, or I'll shoot her."

The barrel of the pistol looked like a tunnel with no light at the end of it. Kristen swallowed, her throat turning dry.

"Don't hurt the woman!" Terrence glared at the man holding the gun. The gunman turned the weapon, pointing it at Jeffrey's temple instead.

Kristen's knees went weak.

Terrence drew his own gun and hit Jeffrey over the back of the head. Her husband hit the ground with a thump. Kristen dropped down beside his still form.

"Why did you have to do that?" She scowled at him.

He wiped his jaw and shrugged. "He started it." He turned to his men. "Now get up and let's get moving." He grabbed her arm and jerked her to her feet.

"I'm not going anywhere with you." Her arm already going numb. "I need to see that this man is all right."

"Him?" Terrance narrowed his eyes. "I thought he was trying to kidnap you."

"And that's why you pointed a gun at me?" Kristen said.

The larger of the two soldiers started to examine Jeffrey's clothes. What if they realized he was a southern officer? She had to do something, fast.

"Terrence, can we just go now? I can't bear to see all that blood."

Shaking his head in disgust, Terrence nodded toward one of his men. With a grin, a soldier kicked Jeffrey's motionless body.

Kristen flinched but pasted on a smile. She needed to get the men away from Jeffrey before they did any more damage.

"Terrence," Kristen said. "I'd really like to go back to the party." She smiled up at him, hiding her shaking hands in her skirts.

"Are you sure?" He peered at her. "I could always just take you home."

Shaking her head Kristen took a deep breath, hoping her smile looked sincere enough. "I really think that another dance with you is what would help me forget all this awfulness."

"Anything your little heart desires." Terrence held out his arm.

She took it, forcing herself not to look back at Jeffrey.

"What about him?" One of the soldiers called out.

"Do whatever you want." Terrence waved his free hand, leading Kristen away. "Just be sure and clean up after yourself."

She heard the heavy thuds from the men kicking Jeffrey. They laughed at his grunts. *Bastards. What kind of men found enjoyment in beating the life out of another human being?*

"Terrence, could you please make them stop?" Kristen said. "I can't stand the way that man moans. It's getting on my nerves."

Terrence took a deep breath. "If you insist. I know how delicate a woman can be." He turned to his men. "That's enough boys. Let's get back to the party."

Relieved when the other soldiers finally joined them, Kristen asked Terrence to release her.

"You're still weak," Terrence said.

"I *am* not." Kristen ground her teeth together. "I'm just fine. Now will you please just let go of me?"

The other soldiers snickered when Terrence let go her arm. He gave them a look that wiped the smiles off their faces.

Kristen wanted to look back at Jeffrey, but she knew it might mean his death. Terrence must have noticed her shiver because he removed his coat, laying it gently across her bare shoulders.

"Thank you." Kristen ground her teeth again in frustration. She heard the sounds of the party coming from the house before she saw it. The music and noise created a festive atmosphere, although she didn't feel festive at the moment. She imagined Jeffrey dying from internal bleeding, while she pretended to dance gaily and enjoy the rest of the evening.

Terrence held out his arm for Kristen and escorted her through the wide doors to the party. Music, food, cigar smoke, and perfumes permeated the air. Kristen stomach, still shaky from the trauma of seeing Jeffrey nearly beaten to death, started to turn over on itself. Every dance seemed like it would go on forever.

Desperate to retrieve her husband and administer first aid, Kristen pasted a smile on her face, her mind concocting a way to depart the party — alone.

Terrence glared at any officer that headed their way. How would she ever get away?

A smiling young man stepped up to the dancing couple.

"What is it?" Terrence said, his face hard.

The boy gave a sharp salute. "I have a message from General McClellan for you, sir."

Terrence took the piece of paper from the boy's shaking hand.

Trying to read the note, Kristen leaned against him. He smiled down at her, his eyes running down her dress. She realized she had pressed her breasts against the man's arm. Kristen could only imagine what he must be thinking, but she had to see the note. From her scant knowledge of history, she knew that General McClellan was in charge of the whole Union Army. Were the Northerners going to attack soon? How was she going to get the note away from Terrence long enough to read it and get back in time to save Jeffrey?

Terrence finished reading the note, saluted the young soldier, and slid the paper into the back pocket of his uniform. He turned to Kristen. "I think we have time for one more dance. You're not too tired are you?"

Robin Landry

She smiled and shook her head.

I'd rather hit you over the head with a lamp so I can get back to my husband, but no, I'm not too tired.

Terrance swept her into his arms and circled the dance floor until she thought she might be sick.

She just needed to reach into Terrence's pocket, secure the note, and return to Jeffrey before he died. Why had she ever volunteered to be a spy? It had brought Jeffrey into this predicament. How would she ever get them out alive?

Twenty Nine

Kristen's **golden opportunity** came when Terrence asked her if she'd like a cup of punch. She gave him a smile, then made her way to one of the corner chaise lounge chairs behind a discrete silk curtain.

Terrance excused himself. He returned a moment later with two cups of punch. He smiled, sat down beside her, and handed her one of the crystal glasses.

"Will this take away my headache?" She held the delicate cup with one hand and rubbed her forehead with the other.

Terrance smiled and reached into an inner pocket of his uniform. He drew out a thin, silver flask and opened it. Kristen held both glasses as he poured a clear liquid into them. The punch now smelled like rubbing alcohol, perfect for her purposes.

Sipping her drink, she watched Terrence down his in one gulp. He poured more alcohol into his empty cup and swallowed again.

"I do like a man who can hold his liquor." Kristen smiled.

Grinning, Terrence poured himself another. She pretended to drink from her own cup. Her escort did not seem to notice.

"May I get you more?" He raised an eyebrow.

"Please." Kristen waited until Terrance turned his back and then poured her drink into a potted palm tree next to the bench. "Sorry," she whispered to the plant.

Her date returned in less than a minute. He carried two half-full glasses, which he topped off from his flask. Kristen again sipped at her own drink, but this time the liquid tasted like it could strip paint off the wall. She had no desire to sip anymore. She needed to keep her wits about her.

Terrance downed his third cup and turned to her with hooded eyes and a half smile. Although disgusted by this man, she kissed Terrence, gritting her teeth to keep his tongue out. He groaned aloud, his hands roaming all over her body as she finally allowed him to deepen the kiss.

Kristen's hands roamed over his body, but only to search out the note he'd tucked onto his pants pockets. She had to get that note. Her fingers moved deep into his right, front pocket. No luck.

Hidden from the rest of the party by the heavy curtain and dim lighting, Terrance seemed to think he could do as he pleased. Kristen certainly encouraged the passionate young man. His moans grew louder. She dug into the left, front pocket. She hoped nobody would hear them.

Finding both front pockets empty, Kristen ran her fingers down his back, seeking his left, back pocket. The moment she touched it, Terrence pushed her away. She could not look at him. *Does he suspect what I've been doing?* Her heart pounded in her chest and her hands felt like ice.

"We need to find a place more private," Terrence said in a husky voice.

"I'm not sure I'm ready for that."

"I think you are," he whispered, his mouth moving down her neck.

One last chance, Kristen thought. She had to think fast, but she could barely catch her breath. Sliding her hands down his back, she touched the pocket of his trousers. The heat emanating from him made her hands pause.

"Don't stop."

Please let me find the note before it's too late.

The gods of the Southern cause must have heard her, because she felt the folded piece of paper between her fingers. She pulled the paper out but Terrence had moved his mouth to her neck again. She felt a sharp bite.

"Ouch!" Kristen pushed him away and slid her hand under her gown searching for her own pocket.

Terrence's mouth fell open. "I thought you liked it a little rough."

"Where in the world did you get that idea?" Kristen smoothed out her gown. "I'm surprised you think I'm that kind of woman!"

"But—"

"I'd like the carriage brought around so I can go home."

Terrence worked to focus his eyes.

Kristen knew her chance to escape had arrived. "And I would prefer to go back alone."

A confused expression came over his handsome face. "Did I offend you in any way?"

"Well, you're certainly not acting like a gentleman," Kristen said. Her husband's life was at risk. She did not have time to be polite if she intended to get back to him in time.

"I'll get the carriage for you." Terrence's voice slurred.

"Be quick about it, I've had enough of your ungentlemanly behavior for one night."

Shaking his head as if to clear it, Terrence left her to search out the coachman. Unable to wait any longer, Kristen moved out of the cove and sped through the throngs of dancers and waiters asking her if she'd like more champagne. She finally made it through the large, front door.

She stepped off the bottom step, a coach slowing to a stop before her. A familiar voice called out, one that she wanted to ignore.

"Kristen!"

Terrance had found her. Now she would have to return to Mrs. Green. She would go back to the mansion and leave at the first opportunity. She could do nothing for Jeffrey at the moment.

"Where were you going?" Terrence said. The coachmen helped Kristen into the carriage.

"I just needed some fresh air." Her chest tightened in frustration.

"The streets are not safe at night for a woman to be out by herself."

As if I'd be safe with you, cowboy.

Kristen took a deep breath, not trusting herself to speak. The ride back to the mansion took only a few minutes. The carriage stopped at the side door and the coachman jumped down. Terrence nearly fell onto his face, so the coachman ran to the opposite side of the coach to help him out of the carriage.

"This will just take a minute." The coachman called to Kristen, closing the carriage door on her.

"That's fine. Thank you for taking care of him."

She watched the coachman half-carried Terrence into the house. The door opened and light streamed into the yard. The coachman hurried back to the carriage and put out a gloved hand. Kristen stepped out of the carriage holding his arm until she entered the front door of the mansion.

Once inside, she turned and thanked the coachman and the door closed behind her.

Thankfully, Terrance was nowhere in sight. Seeing a small lamp on the hall table, she picked it up, held up her skirts with her other hand, and rushed up the wide staircase.

Now all I have to do is give Mrs. Green the note and then find Jeffrey. Kristen could not even entertain the idea that she might be too late.

Thirty

Kristen tiptoed into the guest room. She pulled a shawl out of the middle drawer of the bureau, put her evening bag on the bed, and packed a travel bag. Next, she made her way down the stairs, stopping to hold her breath at every creak the house made. Once she made her way into the kitchen, she stopped to listen for any signs of life stirring in the big house.

Were the coachman and the butler gone? Would anyone try to stop her if they saw her taking items from the kitchen? She could not think about that. She had to get back to Jeffrey before it was too late.

Kristen placed the items in her travel bag, put food in her shawl, and tied it so she could sling it over her shoulder. She retraced her steps along the hall, leaving the mansion through the side door. She hurried through the yard to the main entrance and down the street. She turned left, counted the blocks and rushed toward the mansion where the party had been only a few hours earlier. Although the yard still blazed with light, the house seemed quiet. Two more blocks and she would be where she had last seen her husband.

Where is Jeffery? Kristen double checked her surroundings — certain she had found the correct alley. She looked down at the cobblestones and found nothing but a pool of blood.

"He has to be here somewhere." The alley looked empty, except for a row of garbage cans and a few wooden boxes stacked haphazardly beside them.

Barely more than a whisper, a voice called out to her. "Kristen?"

"Jeffrey?" Kneeling down, Kristen saw a dark shape between two of the garbage cans. Throwing boxes and trash away from the cans, she dug until she reached Jeffrey, lying on the pavement. *Oh, thank God, please let him be okay.*

"Kristen?"

Jeffrey's clothes were damp and sticky. She recognized the sharp, coppery smell of blood. How much had he lost? In the dark alley she could barely see her hands in front of her. She would have to move him somewhere into the light to see his wounds.

She slipped her hands under his arms and pulled with all her might. She could only drag him a couple of feet, but it was enough. In the dim light of a nearby gas street lamp, Kristen realized Jeffrey had lost a lot of blood. She needed to get him someplace safe. Mrs. Green's house would not be safe if Terrence saw him again. He might even recognize Jeffery as a Southern officer and a sworn enemy.

"How in the world am I going to get you back to your army?"

"Diablo."

"Diablo?" Kristen said with a frown. Was her husband having some sort of near-death experience? "Are you sure you don't see a tunnel with a light at the end of it? I'm pretty sure you haven't done anything horrible enough to get you sent to hell."

An irritated tone crept into his voice. "My horse." Jeffrey's voice came out as a whisper. His swollen eyes stayed closed.

"Oh, right. Of course, that's the name of your...never mind." *Why's he talking about his horse at a time like this?*

"Wh-wh-whisper..."

"What are you trying to say?" Kristen leaned closer. "You want me to whisper? There's no one here but us," Kristen said. "Jeffrey, I'm keeping my voice as low as I possibly can."

"Whistle," Jeffrey managed to croak out. "Just whistle!"

"You want me to whistle?" She could not believe he wanted her to whistle a tune at a time like this? What was wrong with him?

"For my horse." He collapsed in her arms.

"Oh, right." She understood at last. "You want me to whistle for your horse." Now If only Diablo could take them where they needed to go. Unsure of how to whistle, Kristen curled her forefinger and thumb, put them in her mouth, and blew as hard as she could. A loud shriek split the night air.

Within seconds the sound of hoof beats clattered down the alley. Too dark to see if the huge black shape charging toward them carried a rider, she threw herself over Jeffrey.

The pounding hooves came to an abrupt stop, just inches from Kristen's head. When she felt something sniffing at her hair, she raised her eyes.

"Diablo! Oh thank goodness, it's you." She smiled. "Definitely something I never thought I'd be saying."

Now, she had to get Jeffrey into the saddle. "Too bad you can't lie down like a camel."

The horse blew air out his nose as if to answer her.

"I guess it's up to me." Rising to her feet, Kristen put her hands under Jeffrey's arms and tried to raise him to a sitting position. Every time she got him into a sitting position, he fell back over.

"Damn it."

She panted from the effort of lifting the dead weight of her husband. "I wish you'd help," she said breathless.

Jeffrey stirred and opened his eyes. "Yes, my love?"

Kristen gritted her teeth. "No, your wife. Now give me some help before someone comes back here and finds us."

Jeffrey closed his eyes, then tried in vain to get up. Fresh blood dripped out from under the front of the shirt from his struggle.

"Just lay back for a minute." She reached underneath her dress and ripped several long strips from her pristine-white, cotton petticoat. She folded one of the pieces of material to make a bandage, and used the rest to wrap around her husband's waist. The long and wicked wound bled enough to cause her concern. In his already weakened state, she did not want him to lose any more blood. Still, getting him onto the horse would be hard.

Diablo stood restless and snickered as Kristen tried to get Jeffrey to stand up. He fell onto one of the wooden crates, which gave her an idea.

"Just sit there." She grabbed one of the crates and pushed it toward the horse, setting it next to his left, front leg. "This could work."

"Kristen, do you know I love you?" He murmured into her neck as she tried to lift him to his feet.

"I thought you hated me." She struggled with his heavy body and felt his forehead. *He's hot with fever!* Hours had passed since Jeffrey took the beating, and she still did not know the extent of his injuries. She would not rest easy until she examined him more closely. If his wounds included a brain injury, it might already be too late.

"I could never hate you, because I love you," he said.

"That's wonderful," she said, breathless from her exertions. "Now, if you could just help me a little bit."

"I have to tell you something before I die."

"You're not going to die, at least not yet."

"Kristen," Jeffrey said, his voice groggy. "I know I'm going to die because I've seen an angel."

"You have?"

Jeffrey gave a weak smile. "I know I'm going to die, otherwise God wouldn't have made you the angel you've been for the last few weeks."

"Me?" Kristen almost could not keep from laughing. "I am no angel. Now, can you step up onto this box and put your foot into the stirrup. Do you think you can do that for me?"

"Yes, you're an angel." Jeffrey then lifted his foot into the stirrup, and Kristen pushed him up into the saddle. After a lifetime of riding, he rode without effort.

Kristen tore the metal hoops out of her petticoat and dropped them on the ground. The sun peeked over the horizon as she climbed on the box and swung her leg over the saddle behind Jeffrey. To escape any watching eyes, they needed to move quickly. Mrs. Green might already be looking for her. What would happen when she found the guest room empty? Pushing such thoughts from her mind, she kicked her heels into Diablo's side.

"Come on boy. It's up to you now."

The big horse did not have to be told twice. He took off at a fast trot, she only had to hang on and keep Jeffrey from sliding off. Riding through the alleys made it easier to avoid people except for the occasional shop owner that opened his door.

Out of town in minutes and on the back roads of Maryland, Jeffrey rode along in silence. Kristen kept one arm wrapped around his waist and one hand on the reins. Diablo seemed to sense the need for a smooth ride. He carefully maneuvered along the deer path that wound its way through the thick brush.

Once they were far enough away from town to be safe, she would stop to examine her husband's wounds more carefully. She knew Jeffrey's chances might not be good. He might not regain enough strength to fight again.

Pushing negative thoughts from her mind, Kristen pulled the reins hard enough to lead Diablo into a nearby patch of trees. She did not want to be seen on the road by any curious passersby, whether civilian or soldier. Since many of the Southern soldiers also wore navy blue like the Yankees, how would she know who to trust? The little knowledge she could recall from high school history hadn't disclosed that fact.

Tired and weary from stress and lack of sleep, she brought the horse to a stop, slid off, and nearly fell. Without support, Jeffrey began to lean to one side. Kristen reached up to catch him, but only managed to break his fall. Together they tumbled onto a thick carpet of new spring grass and rolled until they hit the trunk of a huge tree.

Jeffrey groaned as she struggled to get off of him. Her long skirts tangled around her legs made it impossible to move. She lay still on top of him and considered the best way to get them untangled. After she caught her breath, she tried to sit up. Something around her waist held her back. Had her skirts traveled up? Kristen put her hand behind her and discovered his arms wrapped around her in a steely grip.

"You're going to have to let go." Her face hovered only inches away from his.

Jeffrey lifted his head to touch her dry mouth with his. His lips hot with fever, kissed her with a desperate intensity. Kristen could not have pulled away if she wanted to. It felt good to know he had energy and strength to kiss and hold her—better yet, that he wanted her—at least in his fevered state.

Kristen forced herself to pull away. "Jeffrey, I really need to care for your wounds."

"Mmm." His mouth lifted again, seeking hers.

Kristen pushed against his chest with all her strength and sat up. "You're not going to be any good to me dead. Now, let me see how badly you've been hurt."

With his eyes still closed, Jeffrey lay back with a smile on his face.

Kristen unwound her skirt and stood over her patient. She walked over to Diablo. He tore large chunks of fresh grass out and chewed.

"You are such a good boy," Kristen cooed, stroking the horse's long nose. "I can't believe I was ever afraid of you. Now if you would just hold still for a minute."

Across the saddle she had tied her travel bag and the shawl with food. In addition to a loaf of bread, some cheese wrapped in cloth, and some dried beef, she had taken a bottle of whiskey. With the bundle in hand, she sat down beside her patient, unbuttoned his plain, cotton shirt, and pulled back the strips of cotton she had wound around his waist earlier that evening. The gash across his stomach was long, but not too deep. It seemed to have bled out, leaving an angry red line.

Tossing aside the soiled pieces of petticoat, Kristen tore a new piece off another layer of her petticoat. "It's a good thing women wore a lot of clothes."

Unfortunately, he had to heal without the benefit of modern medicine and a clean hospital. She would do almost anything for a good antibiotic and a smooth riding car instead of a horse. Everything in the 19th century seemed to be in slow motion. Cooking took longer, getting places took longer, and healing would take much longer than normal. Nothing she had seen so far ever happened fast.

Kristen soaked the cotton she'd torn from her undergarments

in the whiskey. The alcohol would keep Jeffrey's wound from infection. First, she applied the material to his skin. Luckily, he slumbered deeper than normal. Only his muscles flexed when she rubbed harder.

Kristen could have watched Jeffery's body all day long. Never before had she seen such a fine display of masculine form. Everything about him appeared to be perfect, from his wide shoulders to the defined pectoral muscles with the trail of dark hair... Just looking at her husband had the power to take her breath away.

She surveyed her work and took a deep breath. "That's the best I can do."

How much damage had been done? With careful fingers Kristen parted the thick black hair on Jeffrey's head. Blood and dirt matted most of his hair which made it hard to see his scalp. She would have to remove the blood to see exactly how badly he had been hurt. Knowing how profusely the scalp could bleed, she did not think the bump he took was all that serious. Ripping another piece of cloth from her undergarments, she rubbed the scalp area with the most dried blood on it, which started it to bleed again.

He moaned in his sleep and turned his head away from her.

"You're going to have to hold still, if you want me to help you."

Kristen continued her probing. The gash, deeper than she had first thought, had left the flesh around it already an angry red. Infection was a reality.

Reaching for the bottle of whiskey, Kristen put it to Jeffrey's lips to get him to take a drink.

She took a deep breath and poured a generous amount onto Jeffrey's head at the site of the wound. The moment the whiskey hit his scalp Jeffrey sat up, his eyes wide. To his credit, he did not cry out, but she could tell that his scalp stung far more than he would admit.

"I'm sorry I had to do that."

"Are you trying to kill me, woman?"

"I thought a little whiskey on your wound might help."

"Try it in my mouth, next time."

183

She could not help but laugh, the tension of the night melting away. However, Jeffery did not find the remark funny — the look on his face priceless.

"I see you're not feverish anymore."

A slow smile spread across his handsome face. Even through the pain his gray-blue eyes sparkled. "I never was."

"Really?" Kristen wanted to ask him if he remembered what he'd said earlier. She decided against mentioning it. Some things are better left unsaid.

"Why? Did I say something I shouldn't have?"

"No, not really." Kristen hated the heat rising in her cheeks. Why did she have to show her feelings so easily? "I could use something to prevent infection." She swiped at a bee buzzing around her head. "I guess I shouldn't have put us in the middle of all these flowers."

"You could use honey," Jeffrey said. "With all these bees around, there has to be a hive nearby."

"Honey? Are you hungry?"

Jeffrey shook his head. "Lila was always using honey on my cuts when I was a kid. She did the same thing when I watched her tend to the slaves."

"I've never heard of using honey." Kristen frowned at the large bumblebee still circling. "But it's worth a try." She scowled at Jeffrey. "I wouldn't want you to die, even though I'm sure you're too stubborn to do any such thing."

Standing up, she looked around. "So where do bees keep their honey?"

Jeffrey's eyes went wide. "But you can't get it."

"I thought you said we needed it? So that means I'm the one who has to go get it, since you're not in any kind of shape to go climbing trees, or wherever it is that bees keep their honey."

Jeffrey sighed. "I'll be fine, and it's too dangerous, so just forget I said anything."

"I'm not going to forget you said anything. If you think this is going to work, and if Lila did it I'm sure it will, then you just need to tell me how to find honey."

"You always were stubborn," Jeffrey said, grumbling under

his breath.

"I heard that."

Jeffrey took a deep breath. "We need a fire, and then you'll need to follow the bees back to their hive."

"Sounds like fun." Kristen had no idea how to follow a bee, but if it would save Jeffrey's life, then she was willing to give it a try.

"I know you're afraid of bees so why don't we just forget this."

"I am?" Kristen frowned. "Oh, that's right, it must've slipped my mind. But, since you can't go anywhere because you might have a concussion, I'll have to go. Just tell me how to find a beehive."

"A concussion? What's that?"

Kristen took a deep breath. "It's just something I read about. Like if you get hit on the head, you're not supposed to do anything strenuous for a day or two. If you don't listen to me, you're going to make yourself sick, or you might even bleed to death if you open up your wound again. Now, tell me where to find the bees and I'll get you some honey."

"You always were a stubborn woman."

"I know. It's part of my charm." Kristen smiled. "Can the fire wait until I come back with the honey?"

Jeffrey laughed but the look on her face brought him up short. "Kristen, you need a fire so you can take a smoking branch with you to the beehive. Smoke puts bees to sleep."

"Why would I want to put the bees to sleep?"

"So they don't sting you to death?"

"That would be unfortunate."

"Kristen, the bees are not going to appreciate you taking part of their hive."

"Oh, I hadn't thought about that."

Jeffrey stared at her not saying a word.

"What?" Kristen said. "Why are you looking at me so strangely?"

"Don't you remember why you're so afraid of bees?"

"I might've forgotten." She had no recollection of why she should be afraid of bees, since she had never been afraid of bees in her entire life. Then again, this was not her life.

Jeffrey sighed. "Last year your horse reared up, throwing you against an old stump that had a beehive in it. You were stung all over your face and neck." Jeffrey's eyes narrowed. "Surely you haven't forgotten how frightened you were." He paused. "Although, I'm not sure you were as frightened by the pain of the stings as you were at the thought of your face being permanently disfigured."

"I would never be so vain." Kristen brushed off her skirt and looked around for the phantom beehive.

Jeffrey made a choking sound.

She turned to her husband lying helpless at her feet, and glared down at him. "If you laugh, Jeffrey O'Connor, I swear I'll stitch up that hard head of yours with a sharp stick and the rope from your horse."

He shook his head. "I would never laugh at your beauty, my dear. Nor at your wish to preserve it."

Still glaring, Kristen nodded. "Thank you. I am not vain, at least I'm not now, and I don't appreciate you insinuating that I am."

A smile tugged at the corners of his mouth. The deep creases in his cheeks rendered her husband so dear to her a strange tug happened in her heart. How could she love another person this much? Even with all her medical training, she felt certain that her heart would stop beating if she ever had to leave this man. She had read that couples who had been married for most of their lives, often died soon after the other had passed away. Until now she hadn't understood. Strange as it seemed, Jeffrey was her other half—better half. Around him, she wanted to be better, stronger, and braver than she had ever been before.

Kristen took a deep breath and composed herself. "So do you have any idea where this beehive might be so I can get you fixed up, and we can get moving?"

Jeffery smiled and his blue eyes laughed. "I would guess that a beehive is right there," he said pointing to a dead stump in the middle of the meadow.

"Great, I'll be right back." Kristen raised her skirts and rushed to where Jeffrey had just pointed.

"Without a fire?

"I'm not afraid of bees," Kristen shouted over her shoulder. *Surely I could handle a few bumblebees. All I have to do is grab a piece of the hive, break it off, and run back. Besides, bumblebees didn't sting or at least that's what I read somewhere. Or maybe they could only sting you once. I hope that isn't just an old wives' tale.*

Jeffrey's swearing coming from behind her only made her walk faster. She had to raise her skirts high to get through the long grass. Wildflowers bloomed everywhere around her, their heady perfume filling her senses. The warm sun on her back helped her forget how tired, hungry, and worried she had been. For all her complaints about the transportation and medical deficiencies in this lifetime, she enjoyed the wonderful slow daily life—too much to allow anything to interfere. "And," she whispered to herself, "being in love for the very first time."

She wanted to run back to Jeffrey and make love to him like a pagan to celebrate the coming of spring with the promise of a warm summer. However, that was impossible. First of all, his injuries, and second, what would be gained if she indulged her pleasure? She might cause him to fall in love with her only to leave, giving him back to the other wife who hated him and would crush his soul one more time.

Kristen let go of her troubling thoughts as she neared the old stump. Bumblebees flew lazily around it, entering and leaving a large, rotted hole in the front of the remnants of the dead tree.

All I have to do is reach inside and grab a handful of honey. It will only take a second and the bees probably wouldn't even notice me.

Kristen let go of her skirts, took a deep breath, then reached her hand into the hive. The bees still buzzed around the entrance, seemingly unaware of her presence.

"That's right, little fellas. Just go about your business. I'm only going to borrow a little bit of your honey for a good cause."

Kristen reached her hand into the hole until she touched something sticky. So far so good. She kept digging until she found something solid. Something wiggled in her palm. Ignoring the urge to let go, she tightened her grip and pulled her hand out.

Yes, she had found honey but it came with a swarming black cloud. It took only seconds for her to realize the black cloud consisted of hundreds of angry bees.

Kristen turned and ran but the black cloud enveloped her, vigorously defending their home. Like being stabbed by a thousand needles at once, the unbelievable pain left her arms on fire.

Blinded by the swarm that seemed determined to kill her, she screamed in pain until a bee flew inside her open mouth. Now choking, Kristen ran mindlessly until she heard a voice call out.

"Kristen!"

She tumbled toward the voice, into a pair of strong arms that wrapped around her and brushed at her arms and face.

"You're okay now."

Jeffrey's voice soothed her, but she could not see and the pain grew worse.

"Just let me put this on you." Jeffrey held onto her as she sobbed.

Something cool touched Kristen's face. It felt so good she nearly wept, but her eyes were sealed shut. The sensation travelled, bathing her arms in a cool wetness that stopped the stinging. She moaned out loud.

"You're going to be just fine."

"Thanks," she said in a choked voice. She could barely talk. Maybe the bee that flew into her mouth had stung her.

"Can you see?"

Her eyelids felt as if they had weights on them. "I can't even open my eyes."

Jeffrey put his arms around her, holding her tightly. "It's okay," he said. "I'll take care of you until the swelling goes down and you can see again."

Kristen could not seem to help herself. She cried, soft at first, and then with great heaving sobs.

"Kristen, what's wrong? The pain should be gone now. There's no reason to get so worked up again."

"What's wrong? Are you kidding?" she said between sobs. "I'm the one who's supposed to take care of you. Now I'm blind, we're stuck in the middle of nowhere, and your head is probably going to get infected. The gash across your stomach is probably going to get infected too and—"

"And what?" Jeffrey said, his voice light with amusement.

"And—and I'm hideous! And I just finished telling you that I'm not vain. I have no reason to be, but I was just getting used to being beautiful—" She stopped, realizing what she had just said.

The arms that held her began to shake.

"You're not laughing, are you? Good, because this would not be a good time to laugh."

"I can see that," Jeffrey said. The shaking of his arms grew even more pronounced. Jeffrey finally laughed out loud.

Kristen pulled away, furious at his total lack of sympathy. Spinning away from him, she took a blind step forward and hit her head on a tree trunk. Hurt and humiliated, she collapsed into the tall grass.

Jeffrey sat beside her and pulled her onto his lap. Unable to see anything, she struggled to get away until she heard him groan.

"And now I'm hurting you!"

"You wouldn't if you'd just hold still."

"I'm so sorry." Kristen could not see to get away, so she let him hold her in his lap.

"Sorry for what?"

"For hurting you, for not listening about the bees—for just about everything."

Jeffrey chuckled. "I've never seen you run so fast."

"I never had a reason to before."

"I won't say I told you so."

"Good, because I'd hate to hear it."

They both laughed.

"You're going to just have to trust me for the next couple of days." The sincerity in his voice made Kristen want to kiss him.

Surprising how blindness could make a person feel so vulnerable. She found that she did, in fact, trust her husband more than she ever trusted anyone before in her life. He would keep her safe from all harm, be it snakes or enemy soldiers.

"You feel up to saddling the horse?" she said.

Jeffrey chuckled again. "My head is going to be just fine. I can put some moss on it. And that should hold until we get back to camp."

"Moss?" Kristen reached up to feel her husband's head. "You mean moss works as well as honey?"

"Sure. It's just that, whatever honey you don't use on my head, we could just eat."

"You could've saved me a lot of trouble if you had told me about the moss," Kristen said touching the tender skin around her eyes. The mud that Jeffrey had rubbed on her face had started to dry. "At least my complexion is going to look really good."

"And you said you weren't vain."

"Hm. Well maybe I just don't like having dirt all over my face."

"Oh."

"Where is your horse? We need to get back to camp." Kristen stood up and reached out her arms to feel for the horse.

Why had not Jeffrey moved? She hated not being able to see. "Jeffrey?" She heard chuckling again. "Why aren't you doing anything?"

"Because our horse is long gone," Jeffrey said. "Turns out he doesn't like bees either. Not after a whole swarm came at him."

"But he'll come back, won't he?"

"I can't really say."

"Now what are we going to do?"

He stood up. "We're just going to have to walk."

Before Kristen could object, Jeffrey took her arm and led her through the tall grass. She tripped over rocks, clumps of grass, and falling branches until they finally reached the road. However, the dirt road had deep ruts that held water. Kristen stumbled over the ruts, the water soaking her skirts almost up to her waist.

"But it's at least half a day's ride back to camp."

"I know."

"Then it will take us at least two days to walk back to camp."

"One and a half to be exact."

"But we don't have any more food or water." Kristen tried to open her swollen eyes, they remained glued shut. She had no choice but to hang onto her husband's arm and stumbled blindly along the uneven roadway.

"I see a farm up ahead. We can rest there for the night."

"What?" Her shout set off a flock of quail crossing the road.

Jeffrey stopped. "Kristen, what's wrong now?"

"What if there are people at the farm? I can't let anyone see me like this!"

After a moment of silence, Jeffrey started to shake again.

"Jeffrey, what's wrong? Is it your head? Are you all right?"

The shaking increased and he let go of her. She waved her arms around wildly, trying to find him. "Are you all right? What's wrong?"

Turning around in a circle to search, she tripped and fell to the ground. A burst of laughter told Kristen that Jeffrey was just fine. Like a dam that had burst, peals of laughter rolled up in waves.

"You are despicable. How can you be laughing at me again at a time like this?"

Jeffrey said, "You don't want help of any kind because of the way you look?"

Kristen turned away. "I'm not speaking to you."

"Kristen, we have to find help."

"I know that." She hated the way her voice sounded. Sure, her once beautiful hair, now barely chin-length. Her swollen shut eyes probably also had last night's makeup smeared all over her face. And mud covered her from head to toe.

The visual it brought to mind turned the situation so ridiculous that Kristen laughed long and hard. She fell onto her back and turned her face to the sun, letting it warm her. Never before had she allowed herself to feel the sheer joy of living.

Thirty One

Jeffrey watched his wife turn her face to the sun, something she had never done before. The look on her face made him realize that she might truly be different. She might look the same, but the woman lying in the tall, spring grass with her mouth open wide and laughter pouring out of it had changed. He did not know how or why, but her behavior was profoundly different now.

He could have gazed at her all day, enjoying the way her full lips curved back in merriment. Right now, he thought only of throwing himself down on top of her and drowning in the joy pouring from her so easily.

Whatever trick the gods had pulled to change his wife, mattered not to him. He vowed to put his former distrust aside and enjoy this woman. Who knew what tomorrow would bring? The war would surely take him before Kristen could change back into the woman she had been only a few short weeks earlier.

First, he had to see about getting her some help. Jeffrey did not know if the swelling from the bee stings would go down in a day, or if her eyes would be damaged permanently. If the farmhouse ahead had a woman who knew her cures, maybe something could be done for Kristen soon. Setting aside his lustful thoughts, he reached down a hand to her.

"Come on, Kristen. It's time to go."

"I want to stay here forever." Her voice still rang with merriment.

"I'd rather get something to eat." Jeffrey knew what motivate her. "And my head is really starting to hurt."

"What?" Kristen grabbed Jeffrey's hand and pulled herself up. "Let's get going so I can take care of you."

He chuckled under his breath. His head had been hurting ever since he'd taken the first hit. He purposely brought it up now to get her moving. She seemed bent on putting her own needs aside to help him. Suddenly, Jeffrey realized the change in his wife — she no longer cared only for herself. Now, for some reason, she actually thought of others first.

They walked along in companionable silence for nearly an hour before they reached the farmhouse. Jeffrey explored his thoughts of how and why his wife had changed. He would have given a year's pay to know exactly what had changed her, but he would not complain. He liked the changes. He had no desire to tempt fate. Better to just keep quiet and enjoy the present.

They walked through acres of newly turned fields ready to be planted, until they came to a large, white farmhouse.

The white porch wrapped around the house where two young children played under the watchful eye of their mother. He could see her through the kitchen window rolling out dough.

"Good evening, ma'am," Jeffrey called out. The woman frowned.

Jeffrey stood just outside the front gate holding onto Kristen's arm. "I could really use some help for my wife, ma'am."

The woman brushed the flour off on the apron covering her long skirt. "What in the world happened to her?"

Jeffrey squeezed Kristen's arm when he felt her stiffen.

"I thought you said I didn't look that bad," she whispered, digging her fingers into his arm.

"You don't," Jeffrey said. He gave a grimace but did not try to pry her hand loose.

The woman narrowed her eyes but moved aside. "Why don't you two come into the house?"

Jeffrey smiled at the woman's hospitality, and led Kristen along behind him. "My wife's efforts to get some honey was interrupted by an angry swarm of bees." Jeffrey said.

"Sounds like quite a story." The woman paused and then smiled, as if deciding the two were harmless. "Come on in here and get yourself something to eat. It looks like you could use it."

"Nice to meet you." Kristen lifted her skirts and felt her way up the porch stairs.

Both children ran to hide behind their mother's skirts.

"I'm Captain O'Connor, and this is my wife, Kristen."

"Emily Jenkins. My husband is Jed. He'll be home soon." She looked down at her children. "Now go back out and play, boys."

The larger of the two boys peeked out from behind his mother's skirts. He stared at Jeffrey. "Is he a real soldier?"

"I would expect so," his mother told him. "Now you boys go back outside and play. I need to see to these folks until your daddy comes home."

The boys moved past Jeffrey, their eyes wide. He smiled down at them, which caused them to run out the door giggling.

"What makes you think I'm a soldier?" Jeffrey said. "I'm not wearing a uniform."

Emily shrugged. "There have been many, many men coming by here lately to join the fight. It's the way you stand," she said pointing at the gun at Jeffrey's side. She shook her head. "Why do men think war is something glamorous?"

"A lot of men think that way," Jeffrey said. "It only takes one battle to show them otherwise."

The woman nodded. "Your Mrs. needs some attending."

Jeffrey nodded, his hand still on his wife's arm.

"I tried to steal some honey from the bees," Kristen said, speaking up for the first time.

"Kind of figured that." Emily took Kristen's other arm. "Why don't I get you a nice bath and some clean clothes. I know you'll feel a whole lot better without all that mud on you."

"I would love that."

"Don't go thanking me too soon. Anything I give you to wear is going to fit you twice over again." Emily chuckled as she led Kristen up the stairs. She called out over her shoulder. "You can bring up the boiling water."

Jeffrey looked around the kitchen. A large, iron pot hung over the fire, filled with water just ready to boil. Throwing a dish towel over the handle, he made his way up the stairs with the pot. When he reached the top of the stairs, he saw the two women in the bathroom.

She instructed him to pour the water into a large tub already half-full of water.

"I was about to give my two boys their weekly bath, but I'm certain your wife needs it more."

He nodded. He had hated his weekly bath as a boy more than anything, never seeing the point of washing off the dirt of his adventures.

"I think I might have something for your wife's eyes too." She swept down the stairs. "We need to get that swelling down."

Kristen stood in the middle of the room. She turned her head toward Jeffrey, as if she could see him.

"I'll be back when you've finished." He turned and left the room.

Thirty Two

Kristen could hardly wait to slip into the warm bathwater. Unbuttoning the tiny buttons that ran down the front of her gown seemed to take forever. Next, she took off her muddy boots, stockings, and the remains of her petticoats.

Feeling for the edge of the tub, she slipped her leg into the warm water. It felt wonderful. She heard the door open and the sound of Emily's heavy footsteps.

"You just lie back and relax," Emily said. "I have just the thing for your eyes."

Something cool enveloped her swollen eyes. The relief was immediate. "What did you put on my eyes?"

"Just a couple of cucumbers from the garden. It's something my mama taught me to do when my eyes get tired." She gave a great sigh. "Like mine seem to be most of the time lately."

The doctor in Kristen came to attention. "I can take a look at your eyes when my sight comes back, if you'd like."

"Your sight should be just fine by tomorrow."

"Thank you so much for everything you've done for us."

"It's been my pleasure. Now you just soak here for a while and let those cucumbers do their work. I'll be up in a little while to help you wash your hair."

With a sigh, Kristen slid further down into the tub, letting the warm water soothe the stings on her arm and her neck. Almost asleep, she felt someone stroking her hair. "Thanks again for everything, Mrs. Jenkins."

Gentle hands rubbed her head, spreading a lavender smelling soap into her hair. "That feels wonderful."

Strong hands moved down her shoulders, massaging her tired muscles. When they moved lower, Kristen bolted upright out of the water. "Mrs. Jenkins?"

"No, it's me." A deep voice answered.

"Jeffrey?"

"Yes, it's your husband. Mrs. Jenkins had to take care of her two boys, so I volunteered to help you wash your hair."

"Your hands are not in my hair."

"No, they're not," Jeffrey's husky voice said.

Kristen could have asked him to remove his hands, but something stopped her. Rather than identify that emotion, she remained silent instead.

Tension filled the air. She'd never felt more sensuous, and electricity tickled her skin. The warm water swirled around her and the scent of lavender filled her nose. It made her want to cry out loud with joy. *Who is this man who has such power to move me?*

Although she could not see, Kristen imagined the sharp planes of his face. She visualized his hawk nose, the deep crevices in his cheeks, and the irresistible dimple in his chin. It made her want to reach up and caress every inch of her husband's face.

Several minutes passed with the enjoyment of his hands gently rubbing and squeezing the soap out of her hair. No hairdresser had ever made her feel like this, or she would have gone more often.

"About done, Mrs. O'Connor?"

"I think so." Kristen hoped she had not been moaning.

"I have some clothes for you." The large woman came bursting through the door with an arm full of dresses and petticoats. "Pardon me." She smiled at Jeffrey. "I was wondering where the Mr. had gone."

Jeffrey stepped away from the bathtub. "I'll pay you back for everything."

Kristen would have given anything at that moment to be

able to see his face. She thought he might be embarrassed, but it did not show in his voice.

"Here's your towel, Mrs. O'Connor."

Kristen felt the rough cloth pressed into her hand. "Thank you, and please call me Kristen."

"Only if you call me Emily."

Kristen stood and wrapped the towel around herself. It smelled as fresh as the outdoors. She inhaled deeply, letting Emily help her dry off. The older woman then helped her into a dress, a few sizes too large.

Once dressed, Kristen made her way downstairs. The rich smell of simmering chicken wafted up the stairs. Laughter drifted up from downstairs as well. She carefully made her way into the dining room. The swelling around her eyes had gone down considerably. She could now make out shapes through the tiny slits of her eyelids.

"Hurry up before it's all gone."

Kristen spotted the shape of a large man sitting at the head of the table.

"This is Kristen O'Connor, the captain's wife," Emily shouted above the noise at the table.

The two boys teased each other and laughed uproariously. Jeffrey stood and held out a chair for her, a sheepish expression on his face. She sat, grateful she could see enough to sit without falling.

The young boys halted their poking of each other for prayers, then dove into their plates of fried chicken, mashed potatoes, gravy, and biscuits, as if this might be their last meal.

Kristen took her first bite and sighed. The food tasted so wonderful. Maybe the atmosphere created by the happy family, or maybe the generous portion of fresh butter on her biscuits, or the fact that she had not eaten for many days. Whatever the reason, everything tasted amazing. Was it the time period? "Emily, your cooking is absolutely delicious."

"You got some gravy running down your chin."

"Oh." Her face grew warm as her fingers searched to swipe the mess away.

"I do like a woman who isn't afraid to eat," Jed, boomed. He looked over at his wife and wagged his bushy eyebrows.

"Jed, you're so bad," Emily grinned like a schoolgirl.

The rest of the dinner they ate and drank homemade beer. Jeffrey told stories of his time in the Mexican American war. The boys begged him to recount just how many enemy soldiers he had killed.

Jeffrey shook his head. "It's not really fun killing other people," Jeffrey said, his eyes downcast.

To Kristen, the tone of his voice almost sounded as if he spoke to her alone. For the first time, she realized that he did not want this new war. She felt for him, but knew that as a man, especially one from the South, not much could be done to avoid the war. A man's honor meant everything in this time. At least it did to a man like her husband. Her heart swelled, realizing how much she admired her newly acquired husband.

After dinner, Mr. Jenkins offered a pipe to Jeffrey. He sat in front of the fireplace and lit a smaller one for himself.

When the two boys found out that Jeffrey trained the sharp-shooter division, they pestered him until he promised to take them out shooting in the morning.

The thought of teaching an eight and ten-year-old to shoot dangerous weapons horrified Kristen. Emily and Jed smiled indulgently at their boys—approval mixed with pride.

I have to remember that I'm in a different time.

When dinner was over, the table cleared, and the dishes done, Emily wiped her hands on a dishtowel and said, "It's time for you boys to get on up to bed. The captain will expect an early start tomorrow morning."

They started to object but Jed growled a warning. "You boys mind your mama."

Looking at their mother they grinned. "Sorry, Mamma," they said in unison.

Emily turned to Kristen. "I have a spare bedroom made up for the two of you. The bed might be smaller than you're used to, but it's very comfortable."

For the first time Kristen realized that as a married couple, Emily would assume she and Jeffrey would share a bed.

"Your hospitality is gratefully accepted," Jeffrey said with a smile. "Any bed will be fine with us. After two nights on the ground, I'm sure my Mrs. will be particularly grateful."

Emily returned Jeffrey's smile, then looked to her husband. "Time you and I went to bed too, husband."

Kristen could barely see the Jenkinses but she felt the warmth flowing between the two of them.

"Just up the stairs to the right," Emily called out as she climbed the stairs. Her husband put out his pipe and followed his wife, leaving Kristen alone with Jeffrey.

"I can sleep down here." He opened his palm toward her.

Kristen shook her head. "I don't think that would be the best idea. The Jenkinses think we are as happily married as they are."

Jeffrey did not answer, but she felt sure that the sigh he gave could be heard all the way up the stairs.

"If we don't share the room they've offered us, they might take it as an insult. Maybe there's a couch in the room that one of us could sleep on."

"You can have the bed of course," Jeffrey said. He stood up and stretched. "I'm used to sleeping on the ground."

Kristen stood and faced her husband. "We're both adults, so we'll share the bed. We can act mature about this."

Jeffrey shrugged his shoulders. He offered Kristen his arm. "I'm willing to try if you are."

"Of course." She linked her arm through his. She could now see well enough to climb the stairs by herself, but she enjoyed the feel of pressing against her husband.

She breathed in the male scent of him. He smelled of horses, tobacco, and something else definitely male that excited her senses.

A handmade quilt of bright colors covered the bed with two large, down-filled pillows. As inviting as the bed looked, it was only a little larger than a twin bed.

Kristen tried not to look at Jeffrey. The room seemed to grow smaller and smaller. Her cheeks heated up, imagining his large frame sprawled across the tiny bed.

Thirty Three

"**I can sleep** on the floor," Jeffrey said.

"I already told you, that wouldn't be necessary." Kristen hoped her voice sounded steady because she felt anything but calm.

"I can help you with your dress." Jeffrey moved around behind her.

"Thanks." Kristen felt ridiculous. *How can I be feeling shy with a man I've already been intimate with?*

Wearing only the long, cotton shift left for her by Mrs. Jenkins, Kristen climbed into bed. She buried herself under the mound of blankets and closed her eyes. A gentle probe with her finger told her that the swelling had gone down, leaving her eyes almost normal. If she wanted to, she could have opened them almost all the way. She chose to keep them closed, since Jeffrey was undressing at that moment.

The bed moved as he joined her, his weight making the mattress dip down in the middle. Kristen could not help but fall into her husband's warm body. Fighting off the impulse to wrap her arms and legs around him, she gritted her teeth and pretended to sleep. *How am I going to get any rest?*

His wife's soft body lay against his rigid one. He kept his hands clasped tightly across his stomach, revisiting the urge to kiss her. His lips held a tight line, barely breathing. He almost groaned when she shifted positions in the tiny bed and rubbed up against his side. Never had he wanted her more. However, he knew better than to touch her. She could become cold and reject him at any moment, cutting him to the bone again.

Certainly, she had been different these past few weeks, and he'd tried his best to keep his feelings at arms' length. But it was becoming harder and harder to do so. Something about his wife pulled at his very soul.

Determined to resist the physical temptation Kristen presented, Jeffrey closed his eyes and willed his body to relax. His flesh ignored him. Every breath his wife took registered in his mind and his body, his desire grew until he suddenly sat up in bed and threw the covers off. He stood by the side of the bed wondering what to do about getting through the night.

"Is something wrong?" Kristen asked in a sleepy voice.

The sweetness in her voice nearly undid him. Part of Jeffrey believed her sweetness contrived, but he could feel the warmth wash over him. His body raged, while confusion ruled his mind.

"I just can't seem to sleep." He could not keep the gruffness out of his voice.

"I can't either," Kristen said. "But if you come back to bed, I promise not to toss and turn so much."

Jeffrey almost laughed out loud. Did she really think the reason he could not sleep was her fault? Because she moved too much? *No*, he wanted to say, *I like when you move around, I just want to be on top of you while you're doing it.* Instead of saying what he thought, Jeffrey just shook his head and walked to the window.

A full moon hung in the sky, sending moonbeams to light the large barn and the fields beyond. The warm air smelled of fresh grass, flowers and the promise of new life.

Jeffrey wished she could be a part of that world. How he wished he could look forward to a son or daughter to share the fortune he had acquired during his life. A strong son like one of the Jenkins's boys, or maybe a daughter with thick, dark curls like her mother.

"Are you coming back to bed?"

Shaking off his regrets, Jeffrey looked back at the bed where his wife lay. She looked so beautiful with her dark hair fanned out across the white pillow.

Had she really changed? Jeffrey did not believe a person could change so completely, but he wondered if his wife had. Was this change just wishful thinking on his part?

"I should sleep on the floor." He let out a long, weary sigh.

"I'd rather you sleep in the bed."

The tone of her voice made Jeffrey's decision easy. It held promise and an unspoken invitation. With a sigh, Jeffrey turned away from the window and slid beneath the covers again.

"I'm cold," Kristen said.

"The bed feels warm to me."

Kristen's slender arms reach out and wrapped him in a tight embrace. Her warm lips touched his neck and Jeffrey's body responded.

"Kristen, we can't—"

"Jeffrey—"

"No!" He froze. "I've used you in the past for my own base needs, but this has got to stop."

"I need to tell you something." Kristen said, her voice choking.

"What? That you found someone else, and you've been kind to me out of pity?" Even as he said the words, Jeffrey assumed that he finally knew the truth. His wife had changed, she'd fallen in love for the first time and it had softened her. Unfortunately, he should have known it would not be him. "So who is he?"

"I've no idea what you're talking about."

"The man, who is he? The one who has you acting so differently?"

"There is no other man and that isn't what I want to tell you."

Kristen's grip loosened. She pulled away from him and buried her face in the pillow. Her body shook.

He wondered if she cried because she did not know how to tell him? He'd caught her flirting with every man who glanced her way in the past. Jeffrey had never really wanted to believe that Kristen would fall in love with someone else. He believed his wife incapable of loving another human being, at least not as much as she loved herself.

"Kristen, I can take it. Just tell me the truth and we can get on with our divorce. I'm not going to hold you to me, if it's not where you want to be." Jeffrey suddenly felt very tired. *I hope I die bravely in the war, because I'm ready to go.*

"But that's not it." Kristen said, her voice muffled by the pillow. "What I have to tell you is so complicated that it's something you're never going to believe." She pulled away from him, sat up, and looked him straight in the eye.

For the first time Jeffrey noticed that the swelling had almost gone from her eyes, although they were now swollen with tears.

"I've been different for the past few weeks because I *am* different."

"You mean you decided to be someone else?" Jeffrey ignored the urge to laugh, because he could see the sincerity in her eyes.

"No," Kristen said. "What I'm trying to say is that I *am* someone else. The wife you once knew is gone and somehow, don't ask me how, I've taken her place."

"Wait a minute," Jeffrey said sitting up. "Are you trying to say that you've possessed my wife's body?" Was his wife losing her mind?

"I know it's hard to believe and you can hate me for taking advantage of you while I pretended to be your wife." Kristen cringed but continued. "I should've told you the first day and then none of this would've happened."

"Kristen, I know this has been rough on you — the war and all — but it's no reason to get so upset. We can find a good doctor for you when we get back to camp."

She slapped his hand away. "I'm not crazy, and I'd appreciate you not treating me like I *am*. I'm from the year 2018, and I'm in my third year of residency as a doctor, and the last thing I remember is lying down on a couch, and having a psychic regress me to one of my past lives."

*K*risten paused to catch her breath. She couldn't see his face in the dark room, and since he said nothing she decided to continue. "I woke up dressed in unfamiliar clothes, lying on the couch in a room filled with antiques and you sitting beside me."

The silence stretched on as her eyes adjusted to the darkness. She took a deep breath. "Do you believe me?"

Jeffrey frowned and stroked his chin. He had three-days-worth of stubble that to Kristen's eyes made him look dangerous, and if possible, even more desirable.

Time had no meaning as a rush of years spent loving this man passed like a wave over her. She could not tear her eyes away from his.

Finally, he broke the silence. "I'd like to believe you." He opened his mouth, closed it, then spoke again. "Mostly because you're my wife and I owe you at least that much." He shook his head. "But, Kristen, you look the same as you always have. We've been married for three years and we've known each other for ten. You don't look any different than you ever did although . . ."

"Yes?" Kristen arched a brow. Surely, there must be something about her inside that made the outside look slightly different.

"I just don't know, Kristen. I'm going to need proof."

How could she prove this switch to him? Then an idea formed in her mind. The previous wife had no medical knowledge. Kristen smiled as her excitement built, while she decided what to say first.

"Jeffrey, I can prove to you that I'm really a 21st century physician. Just listen." She moved her leg out from underneath the cover. She pulled up her nightgown to expose her leg. Kristen smiled at him. "Can you see?"

Clearing his throat he nodded.

"Good, I'm going to tell you what I know about the leg. First, we have the gluteus maximus," she said pointing to her bottom. "Then we have the gluteus medius, gluteus minimus, herpetiformis, obturator internus, gemellus superior, gemellus inferior, quadratus femoris, and the obturator externus."

Jeffrey blinked.

"Those are the Latin terms for the muscles of the leg." She pulled her nightgown back down. "I can continue with the entire muscular system if you'd like."

Still looking at her leg now covered with a thin cotton nightgown, Jeffrey shook his head.

"I can also name the bones of your hand," she said taking Jeffrey's hand in her own. "This is your corpus." Kristen ran a finger along his wrist.

Happily, she noted that her touch seemed to disturb him—for the better she hoped. "You have one center for each bone and they're all cartilaginous at birth. Next is the corpus, which is two centers for each bone, one per shaft, one for digital extremity, except—"

"You can see now?" Jeffrey pulled his hand away.

"Yes, Emily's medicine worked miraculously. I need to ask her what kind of herb she soaks the cucumbers in." Kristen twisted her hands in her lap.

"Either you're not lying about being a doctor, or you memorized a whole lot of Latin just to impress me." Jeffrey leaned back against the headboard. "It's not the Latin that's convincing me though," he said.

"It's not?"

"No, it's the way you treat me," Jeffrey said closing his eyes. "Even the first afternoon when you came in from riding with the governor. I took you by force and you responded with love. You made me ashamed of myself."

"Oh, Jeffrey." Kristen said moving toward him.

He moved away. "Let me say what I have to say." He ran a hand through his hair.

"I guess I knew you were different ever since that day in the parlor when you fainted. I didn't know how, and I didn't know why. I actually thought you'd invented a new way of torturing me." He lowered his voice. "I thought you wanted me to fall in love with you all over again so you could drive me out of my mind when you finally decided to tell me that it was all a sham—our marriage, your love for me, everything—nothing but an elaborate ruse to throw my love for you in my face."

Kristen wanted to cry when she heard the heartbreak in her husband's voice. All of his strength and passion had been used against him. Why? What had been his wife's reasoning? She would probably never understand, and it did not matter anyway.

"I would never do that," she said, her voice soft.

Jeffrey was silent. Time seemed to be suspended as they looked at each other. Finally, he reached out a hand to her. "I don't think you would," he said.

Kristen fell into his arms. Everything felt so right and she never wanted to leave this man who offered her his life, even under these confusing circumstances. He risked being hurt again by a woman who claimed to be from a different century and now inhabits the body of the wife he had grown to hate.

She knew that if things had been turned around, she would not have wanted to risk her heart. Her eyes filled with tears, from both sadness and the heart-wrenching happiness she now felt.

Jeffrey's strong hand stroked her back. It should have been her giving *him* comfort. His generosity astounded her. Kristen wanted to give something back to him for his belief in her, for everything he had done since she entered his life. Her body was the only language she could use to convey the depth of her feelings.

The stroking on her back intensified. Kristen responded by pressing closer to her husband's hard chest. His heart beat faster. She looked up and Jeffrey's lips moved closer. She slid her arms around his neck and kissed him like she had never kissed anyone in her entire life.

Thirty Four

*J*effrey fell off an emotional cliff. His head buzzed and his body burned as his lips met those of his wife. He knew this relationship with Kristen represented home. No longer concerned about the reasons why his wife had become suddenly different. What did it matter? Tomorrow she could cut his throat for all he cared, just as long as he had her tonight.

As his hands rose up her neck, he could feel her slender, delicate throat, fragile in spite of her tough talking. He could actually see himself starting a life with her—at least the woman she was now.

More than anything, he wanted to believe the story his wife had just told him. He wanted nothing more than to send up a silent prayer to heaven to give thanks for his good fortune, no matter how it had come about.

The universe could be a strange place. Maybe he should not question it.

Moving down from her throat, he pulled the neck of the night-gown she wore down over her shoulders until she was naked to the waist. The moon created just enough light for him to see her clearly.

Jeffrey felt himself start to lose control. He gritted his teeth and buried his face in her hair. The lavender scent wafting up from her velvety soft curls only made it more difficult to get his senses under control again.

With his control at the breaking point, Jeffrey moved his

mouth lower until it found his wife's breasts. Nestled between them, he felt something cold and hard against his mouth. He stopped and looked up at his wife.

"You're wearing the locket."

"Why wouldn't I?" Kristen said, her voice barely above a whisper.

"Because you told me you hated having any kind of remembrance of me." The memory made Jeffrey's chest tighten.

"I did?" Kristen gave a little chuckle. "I'm not that woman, remember? I love having you near my heart."

In that moment Jeffrey truly felt that the woman in his arms might not be the woman he had married. For some reason, known only to fate, he'd been given a second chance. He could love the woman in his arms with all his heart, unafraid of what she would do with that love.

His heart constricted. Surely, he had been granted a precious gift and he intended to enjoy it while it lasted.

With a sigh, Jeffrey determined to show God how much he appreciated the gesture. He vowed to love his wife with every ounce of his being, for as long as he lived. Maybe the war would cut that time short, but with whatever he had left he would love her as no woman had been loved before.

When morning came, Jeffrey still held onto his wife. He felt her awaken as the bright sun came through the window. His body re-awakened with desire by the hands she ran over him.

Jeffrey thought he might die of pleasure from her touch. Never had he felt so much for a woman. Only the rumbling of his stomach, lying in her arms an hour later, reminded him that he had not gone to heaven, and had duties to perform.

"If I hadn't believed you were someone else last night when you first told me," Jeffrey said, "then I surely do after this morning."

Snuggling into her husband's arms, Kristen sighed. "What made you finally realize that I was someone new?"

Jeffrey tightened his hold on her. "You might be crazy, but you *are* my wife, no matter what the circumstances."

"I am?" Kristen sat up in bed. The covers fell away from her, leaving her gloriously naked.

Jeffrey found it hard to breathe. A soft knock on the door broke the spell. He ground his teeth. "Yes?"

"You folks ready for breakfast?" Emily Jenkins called out.

"We'll be down in a minute," Jeffrey said.

Kristen frowned. "Why didn't you tell her we'd be down in half an hour?"

"Wife! We can't keep our hosts waiting." Throwing the covers off, Jeffrey took one last look at her before sliding out of bed to put on the clothes he had left lying neatly folded on the floor the night before.

Kristen came to stand beside him as he buttoned his shirt.

"You really need to get dressed and stop distracting me."

With a smile, she went to where her own clothes lay. "I'll need help."

Taking a deep breath, Jeffrey steeled his resolve and started to button up the back of Kristen's dress. He hoped there would *be* a future for them, where time would not be a luxury. He concentrated on fastening her buttons, instead of tearing them open again.

Thirty Five

Kristen loved the sound of the noisy breakfast table. The two boys tore into their breakfast as if it would be their last. For the first time in her life she realized she wanted children. She glanced over at Jeffrey and smiled, picturing what a child with him would look like.

Maybe a boy would come first, with hair as black as a raven's wing and eyes as intense as his father's. It would be wonderful to have a sweet girl, with curly black hair, wearing the same determined look as her father's, when he concentrated on a task.

She smiled and put a hand on her flat stomach. Lost in her daydreams, she did not notice that everyone stopped talking. Even the two boys had stopped teasing each other. All eyes focused on her.

"What?"

"Is everything all right?" Emily said. "You're not sick, are you?"

From the look Emily gave her hand lying across her stomach, Kristen guessed the woman's thoughts. Apparently, so could everyone else because laughter erupted around the table.

"Are you going to have a baby?" One of the boys asked.

Her face grew hot. Kristen stole a look at Jeffrey. His face had gone white. *Does he not want children?*

Kristen shook her head, giving a weak smile. What could she say? Jeffrey did not want children with her. She was not even the woman he married, and with children he would be trapped with

215

her forever.

Why didn't I take precautions? Can I even do that in this day and time. But if I get pregnant, I'll be changing history. Why didn't I think of that?

From now on, she would have to use some sort of birth control. From the look on Jeffrey's face, he wanted her to use something too. He did not appear as if he wanted any children. Sadness washed over Kristen for what might have been.

After that uncomfortable moment, the table talk picked up again. When the boys finished, they followed their father out the door. Kristen caught their excited chatter over whose turn it was to milk the cows.

"I have your dress washed," Emily said. She stood up to clear the table. "I hung it by the fireplace overnight, so it's almost dry now."

"That was so kind of you," Kristen said and then her mouth dropped open. "Oh, no!"

"Kristen, what's wrong?" Jeffrey said turning to stare.

"I had something in the pocket." Kristen's stomach lurched and she quickly stood. "May I see my dress?"

"Certainly," Emily said with a puzzled look on her face. "I'm just about to hang the laundry on the clothesline."

"Kristen?" Jeffrey reached for her arm.

"I'll tell you in a minute." Kristen pulled out of Jeffrey's grasp and hurrying after Mrs. Jenkins.

In the washroom, Kristen picked up her dress from the basket of wet clothes. Her frantic search through the pockets came up empty.

Mrs. Jenkins frowned as she watched Kristen. "Are you looking for something?"

"Oh, just a piece of paper," Kristen said in a distracted voice. It was gone. Somehow she had lost the note she had stolen from Terrence that told of the Union army's next move. Now everything she had been through was for nothing.

Jeffrey came up behind her frowning. "What's wrong?" He turned Kristen around.

"I can't believe I was so careless." Her eyes filled with tears.

"It can't be that important," Jeffrey said. "Let's just worry about getting back to camp."

"You can't believe just how important this is," Kristen whispered under her breath, watching Mrs. Jenkins gather the clothes to hang outside to dry. "I stole the Union Army's plan for their next attack!"

"You mean this?" Jeffrey held up the piece of paper she had been searching for.

Kristen stared in disbelief. "How did you—?"

"Let's just say it's safe, and we need to get the information to General Beauregard as soon as possible."

She glared at Jeffrey, but he spun on his heel and left her alone with Mrs. Jenkins.

With a sigh, Kristen turned her attention to her confused hostess and smiled. "Let me help you with those." She took the basket.

Together, the two women spent the morning hanging clothes on a line that stretched between the house and a large, graceful oak with spreading branches.

As soon as Kristen's clothes dried in the hot afternoon sun and they packed some food for the journey, they readied the Jenkins's horse for their departure. Without Diablo they would have to ride together again, because the Jenkinses could not afford to loan them any more of their horses.

After thanking their hosts and kissing each of the boys, Kristen mounted behind Jeffrey on the horse. He rode in silence urging the horse forward, so she wrapped her arms around his waist and held onto him.

They did not speak for nearly an hour. Kristen leaned against Jeffrey's wide back and closed her eyes, exhausted from having barely slept the night before. Those thoughts brought back such passionate memories she wondered if Jeffrey could feel the increased heat of her body through his thin, cotton shirt.

What had changed? Why was he being so distant? On those thoughts, Kristen fell asleep. In her dream she saw her husband surrounded by their children. The horse came to a sudden halt. She jerked awake, grabbing tightly at Jeffery's shirt to keep from sliding off.

"We'll stop here, but only to eat," Jeffrey said in a tight voice.

"Sure." Kristen shook her head, trying to clear the sleep fog. Visions of happy, dark-haired, blue-eyed children filled her with happy thoughts. She put a hand on her waist.

"Are you all right?" Jeffrey said.

"Of course, why do you ask?" Kristen frowned.

"We have to get back to camp." Jeffrey did not answer her question. "The message you stole is very important."

"Good, that means that my spying was a good idea."

He turned to her and his eyes narrowed. "The message is important. For you to put yourself in danger was not a good idea."

"But we wouldn't have that message if I hadn't been a spy."

"Look, Kristen, we have many people spying for us, and yes, a lot of them are women. That doesn't mean someone like you should be doing it," he said, his eyes narrowing. "Do you realize how easily you could have made a mistake?"

"But I didn't."

"Only because I got you out before you had a chance to."

"I handled it just fine." Kristen put her hands on her hips and glared at him. "I made it through medical school, so believe me, I can handle the 19th century."

Jeffrey gave a short laugh. "Like you handled the bees?"

Kristen's mouth dropped open to protest, but she closed it and reconsidered for a moment. "In my time, we have a civilized way of getting honey. We buy it in the grocery store—in a jar."

"Oh?" A smile lifted Jeffrey's lips. "I suppose you have all your food already cooked?"

"No, not all of it."

"Good, then you know that we need firewood to cook the food that the Jenkinses gave us."

Kristen turned on her heel and headed toward a small patch of trees. She knelt to gather branches to start a fire. How did he always turn things around on her?

Around Jeffrey she felt like a naughty child instead of the well-trained doctor she would be in her own time. She picked up branches, breaking them into smaller pieces with more fury than necessary. She looked around for more. A sudden movement caught her eye, but before she could turn around, something wet dropped into her hair.

Dropping the branches she so carefully gathered, she cursed and ran back toward the road where she left Jeffrey. Whatever had wrapped around her hair had let go, but was now running after her. She heard the pounding behind her and felt the hot breath on her back. Kristen ran for Jeffrey, screaming. When she saw him she collapsed into his arms.

Thirty Six

*J*effrey dropped Kristen to the ground and reached up to catch the horse with both hands. "Easy, boy."

Kristen pushed herself off the ground spitting out grass and dirt. "Why did you drop me?"

Jeffrey ignored her as he tried to catch hold of Diablo's bridle. "Easy, boy, everything's just fine. You're going to be all right now."

"Well I'm not going to be all right. You just dumped me onto the ground!" Kristen got to her feet and brushed off her clothes.

Jeff turned from his horse with a sheepish expression. "I had to catch my horse."

"I can see that." Kristen arched an eyebrow. "I'm happy you were successful."

"Well, I'm sorry," Jeffrey said continuing to rub his horse's forehead. "Thanks for finding him for me."

"Sure, anytime." Kristen walked up to the big horse and looked him in the eye. "You didn't have to scare me to death," she whispered into his twitching ear.

"We can get back to camp by nightfall now," Jeffrey said. "I'll ride Diablo bareback, and you can ride the Jenkins's horse."

Disappointed to not be riding on the same horse next to her husband, she consoled herself with thoughts of sleeping under the stars with Jeffrey. She smiled at the big horse.

*H*appy to have his horse back, Jeffrey rode in content the rest of the way. Once he and Kristen reached the army camp, he sent one of his men to the Jenkins's farm to deliver their horse.

General Beauregard learned the Yankee's movement thanks to Kristen's stolen note delivered by Jeffrey. Later, other spies, and local newspaper articles confirmed the Union Troops movements. Their next move would be a small creek called Bull Run. The Confederate Army would wait there to fight the first real battle of the War Between the States. General Beauregard had been in charge of the soldiers that were taken at Fort Sumter, the battle that had started the war. Now he supervised the troops who would fight the first battle.

Excitement permeated the air, recruits placing bets on how long it would take for the Yankees to start running once they recognize the force of the Confederate Army. Everyone enjoyed the diversion except Kristen. She remained in her tent with her roommate, not her preferred companion.

Amy barely showed, yet she glowed with happiness. Her young husband told his wife that the war would be over just as soon as the officers let him have a go at the Yankees. Kristen wanted to cry when she heard such talk. She prayed Amy would not become a young widow with the child.

July 20, 1861, the battle would start tomorrow. Kristen could hardly believe she would witness history as a participant.

In the weeks since she and Jeffrey had returned to camp, she had been unable to talk with him alone. She cooked for the officers during the day, while her nights seemed long and lonely without Jeffrey. That one glorious night spent with him at the Jenkins's place, made her feel more lost and alone without him. Memories flooded her mind at the most inopportune moments.

Just the other night Kristen had mistaken the wrong man for Jeffrey, whispering her desire into the man's ear. When the officer turned, showing her mistake, she dropped the hot potato she held onto ground.

Jeffrey finally entered the tent, but Kristen had not noticed him until he finished eating his food and stood to leave. She had missed a chance to talk to him.

For the life of her, she could not understand why Jeffrey had suddenly turned cold toward her. After the night of passion they shared, she had been certain she would find happiness with her husband. Could it be possible that he actually thought her crazy after her confession?

Tomorrow the first battle would be fought, and Kristen wanted at least to talk to him one last time. Determined to find Jeffrey, she took off her apron and handed it to Amy.

"I've got to go," she said, ignoring her friend's worried look.

One of the women next to Amy nodded. "She needs to see her husband. She might not see him again after tomorrow."

Kristen did not hear anything as she fled the tent. Her thoughts focused on the sight of her husband and the nagging question. *Why does he behave as if he hates me?*

Wandering the fields, she walked past some enlisted men gathered around their fires and cooking their own meals. For men about to enter their first battle, Kristen thought they seemed far more cheerful than she would expect. Kristen's heart tugged at how young many of the soldiers appeared. Their youthful faces so smooth of whiskers, a few recruits actually tried without success to grow some sort of beard. She smiled at the young men she passed, knowing that tomorrow she might be patching up their young bodies with nineteenth-century tools and skills. The more men she saw, the more depressed she became until she finally found Jeffrey off by himself, nearly hidden in a copse of trees. She burst into tears.

"Kristen, what's wrong?" He took her into his arms.

"Everything!" Kristen wailed. "All those men—all those young boys might be going off to die tomorrow, and there's nothing I can do to stop them!" She sobbed into her husband's shirt. Mixed in with her grief, she could not help but notice how wonderful her husband's hard chest felt against her wet cheek, and how enticing he smelled.

"Kristen, this is war. It's what men do. We fight for what we believe in."

"Well it's stupid!" Kristen drew back from Jeffrey's chest. "Don't you know what's going to happen? Thousands are going to die!"

"There's nothing to be done," he said, his voice gentle.

"I know." She tried in vain to dry her tears with the sleeve of her dress. "But it's such a stupid waste!"

Jeffrey sighed and wrapped his arms around her again. Their eyes met. She raised her mouth up to meet his, stunned to have him turn his head away. Hurt beyond belief, Kristen tried to catch her breath.

"You need to get back to your tent," Jeffrey said in a gruff voice.

"Just like that?" Kristen said, hoping her voice would not betray her feelings. "You could be killed tomorrow and you can't even say goodbye properly?"

"I need to be with my men tonight."

"Instead of your wife?"

Jeffrey took a deep breath. "I can't take the chance of you getting pregnant," he said at last. "You don't want children. You've made that abundantly clear."

"I haven't said anything on the subject." Kristen narrowed her eyes, glaring at her husband. "You still don't believe that I've changed. That I'm someone completely different."

"Would you believe me if I told you the same thing?"

She realized that Jeffrey was right. How could she ask him to accept a story as outlandish as the one she'd told him? "I would love to have your child," Kristen said at last, breaking the silence.

Jeffrey did not answer at first. He just continued staring down at her.

Kristen wished she could read his thoughts. Did he think she at least changed somewhat from the woman she had read about in the diary? Certainly, that woman wanted no children. She must have broken her husband's heart again and again. Now she asked Jeffrey to trust her one more time. Would he? Should he?

She received her answer in a crushing kiss that took her breath away. Kristen found herself being consumed by the kiss, branded as if he demanded an answer from her. She kissed him back with all the passion burning in her heart.

Jeffrey pressed her against the rough bark of a thick tree. She wrapped her arms around his neck, melting into his embrace and growing impassioned by his touch.

Kristen wanted him with a greater need than she had ever felt before. She had always maintained some control in part of herself, as a woman was expected to. Now, she just required Jeffery to be as close to her as possible. Her entire mind, body, and soul wanted him in a way that both frightened and soothed her.

Jeffrey groaned and pulled her away from the tree. His hands found the buttons on the back of her dress, unfastening it in only seconds. He pushed the thin cotton away from her back, running his rough hands over her body. Kristen shivered with delight. For just a second, it was not enough.

Jeffrey's hands moved up her neck and pulled the material of her dress down, further exposing her to the moonlight. Kristen threw her head back and moaned out loud.

A voice in the darkness startled them. "Pardon me, Captain O'Connor, sir."

Jeffrey pulled Kristen up against his chest with one hand and tried to gather up her dress with the other. "Yes, Sergeant Randall?"

Kristen could hardly make out the figure in the darkness only a few feet away. The sergeant kept as far away as possible, but the tension in his voice indicated that he had guessed what he interrupted.

"The men are waiting for you, sir."

"I'll be right there."

The figure turned and melted into the darkness.

Kristen laughed. "You think he saw anything?"

Jeffrey frowned, pulling her dress up. "I'm not sure what he might've seen, but I do think he understood the basic idea."

Turning her around, Jeffrey did up the tiny buttons on the back of her dress and then turned her back to face him. "As you can see, I can't resist you," he said in a serious voice. "So I guess I'm going to have to trust the story that you've told me."

Kristen grinned. "Thank you for trusting me. I don't know how or why this is happening, but I do know that I love you.

Please, trust me, and let us enjoy what time we have left together."

"Meet me in one hour in my tent."

"One hour." Kristen reached up and kissed him on the cheek. She almost skipped back to her own tent to collect her clothes for the night with her husband. Amy smiled when she entered the tent.

"You look happier than I've seen you all week." Amy grinned. "I guess that means you've been with your handsome husband."

"That's right." Kristen hugged herself. "And I'm spending the night with him tonight, so you if you want to have anyone over tonight..."

Amy's smile grew wider. "Now that's a very good idea." She frowned. "You don't think it would be bad for the baby, do you?"

"No I don't, so just enjoy yourself."

With not much time, Kristen packed just a few things — her hair brush and a toothbrush, along with her nightclothes.

Hopefully I won't need any pajamas.

This would probably be their last night together, since the war officially started tomorrow. Wanting to make it count but sadness intruded on her excitement. Determined to live in the moment, she shoved all of her unhappy thoughts aside.

Waiting to join Jeffrey, Kristen combed Amy's long, tightly-curled hair, which had grown nearly to the young woman's waist. With her golden skin and huge dark eyes, Kristen thought she could be one of the most beautiful women she had ever seen.

"Tell me about your life, like where you grew up," Kristen said to Amy kneeling down in front of her.

Amy cocked her head to one side. "It was good. Very good. We always had the best of everything on the plantation. My mama wore beautiful clothes, and her hair wasn't kinky and curly like mine."

"I'm sure she was a lovely woman." Kristen lifted a hand full of Amy's hair. "Would you like me to French braid it for you?"

"Is that different from a regular braid?"

"Just a little." Kristen separated the long strands, weaving them in and out of each other to create a smooth French braid. When she finished she tied a ribbon at the end.

Shouting outside the tent caught both of their attentions, they turned.

"What's going on?" Amy asked.

Before either woman could react, Sergeant Randall burst through the doors of the tent. "Sorry to interrupt, but there's been an accident."

"Jeffrey?" Kristen said even as her heart told her the truth.

"Yes, ma'am. The men were getting a little carried away, and one of them accidentally shot Captain O'Connor."

"Carried away?" Kristen cried out, her heart fluttering. She needed to know more, but found that her throat had constricted and she could not speak.

Amy recovered first. "How bad is it?"

The sergeant hesitated for a moment.

Finding her voice, Kristen stared the man down. "What exactly happened to my husband?"

"Well...I don't know exactly, ma'am. You see, the captain was shot in the leg—"

"Oh thank God, that's going to be all right." Kristen's panic left her as her medical training took over. "Take me to him."

"The captain told me just to tell you that he had been shot, he wants you to stay right where you are. The camp doctor is with him now."

"Now you listen, and listen carefully, sergeant. The camp doctor is an incompetent drunk. If you don't take me to your captain there's a chance that the idiot will kill my husband, and you'll be the one I'll hold personally responsible."

The young soldier hesitated for only a moment. "Right this way."

Kristen and Amy hurried after the young sergeant. All of the tents looked the same, but she guessed from the men gathered outside one of them that she had found the right one.

Pushing past the men crowded around the tent opening, Kristen slipped inside the tent. The scene before her almost shocked her out of her training. Jeffrey lay on a cot, naked to the waist, his right leg covered in blood. The doctor leaned over him with a dirty saw in his hands, about to take off her husband's leg. Two burly soldiers held Jeffrey down.

"Stop!" Kristen shouted.

Everyone in the tent turned to look. "Are you drunk?" She could smell the whiskey wafting off the doctor as if he bathed in it. "And what are you about to do to my husband?"

"Save his life, ma'am. Now you get out of here before I have to have one of the men drag you out." He motioned with his head to the soldiers holding her husband down. "Put that woman outside."

At first, no one moved.

"Get that woman out of here!" the doctor yelled in a slurred voice.

"You will not operate on my husband in your condition. You will not so much as put a bandage on him!" Kristen shouted back.

"I said, get this woman out now!" The doctor lifted the saw into position again.

Kristen rushed forward, grabbing the doctor's arm. "You will take your saw and get out of here." She turned to one of the soldiers at the head of the cot. "You need to get them out of here so I can get to work saving your captain." She put every bit of trained authority into her voice.

The soldier hesitated. Jeffrey opened his eyes and stared up at Kristen. She could see the pain along with the trust that he held in her abilities, though he had not much reason to believe in her.

In a weak voice he said, "Private Oldfield. Do as my wife says."

The giant of a man let go of Jeffrey and lumbered toward the doctor. The doctor gave a disgusted snort and dropped the saw on the ground. "It's your funeral." He muttered, turning to leave the tent.

Once outside the tent the doctor yelled, "If she kills the captain, I'll have her thrown in the brink."

Chills ran down Kristen's spine, not from what the doctor said, but the look of trust she had seen in Jeffrey's eyes. He closed them now, leaving her to do her work.

In a modern hospital, Kristen knew she would have a good chance of pulling Jeffrey through this with only a hairline scar. But here in the 1860s, she had only a fifty-fifty chance of saving his leg because the chances of infection were so high.

"I need boiling water." Kristen shouted without turning.

The water arrived in a coffee pot. She found a doctor's bag with instruments next to the bed. Among them she located a reasonably sharp-looking scalpel. She placed the scalpel in the water and turned to face a terrified soldier. He looked impossibly young but responded to her orders as if she were the general. "I'll need some laudanum. Can you get me some from the hospital?"

The soldier hesitated for a moment, his Adam's apple moving up and down.

"Do you need to say something?" Kristen said.

"I'm not sure the doctor's going to give me any," the soldier said, his voice almost a whisper.

Kristen took a deep breath, cursing under her breath. The boy was probably right. She looked around the tent, spotted a bottle of whiskey and grabbed it. She looked down at her husband. "You're gonna have to drink as much of this is you can."

Jeffrey's eyes fluttered open as she raised his head and put the bottle to his lips.

"Jeffrey, can you hear me?"

His lips moved against the bottle. Kristen poured the liquor onto his lips. His throat convulsed as he swallowed.

"That's good." She stroked her husband's cheek. "I'm going to have to get the fragments out of your leg so you don't get an infection."

Jeffrey swallowed more of the whiskey, then closed his eyes again. Kristen would have a very short time to work before her husband regained full consciousness.

"Step back," she said to the soldiers gathering around her. "And you." She pointed to the young soldier at her side. "Hold that lantern higher."

She washed the wound with a small cloth soaked in boiling water. Lead shot peppered his leg from his upper knee to the top of his thigh. Wiping away the blood and dirt, Kristen put the wet cloth aside and took the scalpel from the water. It gleamed faintly in the lantern's dim light.

She had performed surgery before during her residency. The emergency room of the Seattle hospital where she had trained provided many opportunities to work on gunshot wounds.

However, it had not prepared her to cut into the flesh of the person she loved. How she could bear laying the sharp edge of a knife into his flesh, even to save his life? Her shaking hands plunged into the first one hole. Her husband's groan in his groggy state did not help her nerves.

Focusing all of her energy on the job at hand, Kristen put everything out of her mind except extracting of every piece of lead she could see, or feel. The shot had scattered, which made the process long and tedious. Hours passed until finally she no longer required a lantern. Rays of the rising sun shone through the open flaps of the tent. When she put down her tools, her eyes burned and her hands shook from fatigue.

Using the strong lye soap the soldiers supplied, she cleaned up the area where she worked on Jeffrey and wrapped a clean bandage around his leg. She staggered backwards to survey her work.

The young soldier holding the lantern caught her in his arms.

"I'm all right." Kristen wiped her forehead.

"Am I going to live?" Jeffrey croaked.

"Oooh! How long have you been awake?" She gazed at him, wide-eyed.

"For a while now."

Kristen could not imagine the pain that he must have endured.

"I think I'm going to live," Jeffrey said, giving a weak smile.

She nodded, tears running down her cheeks. "I'm so sorry."

"For saving my life?" Jeffrey said.

"I just wish I could've given you something so that you wouldn't have felt the pain."

"Don't fret, wife. You did what you had to do." He sat, then looked down at his leg. Raising his head again, he looked Kristen in the eye and whispered, "You really *were* telling the truth, weren't you?"

Her mouth trembled as she tried to smile. "Yes, I was."

"Then I guess I've fallen in love with another woman," Jeffrey said tracing the trail of tears that streaked down her cheeks.

She wished she could remain in that moment forever, but a voice from behind interrupted her.

"You killed him, didn't you?" said the doctor in a gruff voice.

"No." Kristen spun around to face her accuser. "I did *not* kill him. But you, sir, just might have."

"Young lady," said Dr. Vogler almost growling the words. "I am the doctor in charge of this camp. Since you didn't kill this man—" He glanced over at Jeffrey. "—who is your husband, I guess you can work for me."

Kristen raised an eyebrow in surprise.

"If," the doctor said, "you do exactly as I say."

The air in the tent buzzed with tension. Kristen took a deep breath. "I will work for you, if you refrain from drinking before you operate."

With his blazing red face and hair to match, Dr. Vogler looked as though on fire. Kristen knew she had gone too far, but she would not let anyone endanger the lives of these young soldiers. She had taken an oath to do no harm. She meant to honor that oath, even if it meant losing her job again.

"This war is going to get ugly, just as they all do," Dr. Vogler said. "If I didn't need every available hand that I could get, I wouldn't even consider you at all. As it stands, the battle tomorrow will bring wounds to a great many men. You need to be in the hospital tent in one hour, which is when they'll start coming in." The doctor turned on his heel and left the tent, nearly knocking it over when his head caught the upper left support at the entrance.

"Sounds like it's going to be a good working relationship," Jeffrey whispered with a pained grin.

"He's more arrogant than the surgeons I've worked for in my time," Kristen said in a whisper. "They only thought they were God. Dr. Vogler is certain that he is." Kristen frowned at Jeffrey swinging his legs over the cot to place his feet on the floor. "And where do you think you're going?"

"Today is the day of the first battle. My place is with my men."

Kristen's mouth dropped open. When she finally found her voice, she shouted, "You aren't going anywhere! Did you forget that you just had surgery?"

Standing on his good leg, Jeffrey shook his head for a moment as if to clear it. "I'll admit that I've felt better, but it's my duty to be with my men today."

"But you can't!" Kristen stomped her foot.

Jeffrey scorched her with an expression that indicated nothing she could say or do would stop him. He moved toward her, holding out his arms. Kristen fell into them, but drew back when he staggered against her weight.

"Thank you for all that you've done for me," he whispered into her ear. "I love you."

Kristen shivered at his words. She had saved his life only to possibly lose him during the upcoming battle. Sobbing, she buried her face against his chest. He stroked her back.

"Good luck." She pulled back and gazed into her husband's beautiful, blue eyes

"I've had some very good luck for the past two months," Jeffrey said with a grin. "I'm quite sure it's going to last."

"You can't know that!" Kristen threw up her hands. "Didn't you get hit before the Yankees even fired a shot?"

Jeffrey shrugged. "My bad luck is out of the way now." He gave Kristen a gentle shove. "Now help me get dressed, woman, unless you want the Yankees to be shooting at a naked man."

Kristen found her eyes moving downward. She quickly brought them up to see Jeffrey grinning at her. "You are a disgusting man!"

"Give me my uniform, and I'll be more to your liking," he said with a laugh.

"Oh, I kind of like you this way."

"Captain O'Connor?"

"Come in, Sergeant Randall." Jeffrey pulled the sheet up around his waist.

"The general says the Yankees await us. In fact the whole town seems to be waiting." Sergeant Randall hesitated for a moment.

"Go on." Jeffrey motioned with his free hand.

"Well…" the sergeant said. "Seems there's a picnic going on near the creek. The Yankees from town are all gathering around to watch the battle like it's some sort of entertainment, especially for them."

"Don't they know this is a war?" Kristen said.

Jeffrey shook his head. "They will by the end of the day."

Thirty Seven

Kristen ate her breakfast and listened to the excited talk of the officers. Her heart beat so fast, she could not finish the mush sitting in front of her. She knew General McDowell took four days to reach Bull Run with the Union Army. The Confederate Army had formed an eight-mile line along the creek where the men waited. Jeffrey had left on horseback to lead his men. Now, Kristen waited inside the hospital tent for the wounded men to start arriving.

Would he make it through the battle? And if he did, would he make it through the next four years? She remembered enough about the Civil War to know that it would be a long, bloody fight. *How do I lose him?*

Kristen pushed the bowl of cornmeal away and drained her coffee mug. *I'm going to need more than this if I'm going to sit ringside to the only Civil War ever fought on American soil.*

Despite her dreams of becoming a doctor, she realized for the first time that a career could not replace the other aspects of life she had neglected. Finding love was certainly one of them. Being part of something larger than herself always meant practicing medicine. Kristen now understood family and the love of a good man should also have a place in her life. Life demanded balance. Would she do things differently when she got back to her own time? Once the Civil War started in earnest, would she find herself waking up on the couch in the TV studio?

Kristen ran her hands through her hair and tried not to think

233

about her future, time regression or time travel, or whatever she had done to end up here. The unknown possibilities just complicated her thoughts and her ability to cope with the present.

"Mind if I join you?"

Kristen turned and found Nurse Bitterman standing over her. "I'd love company." She moved over on the bench.

"This waiting is hell."

Kristen sighed. "I don't know if I can bear a single one of those sweet boys coming back all shot up."

"It's what we do." Nurse Bitterman frowned. "Men have to prove their bravery by killing each other and women have to put them back together so they can go out and do it all over again. If we're lucky, after this, they'll wait a generation before starting another war." The nurse looked her up and down. "I must say, you look far better dressed as a woman."

"Thanks." Kristen smoothed out her dress, already stiff with her husband's blood. "I would've changed after the operation, but what's the use?" She shrugged.

"Would've been a waste," Nurse Bitterman agreed. "No use giving the wash women more to do. Once the fighting starts, there'll be plenty to keep them busy." Her eyes closed for a moment as if in prayer. "Mostly washing out the blood."

"I don't even want to think about it." Kristen stood. "May I bring you more coffee?"

The older woman nodded, holding out her empty mug.

*A*lmost seven a.m. on that Sunday the officers left the tent to give last-minute instructions to their troops. Many had gathered in small groups to pray.

Jeffrey sat on his horse looking down at the creek dividing the two forces. Having fought in the Mexican-American war, he had no illusions regarding this battle. His men, mostly young and untested, would learn the brutality of war today. So far they had learned to march, shoot straight, and wear a uniform to impress the ladies.

His men stood in their ranks, some even joking about how

long it would take until the Yankees ran back north. Jeffrey steeled himself to endure the upcoming battle. You go to war because you have to, not because you want to be involved. In his younger days, he might have enjoyed fighting his fellow man in a bloodlust that would fade, leaving behind only death and destruction. But not today.

Diablo whinnied and moved restlessly under him. The movement against his leg sent knife jabs of pain up his thigh. He ignored the discomfort, though his forehead dripped with sweat. The cool morning grew warmer, along with the excitement of the men.

Sergeant Randall rode his chestnut mare over to Jeffrey. With a salute, he said, "Captain O'Connor?"

"Yes?" Jeffrey ran a hand over his thigh—fever-hot to the touch, even through his trousers.

"Are you all right, sir?"

Jeffrey frowned. Did he look weak? He did not feel that tired, but the night had been a long one. "I'm fine, Sergeant."

Sergeant Randall nodded and turned to face the creek and the troops that formed a line on each side. The sharpshooters had positioned themselves high on a hill overlooking the creek, their guns aimed and ready to fire.

Giving his first officer a look, Jeffrey noticed for the first time that Randall's hands shook. As well they should be, Jeffrey thought. He smiled at the younger man. "Any man who isn't scared out of his wits right now is a fool," he whispered under his breath.

"Captain?" Randall turned.

"It wasn't important," Jeffrey said. He pulled a watch from his pocket. The time showed nearly nine a.m. Something would happen soon, he could feel it.

A line of blue-clad soldiers emerged from across the creek. Rifles from the Confederate Army pointed at them. Jeffrey raised his sword for his men to commence firing, which they did with great enthusiasm.

Many Yankees fell and had to be carried back to their fellow soldiers. Some soldiers greeted the reality of war by becoming physically ill. Still they marched forward, spurred on by their leaders. Smoke filled the air as soldiers on both sides reloaded and fired over and over. Each man's face grew black from the powder. Some had streaks of white showing, where tears ran down their cheeks. Screams of excitement and pain echoed in the air from both sides as the armies clashed.

Jeffrey kicked Diablo forward, leading his men into the thick of the fighting. The young soldiers fought valiantly. It tore at Jeffrey's soul to lead his men against soldiers who could have been their neighbors, but they had to kill or be killed. He would sort out his feelings later—if he lived. For the first time in many years he wanted to live. If he could have changed things, he would have taken his wife away from this hell—maybe out west to try his hand at ranching. But it was too late to change his actions now.

Wiping everything from his mind except his men Jeffrey yelled, urging them into the line of blue coats bent on killing them.

*T*he hospital filled fast. Dr. Vogler shouted orders for more bandages, more laudanum, and more help to set up cots. Kristen had never seen so many injured bodies at one time before. The day dragged on as the fight continued. She received reports from some of the wounded men receiving attention. It did not sound good for the Confederate side. The men who had been at the front told her that the losses from the South exceeded those from the North.

Not surprised, because Kristen had already known how it would turn out. She knew that the South would lose the war by 1865, and she also knew Lincoln would be shot. What good would such knowledge do? She could not change anything.

Without a word, she cleaned up the wound on a soldier's stomach. She knew it would kill him, if not today, then a week from now when his ruptured intestines infected the rest of his body. He could die now, in relatively little pain with laudanum bringing him relief from his pain, or later when all the painkillers would be gone and the infection would swell in his belly like a balloon.

"Am I going to be all right, ma'am?" The young man asked, in a heavy Irish accent.

Rather than be honest, Kristen smiled and nodded. Her throat swelled with swallowed tears, making it impossible to speak. She moved on to the next patient.

The young man brought to her on a cot had most of his leg blown off. Someone had tied a belt around his upper leg to try and stop the bleeding.

"You won't have to cut up my leg, will you?" said the boy with a face covered in innocent looking freckles. His blue eyes opened wide with terror as she ripped the remaining cloth of his pant leg off.

Kristen's throat now felt as if she had swallowed a basketball. "Let's hope not," she forced out in a low voice.

The boy tried to smile. It quickly disappeared at the sound of a handsaw biting into bone, coming from behind a nearby curtain.

Kristen washed and dressed the wound, then wrapped it in a bandage before moving to the next patient. With nothing more she could do for him, she moved on. She could not handle watching him get his leg removed in such a crude manner. Tears burned her eyes as she sought to help another soldier who had just been brought in.

*T*he smoke, noise, and general confusion made it so that Jeffrey could barely see what happened around him. The colors of the men's uniforms had become so black with musket powder, sweat, and dirt, that a person could not differentiate which side a person belonged on, or who had shot at whom.

Jeffrey found it impossible to keep his men together. The beautiful spring morning had turned dark. Men shouted and bodies dropped, only to be stepped over by others who would later join the growing pile of wounded. The intensified fighting washed the creek in red from all the spilled blood, as if the creek were a giant artery of the earth herself.

Hours later, when it looked as if the Yankees would win the

day, General McDowell waved his white-gloved hand in victory. The Northerners on a nearby hill cheered. Surely they had just beaten the South, and the war had ended with this battle.

Jeffrey tried to rally his men to continue the battle but a wave of their fellow Southern soldiers, coming toward them in retreat, swept his men away. Diablo reared up at the men pushing against him in their haste to get to safety. Jeffery pressed his thighs against the saddle to hold his seat. A greater pain shot through his leg, his pant leg growing wet with blood as the stitches tore apart.

Yelling at the top of his lungs, he encouraged his men to hold and fight. It did not change the direction of their hasty retreat. In an enormous wave, his men ran from the line of Union soldiers, who outnumbered and outgunned them. Jeffrey turned away from the front line and withdrew from the battle. He needed to gather his men to fight another day.

Turning, he glanced at a nearby hill and saw an incredible sight. On top, in the middle of the Confederate line, a man on horseback stood firm with the soldiers gathered around him. Jeffrey recognized the Virginia flag and the leader—Thomas J. Jackson. Hundreds of Confederate soldiers ran past General Jackson as the man sat on his horse looking toward the Union forces as if no bullet could harm him. To Jeffrey it looked as if the man could hold the entire Southern forces by his sheer will alone.

Jeffrey shouted at his men and pointed at the general with his Virginia company. "Take heart men. We aren't beaten yet. Look at General Jackson on the hill. He's standing like a stone wall!"

Some of his men heard him and took heart. All around the battlefield, soldiers stared at the Virginia troops and their stead-fast leader. The retreating Southern soldiers stopped and turned back to fight again. Jeffrey's men looked at their own leader who also wanted to stay and fight. With his sword out, he marched his horse forward, his men joining him once again.

General Beauregard commanded the men to yell like the Furies. The soldiers obliged him with a blood-curdling cry that cut through the noise and confusion, sending the Union soldiers running.

For a moment the smoke cleared and Jeffrey saw the Washington civilians finally running for cover. The women who had come for a picnic ran off screaming at the bloody fight they had witnessed. Chaos ensued from that point on. The civilians tried to run back across the creek, but soldiers soon caught up with them. Jeffrey watched helplessly as soldiers and onlookers alike flailed in the stream, some drowning during the panic.

Several of the Union soldiers tried to brave it out. They shot over their shoulders while still running for cover. Jeffrey sighed with relief. He had made it through the first battle. He lived for another day. He had the chance to hold his very real and changed wife in his arms again. By some quirk of fate, his wife had become someone he loved and wanted to build a life with.

Still smiling, a stray bullet hit Jeffrey, throwing him from his horse and onto the wet ground. His last thought, regret that he could not hold Kristen one more time. He called out to her just as a wave of blackness overcame him.

Thirty Eight

*A*t first the still, bloodied form appeared to be just another young soldier in need of care. Kristen barely glanced at the man. Blood poured from his forehead, obscuring his features. Hardly noticing him, she focused her attention on another soldier bleeding profusely from a wound on his chest. She knew the lead in the bullets, too soft to exit cleanly, could tear-up a man's body. The bullets smashed against bone, which shattered in their destruction. If internal damage did not kill the man, the lead from the bullets seeping into the bloodstream would eventually do enough damage to get the job done.

Kristen asked for another cup of coffee for her blurry eyes due to a lack of sleep. Rising from her knees at the bed of a critically injured soldier, she gulped the lukewarm brew. She had been an orthopedic resident for three years and never experienced a problem with staying awake.

The waste of these young men's lives bothered her immensely. The ravages of war seemed bad enough, but to kill men you might be related to baffled her. Sometimes, men from the Union side were accidentally carried into the hospital. The blood, musket powder, and dirt made it difficult to determine what kind of uniform a man wore. Adding to the confusion, some of the Confederate soldiers wore navy blue like those of the Union officers.

When Union soldiers entered the tent, Kristen ripped off his uniform so no one knew which side the men came from. As a doctor, she took her duty to heal very seriously. No matter which side her patient had chosen to fight for, she did all that she could to save each person's life.

"Doctor?"

Kristen closed her eyes tight, took a last gulp of her coffee, and turned around.

"Here's a new one, and he's bleeding pretty badly."

"How badly?"

The young woman who had been working beside her all day, looked as pale as her hair. Her face's only color, her red lips from biting them all day. "I don't think he's breathing." She wiped blood out of the man's face. "And he looks as if he's an officer."

Dr. Vogler came into the room. "Put him over with the dead." He gave a quick glance at the still form on the stretcher. "Outside the tent. We need more room for the wounded." He pointed to a row where dead soldiers had been laid out on the grass.

The doctor's casual attitude got Kristen's attention. She dropped her empty tin cup to the ground and hurried to the bloodied man.

"Give me that," she snapped, taking the wet cloth from the woman's hand and wiping the blood away. "I'll not have a life wasted because that doctor is too lazy to come over and check on him." Kristen wiped away the blood. Her heart stopped in her chest. Her head buzzed. She grabbed a nearby tent pole with all the strength she had left in her exhausted body so she would not faint.

Years of training took over. She laid her fingers on the man's neck checking for a pulse, weak, but there. Relief washed over her. He seemed to be in a coma.

"He's alive. Let's see if we can keep him that way." She straightened herself up and faced the volunteer who snapped to attention.

"Let's see what we've got." Kristen heard her own voice but it sounded displaced, like underwater. She wiped the blood from Jeffrey's face. Head wounds bled more than wounds from other areas of the body, but it was disconcerting to see just how much blood flowed from her husband's head.

"You've got to live," she bent close and whispered, searching for the origin of the wound. A bullet had creased the side of his head, starting at the front, ending just above his ear. Not deep and not life-threatening. The wound would probably leave him with a blinding headache that might last a few days.

She almost laughed in her relief. Saying a quick prayer of thanks, she set to work cleaning the wound. Infection worried her at the moment because antibiotics did not exist during the Civil War. *What am I going to use?* She knew from history class, that more men died during the Civil War from infection than their determination to kill each other.

After dabbing away the blood and wrapping a cloth around the wound, Kristen stroked Jeffrey's hair and remembered the night she had shared only a few weeks before. Now it seemed like a lifetime ago. Would they have another chance to love each other? Would the war allow it? She wanted to continue this dream for the rest of her life. For the first time she found herself making plans for the future. After the war, she would return home with her husband and set up a small practice to care for women on the plantation and for those living nearby. *If this is where I'm going to live out my life – if I live my life out in this time.* Never before had she thought of having her own small private practice.

Now she needed to keep Jeffrey alive and get through the next four years. This life meant more than the one she lived in before the regression. This life with Jeffrey had captured all of her hopes and dreams. Before the regression she had never believed that her secret hopes and dreams could coexist with her career. Somehow she had mixed-up her dreams and goals. A movement in her patient caught her attention, ending her daydream. Deep, blue eyes fluttered open. "I must be dead because I'm looking at an angel."

Tears filled Kristen's eyes. "This is no time for jokes," she said brushing away a tear. "How are you feeling?"

Jeffrey gave a tired smile. "I have a headache that feels like it could kill me."

"I might kill you if you give me another scare like that."

Jeffrey tried to sit up. Kristen pushed him back down. "You're not going anywhere."

Collapsing back onto the cot, Jeffrey closed his eyes. "Are we winning?"

Kristen blinked. She realized she had no idea what was happening outside of the hospital. "I'm sorry, but I don't know."

"Can you ask someone?" Jeffrey's eyes opened again. "The last thing I remember was seeing my men running from the Yankees."

A soldier on the bed across the room sat up. "You should've seen it. It was Jackson who stopped those Yanks. He and his Virginia troops stopped them Yankees cold. The general just sat there on his white horse, not moving, not caring if the Yanks were heading straight at him. He just turned to his men and ordered them to shoot for all they're worth. That scared the other side so bad that they started running in the opposite direction. It was a wonderful sight."

The boy laid back down. He wore a white bandage across his eyes.

Jeffrey smiled. "So we won?"

Kristen shrugged. "I guess so."

With a contented sigh, Jeffrey closed his eyes.

The casualties continued to pour into the tent. An officer informed Kristen that the South had won the battle due to the outstanding show of courage displayed by General Jackson and his Virginia troops.

"Stonewall Jackson?" Kristen said.

The officer nodded. "That's what they call him now, Stonewall Jackson. He stood up against those Yankees like a stone wall. Seems he wasn't afraid of anything." The officer shook his head. "With men like that on our side, there's no way we can lose."

Kristen blinked tears from her eyes and wiped them off her cheeks.

"Looks like you could use some rest, ma'am."

Kristen staggered over to a chair and collapsed into it. Her head throbbed and her eyes burned as if they had been scrubbed with sandpaper.

Amy collapsed beside her. "This baby is sucking the life right out of me." She rubbed the small mound of her stomach.

Kristen smiled. "Just be sure you get enough rest. We can let the others take care of things for a while."

Women sympathetic to the South arrived from town to help, now that the fighting had ceased. She showed them what to do to ease the suffering of the wounded. Kristen wondered if the women could not do just as much as she. Even with all her training as a doctor, there still was not much she could do for the wounded. She could clean, stitch, and comfort them, but she could do nothing to fight infections that resulted from wounds not treated with antibiotics.

A great deal of her training concerned diagnosis and determination of which drug therapy to use for each patient. Without those drugs, she was almost as helpless as the good-hearted women who came to assist. They brought with them home remedies of foul-smelling teas and herbs, which she had never seen before. She watched, asked questions, and for the next few days learned a great deal.

She did not know exactly what ingredients the home brews contained, but the women brought them in and administered them to the soldiers. Kristen noted that these concoctions did indeed give the men comfort. White-willow-bark tea brought down Jeffrey's headaches and fever. A poultice of moss, mud, grasses, and various herbs stopped the infection that threatened his leg. More men might have been saved, if only the women had been allowed to continue their work. However, Dr. Vogler considered himself generous in letting the women meddle for even a day or two. He asked them to leave the hospital. "The men needed professional help," he said, "not witches' brew."

Kristen argued with the doctor until he threatened to have her thrown out permanently. Knowing he meant what he said, she stopped suggesting anything and continued asking the women questions about their herbs. She made sure that Jeffrey and other soldiers that could be helped by taking the herbs received them, and she stayed out of the doctor's way.

She flinched when the doctor tended to patients with his grimy hands, but she resisted saying anything. She knew about germs, but she also understood the hopelessness of teaching the doctor something he could not understand. So she watched and winced each time he operated without washing his hands.

"Kristen?"

"Yes?" She sat on the side of the cot where her husband lay.

Jeffrey smiled up at her. "I'm feeling well enough to get back to my men." He tried to sit up but fell back into the pillow.

"I can see that," Kristen said.

"I need to get out before the next battle."

"Because you weren't killed in the last one?"

"I believe in a cause worth fighting for," Jeffrey said, his voice barely above a whisper.

"And dying for?" All the trauma of the past few days had beaten Kristen down. She watched men die, too young to have lived even a fraction of their life yet.

"Women don't understand these things," Jeffrey whispered.

Kristen shook her head. "In my time, women fight in combat right beside the men. So I'd say we do understand these things."

Jeffrey's eyes went wide.

Nodding, she continued. "We fly jets, and command ships. We're doctors, surgeons, lawyers, and other professionals. Women in my time do just about everything that a man does."

"Who takes care of the children?" Jeffrey said.

She twiddled the locket around her neck as if the purple stone in the middle were a crystal ball to give her the answers. "We have daycare centers. People are paid to care for other people's children while their parents are at work."

Jeffrey watched her fingers as she rubbed the amethyst. "I don't have any children, so I haven't had to worry about such things."

Kristen checked under the bandage wrapped around his head and said. "You really should get some rest. Head trauma can be serious."

Jeffrey tried to rise again. He managed a sitting position, then tried to swing his legs over the bed. "I need to be with my men."

In the short time Kristen had spent with Jeffrey had shown her just how stubborn the man could be. She observed his sense of honor and responsibility to his men. She had expected him to join his men before he should, because of his honorable nature. When he stood, she rushed to his side to steady him. He picked up his uniform jacket from the foot of his cot, and with slow, careful movements, put it on one arm at a time.

He grabbed his gun from the floor and buckled it around his waist. He pulled the weapon out of the holster and checked the bullets.

She flinched at the sight of the gun, even though she knew it could save Jeffrey's life.

He turned to her with a weak smile. "No Yankee is going to kill me."

"You don't know that," Kristen shot back. "They've done a good job of hurting you twice so far."

"And you've been there each time to take care of me," Jeffrey said, his eyes softening as he looked at her.

She could gaze into those eyes forever. Did Jeffrey actually feel the same way she did?

As if he heard her ask, he said. "I don't know how or why, but we found each other again. And it's going to take more than a war to keep us apart." He leaned closer and whispered in her ear so that the other men lying in the cots near them could not hear. "I love you."

Never had those three words meant more than now. Kristen's eyes welled with tears. She knew what it had cost Jeffrey to tell her that he loved her. Her husband had given her his heart, even though the woman before her had broken it again and again.

"I love you, too," Kristen whispered back, her voice husky with emotion.

Jeffrey picked up the locket Kristen wore around her neck and lifted it over her head. He pulled out his pocket knife and scratched something on the back of it. Kristen's tears flowed freely watching him.

How could love and pain get so mixed up in a person's heart? She loved him with all her mind, body, and soul. Yet, feeling such love made the thought of him fighting in the war even more horrible. She wanted to beg him to take her away and leave the war behind. She wanted to scream the words she knew she could never say aloud in this time. *The war is a lost cause. Thousands of lives will be lost.* If Jeffrey died, she did not know how she could go on breathing.

Kristen said nothing. She could not get any words past the lump in her throat. Finally, Jeffrey handed the locket back to her. She turned it over and wiped the tears from her eyes so she could read what he had written.

You are my life, he had written. Kristen's heart felt like it would explode with joy.

"Oh, Jeffrey," she said holding the locket against her heart. "Thank you."

"If anything happens…"

He did not have to finish. They both knew exactly what he meant.

Kristen took the pocketknife from Jeffrey's hand. She looked around the tent and found a scalpel. Quickly she carved the same words into the bone handle of her husband's knife and scratched her initials beneath it as well. "There, now you have something that tells you how I feel." Blood rushed to her cheeks. She glanced down.

Jeffrey took his wife in his arms and held her in a fierce hug before stepping back. "I have to get back to my men now."

"I know," Kristen said, tears welling in her eyes again. She wondered how she could have any emotions left after a day spent caring for wounded men and crying about the ones that would die a few days later.

A commotion at the other side of the tent caught Kristen's attention. A soldier she had treated earlier that morning had sat up. The man's uniform that showed him to be a Yankee lay at the end of the bed. The same uniform that she herself had ripped off the man so no one would recognize his part in the battle. She knew that Dr. Vogler would have thrown the man out to die, if he'd known. She had not told anyone of the soldier's true identity.

Awake and aware of his surroundings, the wounded soldier's eyes looked wild scanning the tent and the sea of wounded in cots. Some of the men still wore their gray uniforms. He might have shot some of these patients during the battle.

The Northern soldier seemed to be searching for something, mumbling to himself. Kristen needed to calm the upset man before anyone realized an enemy lay amongst them. She hurried over to the cot and tried to soothe the distraught soldier.

"Lie down, everything is going to be all right," she said in a soothing voice, even though she felt like screaming at the man.

"Let me go!" He shouted, struggling to get out of her grasp. The wounds to one of his arms and both of his legs made him weak enough that Kristen could overpower him. Jeffrey rushed up beside her.

One look at Jeffrey's uniform and the man went wild. "You killed my brother!" He shouted. With his remaining good arm, the Union soldier reached for Jeffrey's gun and brought the weapon up to Jeffrey's chest.

"No!" Kristen pulled the man's arm away.

The weapon, now pointed at her chest, fired.

Kristen felt no pain and assumed she had not been hit. She heard another gunshot and watched the soldier fall back onto the bed. His eyes closed. She tried to push her hand forward to check on the wound now bleeding across the soldier's chest, but found that her hand had not moved at all.

She heard a voice shouting to her, but it faded until she could not hear anything except a buzzing in her ears that grew steadily louder. The tent grew darker and darker, until she had only a pin-hole of vision left. In it she saw Jeffrey's pained face. His sadness washed over her until she could not bear it any longer.

"Kristen...Kristen...Kristen...you can't leave me," he said in a broken voice.

She tried to answer but found she floated above her body. She saw herself being held by the man she had only known for a few months — the man who had become her life.

She floated higher and higher above the scene. Just like a movie, the final scene of a past life from another era. Kristen felt no fear, but she would ache for an eternity without the love of the man now holding her lifeless body. Regret flooded her mind. She wished for something to relieve the intense pain from leaving her soulmate—the man she had come so far to find.

At last Kristen recognized the reason she had gone back in time to experience part of her previous existence. Some loving presence had given her the chance to recognize what she had been missing in her current life. Satisfied with that knowledge, she relaxed and drifted away. Better to have loved and lost...

Thirty Nine

Kristen opened her eyes. Her chest hurt but she drew in warm air. With her hand, she caressed the soft cotton of her blouse. Then, the pain hit from deep inside. Her heart broke at the vague memories, the great loss weighing on her. "Noooo!"

"You're all right," the soothing voice whispered.

Kristen sat up and looked around. The bright light shining overhead made it difficult to see around her. Was this the great, white light people talked about? Should she move toward it?

She shuddered remembering the gun going off so close to her chest. The wonder if she might be bleeding only made the pain in her chest hurt worse.

"Jeffrey." If she were dead, she would never be able to see him again.

"Are you all right?"

Kristen blinked and looked around again. A woman stood over her, blocking the light. *How can I get to the light if she's blocking me?*

"Would you like a glass of water?"

Confused, she looked around. *Why do I need water if I don't have a body? I saw mine from far away as I lay in Jeffrey's arms inside the hospital tent. What in the world was this Angel talking about?*

"Kristen?"

Kristen shook her head, trying to clear it. "Where am I?"

"You're on television." The host smiled.

251

"No!" Kristen moaned. It all came back to her now—the psychic...the couch...the local television show. "Jeffrey," she said under her breath. *Had he actually existed? Had everything just been a dream?*

The psychic said, as if reading Kristen's mind, "You're experiencing one of your past lives in order to learn something."

No kidding.

The psychic continued. "Was your experience a good one?"

How can I answer that question? The earlier time had been the most wonderful, painful, joyful, excruciating experience she had ever had in her life. She felt as if she had lived ten lives instead of just one. It might have been a dream, but she never wanted to wake up from it. She tried to remember all that she had experienced, but already her memory faded.

"I'd rather not talk about it yet." Kristen gave a half smile, sat up, and arranged her clothes. The coffee stain was still there for everyone to see, but she could care less. The pain of losing Jeffrey still so raw it caused an ache in her heart. She wanted to leave this place and go home to have a good cry. Maybe she would not stop crying for weeks, or even months. Who knew how long it would take to heal her broken heart? She did not have enough energy to care.

"Sorry, I don't feel so well." She got up off the couch, stumbled across the studio stage and disappeared behind the curtain.

"Kristen. Are you all right?" Diane said.

Turning and seeing her friend, Kristen said, "I'm fine. I just want to go home now."

"Are you sure you're able to drive?" Diane said trying to keep up with her.

"I think so."

Her friend danced from toe to toe. "Did you really relive a past life?"

Unable to find her voice, she could only nod.

"You have to tell me what happened."

"Later." Kristen gasped and fumbled with her keys. She struggled to unlock the door of her SUV. The car seemed ridiculously large and cumbersome after living in the time of horses and buggies.

She turned to her friend. "Thanks for inviting me. I promise to tell you all about what I can remember of my past life after I have a chance to figure it all out for myself."

Kristen slid into her car, started it, and pulled away. She left her best friend standing at the curb with her mouth open.

Taking a deep breath, she tried to clear her head of every detail and concentrate on driving. However, this task proved to be impossible. She thought about Jeffrey and how she would never see him again. Tears flowed and did not stop for the entire ride home.

Once home, Kristen fell onto her bed. *How am I going to get through the rest of my life?* She had found the great love of her life and learned what had been missing in her own life for so many years. Unfortunately, there seemed to be absolutely no way to manifest her dream lover into her present life.

Forty

The apartment Kristen called home for the past three years no longer brought her comfort. Even with the brightly-colored Van Gogh prints, the white walls looked stark and empty. An aura of loneliness permeated the apartment, filled with objects Kristen had found in second hand shops that might date back to the Civil War period. She ran a finger over a brass statue of a soldier on horseback.

Kristen gazed through the living room window at the blue water of Lake Washington. Beyond the trees, several boats moved across the lake. It pained her to watch many happy families enjoying themselves on this sunny day.

"Families," Kristen whispered looking out the window again. Last month devoting her life to medicine had satisfied her, now her heart ached from the loss of Jeffrey's loving presence. Before the regression she could have gone on to practice medicine. But with the regression she now realized the importance of a personal life.

Too discouraged to eat, she took a long hot bath and spent most of her time in bed. Fortunately, she had a few days of vacation time coming to her, which she took to rest and relax away from people and the hospital.

One evening, she drifted in and out of a nightmare about Jeffrey. This time *he* had been shot. She watched his eyes close. As the sun rose, she witnessed him being brought into the hospital and his body thrown onto the pile of other dead soldiers. She could not stop

Dr. Volger's actions. No one knew he appeared dead rather than unconscious and would awaken in a few hours.

I wasn't there to protect him.

She watched Jeffrey drift in and out of consciousness. She saw him wracked with fever from his infected wounds. He finally died alone, surrounded by the men who fought valiantly under his command.

With a shudder Kristen awakened and wondered about her nightmare. *Had she change the past? Did she change Jeffrey's fate? Would it have been different from the one which she experienced with him? What had been the purpose of her regression? Was the entire series of events simply meaningless?*

Exhausted, Kristen dressed for the hospital on her first day back. Never had she felt so despondent. She could not attribute this feeling to a lack of sleep—she'd had more than enough. She had a new respect for patients suffering from depression.

Arriving at the hospital, Kristen found nothing changed, yet it all seemed different to her. New patients, injured by auto accidents, suffered in much the same way as those injured in battle. The only difference between these patients, their injuries occurred during a time of peace.

Gunshot wounds disabled people of all ages, and they too waited for her help. Kristen went about her job, cleaning wounds, comforting, suturing, and wondering if she even had a future.

"At least it's clean," she said.

The nurse looked up.

"Oh, it's nothing." Kristen looked down at her watch. She had been on duty for a total of twelve hours.

With her shift ended, Kristen went home, but her apartment had lost its appeal. What was home for her anyway? After living in a big, bustling household, and then in a crowded tent surrounded by men and women she cared about, her quiet apartment made her reluctant to leave.

Why had she ever thought she liked living alone? Maybe if there were something to come home to... She brushed that thought aside and jabbed at the elevator button that would take her to the basement parking garage.

"It's broken."

She turned to see her former mentor standing behind her. "Dr. Paine. Nice to see you again."

"After what I put you through the first year of your residency?"

Kristen laughed. "I have to say, I *did* learn a lot from you."

"Yes, you certainly did." Dr. Paine chuckled. "And I hear you're doing very well for yourself nowadays."

"I've had some great teachers." Heat rose in her cheeks. Kristen regretted the former hostile thoughts she had held for her mentor.

"Dr. O'Connor from John Hopkins is going to be giving a lecture at Gibbons Hall tomorrow night."

Is *he asking me on a date?* Her cheeks grew warm. As much as she admired her mentor, he neared retirement.

As if reading her mind, the doctor smiled. "He's the best in his field. Dr. O'Connor will be speaking on a new surgical technique he's perfected."

"I'd love to hear him." Kristen's breath came out in a rush. The elevator door finally opened.

Dr. Paine tapped her on the shoulder. "You're going to be one of our best." He winked at her and walked away.

Kristen moved to her car, glowing from the compliment given by a man she greatly admired. She found herself looking forward to the next evening. For the first time in weeks, she cared about something. If she only had her work, she would become the best surgeon she could possibly be. At least she had nothing to distract her from her career.

Forty One

*T*he crowded lecture hall pulsed with practicing physicians and eager residents anxious to learn about the most current surgical techniques. Kristen never tired of hearing new and better ways to promote healing. Her passion for the healing arts had replaced the gloom of the past few weeks.

Loneliness still hung like an old coat, but she reminded herself that she chose this life many years ago. Her feelings about love had changed because of the brief interlude she had shared with Jeffrey. She had missed much by living a solitary life.

Kristen sat in the front row so she would not be distracted by anyone else. She wanted to fully concentrate on what Dr. O'Connor had to say. The man's last name brought a twinge when she heard it, but there would be no relation between this man and the man she had dreamed of, who had lived over a hundred years ago.

Kristen pulled out a notebook and pen, prepared to write down anything she might want to remember. She wrote the doctor's name at the top of the page.

"O'Connor." *What a strange coincidence?* The man who stepped up to the podium to speak would look nothing like Jeffrey. A doctor with O'Connor's reputation had to be at least sixty years old.

Kristen wished her heart would stop beating so hard. *How ridiculous to have this sort of reaction to a simple name? There's probably millions of O'Connor's in the world, and many of them are probably doctors.*

She took a deep breath and turned her attention to the stage. A white-haired man walked up to the podium.

"See?" she said under her breath.

"Thank you all for coming tonight," the speaker said. He smiled and looked offstage. A young man in a dark suit walked on stage to join the elderly announcer. The two men shook hands, then the older man turned back to the audience. "It gives me a great deal of pleasure to present, Dr. James O'Connor."

Thunderous applause filled the hall. Kristen could not believe what she saw. He stood not ten feet away from her! Dr. James O'Connor, the spitting image of the man who had haunted her dreams and most of her waking hours for weeks. The doctor from Johns Hopkins looked just like her Jeffrey.

"It can't be," she whispered. "I'm just imagining this." She closed her eyes, certain that Jeffrey's image would vanish by the time she opened them again. She counted down from ten.

She opened her eyes and looked at the stage. Still standing behind the wooden podium just a few feet away from her, stood the man identical to Jeffery. He stared back at her as if he, too, saw a ghost.

She held her breath, waiting for him to speak.

Surely then I'll know that it's not the man I fell in love with. Her throat turned as dry as dust. She tried to swallow over her dry tongue threatening to choke off her breathing.

How can this be happening?

The blood roared in her ears, her head spun. If she had not been sitting down, Kristen would have fallen forward and landed on her face.

She did not hear a single word Jeffrey said. The world around her had been reduced to a single pinpoint of light, and that light shone directly on his face. In her mind, the dark suit and the shiny, silk tie had been replaced with a gray uniform and memories of an earlier century.

All through the hour-long speech, Kristen dreamed and remembered, feeling alive again. Her heart raced and chills rushed up and down her body. She could see, hear, and feel nothing but Jeffrey's presence. It felt as if he were speaking only to her. She alternated between bliss and fear. *Is this man like her*

Jeffrey or just a man who resembles him?

She closed her eyes and then opened them again and again, expecting to see someone else at the podium. She feared she would only see a speaker with a passing resemblance to the man she gave her heart to during the Civil War. Each time she opened her eyes, Dr. James O'Connor continued his speech, giving her furtive glances.

Dr. O'Connor shook the hand of the doctor who invited him to speak. Then, smiling, he looked down at the audience. His gaze traveled over the faces until a woman in the front row caught his eye. A bolt of electricity hit him. Time stopped. He stared into a pair of wide, green eyes that gazed at him with a longing so intense it traveled right down to his toes. Something familiar touched his soul. He tried to remember if he had ever met the young woman before. Surely he would never forget such a woman, but try as he might, he could not remember ever meeting her.

The audience's whispers caught his attention. How much time had elapsed? Dr. Lewis stood in the wings frowning at his guest speaker. Dr. O'Connor gave him a slight nod and looked back at the crowd, doing his best to avoid the gaze of the woman in the front.

Impossible!

Something about her felt familiar to him, yet he did not know her. He felt as if they had spent a lifetime together, but equally sure they had never met.

With a quick look at his notes, James pulled his mind away from the woman and back to his speech. With a deep breath, he began. He kept his eyes glued on his notes, avoiding those sea-green eyes—again.

After over an hour, he wrapped up his speech. He felt that he could now safely search for those beautiful, sea-green eyes. For one panicked moment, he thought she'd left. She rose back up after bending down to pick up something. In that split second, James thought he had died and been reborn.

Many in the audience came forward, surrounding him, asking questions, and congratulating him, but he barely heard a word. He thought only of moving off the stage to meet the mysterious woman before she left the auditorium.

When the speech ended, Kristen's heart raced. *Should I leave? Will he think I'm some sort of stalker if I say anything?*

A wave of shyness came over her, and while she might regret it, she bent down to pick up her tote bag. *Should I wait a few minutes? Or Should I stay?*

Her eyes were drawn back to the stage again. Dr. O'Connor still shook hands with his peers. He turned and looked straight at her. Her heart squeezed. She could not trust herself to stand.

Kristen had some experience in dating, but she had no idea why he had just nodded in her direction. She glanced around to see if he might mean someone else, but saw no other young women around her.

James continued nodding to his well-wishers and then smiled at Kristen. Electricity surged through her.

What am I going to say to him? "Hi, you don't know me, but when I was regressed a couple of weeks ago, you and I were married to each other. We fell in love – I was killed – which put me back in my own time. Can we go someplace and have a cup of coffee and get reacquainted?"

Deep in thought, Kristen nearly jumped at her phone vibrating in her pocket. She glanced down at the number. Regretfully, she would not get a chance to meet the man who may – or may not be – her Jeffrey.

She slipped her phone back into her pocket. Her patients needed her. Besides, this man who resembled the man who'd stolen her heart lived here the 21st century, with all the quirks and social maladjustments that made dating in this century so undesirable. *He probably wouldn't be anything like the man I loved.*

Forty-Two

The emergency room in large hospitals is the first stop for traumatic injuries, such as gunshots and automobile accidents. When an ambulance pulled up just as Kristen decided to find something to eat for dinner, she stopped and waited for the doors to open.

Treating those who suffered would never again be something she took for granted. Every injured person belonged with a loved one, something Kristen now understood on a soul level. Her short time with Jeffrey had opened her heart up in a way that insured it would never be closed again.

Kristen took a deep breath and stood in front of the double glass doors that opened to the circular drive of the emergency doors of the hospital. Her elastic hair tie had lost its battle over the last twelve hours, leaving many wisps of hair sticking out. Unaware of how she looked, she concentrated on the ambulance, anticipating the needs of the patient in the vehicle.

Two attendants threw open the doors and a dark-haired man in a suit jumped out. Kristen pushed him out of the way, her whole focus on the stretcher.

"Careful," she said to the two attendants as they lowered the stretcher to ground, activating the legs. She checked vital signs and looked over the elderly woman smiling up at her.

"You look too young to be taking care of me."

Kristen blinked in surprise, a sudden light-headedness hitting her. Something about the woman seemed familiar. *I need to focus. I should have eaten lunch today.*

A deep voice interrupted her thoughts. "Is she going to be okay?"

Kristen turned and for the first time looked into the eyes of the man who'd been in the back of the ambulance. Her heart skipped a beat. She gazed into the gray-blue eyes of Dr. O'Connor.

Shaking off her emotions, she went into the mode she'd been trained for and turned away from him. "I don't know yet, what happened?" She stayed by the woman's side while the stretcher moved through the hospital.

"We were having dinner at the Met to celebrate her birthday. She started to stand-up and collapsed into my arms."

The stretcher stopped at a large room with a male nurse who looked as if he hadn't shaved in days. He pulled a curtain around them.

Kristen nodded and gazed at her patient. She opened the elderly woman's silk blouse and laid her stethoscope against the woman's chest. Kristen sighed in relief. "Her vitals are strong from what I can hear."

Kristen readied to pull her stethoscope away but noticed a gold chain, worn smooth from wear, around the woman's neck. Kristen could just see the top of a locket with a purple stone in the middle of it.

I have to remind the nurses to take care of her jewelry.

She pulled her instrument away and wrapped it around her neck. Kristen turned to see the man who had brought the woman in speaking intently to Kristen's boss.

Why would Paine be down here? I can't believe he hasn't gone home yet.

Kristen turned to the nurse. "Let's get her a room so we can observe her overnight." She gave the two men a nod. *Dr. Paine being down here at this hour must mean that our patient is important — at least to his career — so give her one of the private rooms. And her son appears to already know Dr. Paine. That is interesting. I think I'll make sure this patient is well-cared for myself.*

The nurse had already prepared the gurney for moving. Kristen took the other end of the stretcher and helped push the patient out of the large room, toward the elevators.

At the elevator doors the woman seemed to revive. "You look familiar, dear," she said in a faint voice.

Kristen smiled and patted the woman's arm. "I don't think we know each other."

The woman frowned. "In fact, you look very familiar." She reached a shaking hand to her chest and grasped the locket she wore. "Here, open this for me."

The elevator doors opened and the nurse pulled the stretcher in.

Kristen smiled and lifted the locket out of the woman's hand. "If I look, will you promise to rest until we can see why you fainted?"

The woman frowned. "I asked to drive to the restaurant to prove I wasn't some helpless old lady who couldn't even drive her own car." She shook her head. "Then a car ran a red light while I was going through my perfectly green light. People have no manners anymore. My grandson wants me to stop driving. Just look at how badly today's youth drive."

The nurse, trying his best to appear professional, could barely suppress his laughter. He coughed and looked up at the ceiling.

"I'm sure you do know how to look after yourself, Mrs...." Kristen assured her patient as she looked at the chart for the woman's name.

"O'Connor," she said.

"Mrs. O'Connor," Kristen repeated. Saying the name made Kristen's heart flutter. Her mind made a mad dash around her stored memories, coming up with only one name — Jeffrey.

The elevator doors opened, saving Kristen from her own need to find humor in the old woman's lecture on something she agreed with herself.

"We need to get you settled, Mrs. O'Connor."

"The only thing that needs to get settled is why you look so familiar. And you will know why once you open my locket."

Impressed with the strength of the woman's voice, Kristen smiled and nodded. "We are going to get you into a gown first. Then we can have a closer look at the bump on your head and then I promise I'll look."

Kristen turned to the nurse. "Let's get Alice in here to help me with Mrs. O'Connor." He nodded and left the room.

"Are you going to look now or do I have to have a heart attack?"

"Absolutely. Whatever it takes to keep you from actually needing to be in this hospital," Kristen said with a chuckle. Impressed with the color now present in her patient's cheeks, she didn't want them to get any rosier.

The older woman held the locket up. "You'll have to unfasten it for me—unless I'm allowed to get up and go home."

"I'll get it," Kristen said reaching her hands around the woman's neck and unfastening the latch.

"It's one of the old-fashioned latches. . ."

"I've got it," Kristen said. *How did I know how to do that?*

"I thought you might know how," she said with a sigh. "I am usually right about such things."

Now holding the locket, Kristen barely heard the older woman. The slightly faded picture in the locket was of a woman she knew well. Now, Kristen felt as if *she* were going to faint.

"This can't be."

"And yet it is."

Kristen stared into the eyes of the woman in the photo—a woman she'd been only six months ago. The same one who had loved and lost, only to awaken on a couch in front of a television audience with a heavy heart that lasted until now.

"There you are, grandmother." A tall man with dark hair and gray-blue eyes stood in the doorway of the luxurious hospital room. "Your old friend Dr. Paine assured me that you would have the best of care."

"Hmm—he should. Your father trained him and left him enough money to build this wing in his will."

"Grandmother. . . "

Kristen knew that voice better than she knew her own. "Jeffrey?"

The man turned his eyes from the woman in the bed and turned to look at Kristen for the first time. He frowned. "Doctor?"

"Kristen Bassett, I'll be taking care of your grandmother."

Kristen heard herself say automatically, her mind racing to piece together her reality.

"James, my name is James, but I had a great-grandfather by the name of Jeffrey — Jeffrey O'Connor."

But you're my Jeffrey — I'd know you anywhere. The locket felt as if it were burning into her flesh. Kristen looked down at the photograph, tears forming in her eyes.

"Are you all right?"

She looked up at the man she'd fallen in love with only weeks before. He was more than familiar to her.

James frowned. "Is that my grandmother's locket?"

Her hands shook as she held it out. "She wanted me to look at the picture inside," Kristen said, her voice shaking.

"It's her, James. There's no doubt in my mind. Can't *you* see it?"

Taking the locket from Kristen's hand, James opened it up to the photo. He looked from the photo to Kristen and back again. "There is a resemblance," he said.

"It's more than a resemblance," his grandmother snapped. "And if you weren't so stubborn, you'd see it too."

Kristen gathered her senses and went into professional mode. "A nurse will be coming in to get your grandmother settled for the night." She brushed by James. "I'll be checking on her throughout the night."

James closed the locket and laid it on the table beside the bed. He took a deep breath and then turned to Kristen where she stood in the doorway. He stared at her as if seeing her for the first time. He blinked several times and then frowned. "It's ridiculous," he said under his breath.

"It's fate, young man, now ask her for a cup of coffee before you lose her."

Shaking himself, James looked down at his grandmother. "I have no idea what you're talking about."

"Of course you do, son. Now get this woman a cup of coffee and leave me to my sleep — if it's possible to get any rest at a hospital."

James held up his hands. He turned to Kristen. "Would you like to humor a stubborn old woman and let me buy you a cup of coffee?"

"I heard that."

Kristen found her throat too dry to answer so she merely nodded.

"Lead the way."

Together than walked through the quiet halls of the hospital, down to the noise of the cafeteria. Kristen felt the rightness of walking next to James—Jeffrey in her mind.

I don't know how this happened, but I'm not going to question fate.

James smiled at Kristen as if reading her thoughts.

It can't be this easy. Jeffrey has not just walked into my hospital.

Kristen took a deep breath and smiled up at James, too overcome to do anything but lead the way to the cafeteria where she would either confirm what her heart told her was true or find out that she was in fact, dreaming.

"Would you like to join me for a drink?"

She could smell the cedar, citrus, and something very male. The scent convinced her this man and the man she had met in her dream state were one and the same.

He offered her his arm. Kristen took it and everything fell into place.

"Have we met before?" James said.

Kristen shook her head.

James nodded. "I would've remembered you, and yet... there's something very familiar about you."

Kristen smiled. "Maybe we met in another lifetime."

"I'm sure I would have enjoyed that life."

The world felt right again with James at her side. Kristen gave a short prayer of thanks to whatever power in the universe that had given her a second chance.

They exchanged a smile and walked into the soft Seattle mist, and the beginning of a mysterious new life with each other.

Robin Landry lives in the Pacific Northwest, where the near constant rain for much of the year, allows for guilt-free time spent indoors writing. Her favorite part of the writing process is researching thoroughly the subject of a novel.

Dream Lover was a deep dive into the time of the Civil War, and the idea of past lives and their influence on our current lives.

A certified hypnotherapist, she has regressed many in experiencing their past lives, which can never be predicted but is always fascinating.

Landry turned her attention to writing novels when she married at the end of a successful career as a singer in a rock band by the name of Widow. For seven years she sang, and played guitar opening for larger acts such as Brian Adams, INXS, and Stevie Ray Vaughn. A book of poetry came out of a middle school assignment with her daughter, and a series of Young Adult novels.

Next came a novels in the time travel genre, with Dream Lover finding a home with Mystic Publishing."